Paragon:

An Icon Story

By

Riley Tune

Paragon: An Icon Story 2nd Edition

To the dreamer, and the rebel. To anybody that has greatness inside of them and simply doesn't know which path to take. This book is for you.

I can't thank you enough for buying this book! If, after reading, you find that you enjoyed it, please leave a review on the site from which it was purchased, or any other book review site. I'd love to hear what you think. Also, if you would like to be added to my email list for updates on new projects, cover art previews, and bios of new characters, please see the link below:

http://eepurl.com/coooRH

If you want to learn more about me:

www.rileytune.weebly.com

My YouTube for writers:

www.youtube.com/onewordatatime

CONTENTS

PROLOGUE 1

CHAPTER 1
THE BATTLE OF AGES 21

CHAPTER 2
PURGATORY ACADEMY 31

CHAPTER 3
MY TEACHER'S AN ASSHOLE........................ 45

CHAPTER 4
HOME SWEET HOME.................................... 55

CHAPTER 5
THE PONY SHOW 69

CHAPTER 6
FLEXING MY POWERS 79

CHAPTER 7
EBONY DISTRICT 89

CHAPTER 8
LOBO 103

CHAPTER 9
THE TALK.. 115

CHAPTER 10
R.M.F.C... 125

CHAPTER 11
IMPERIAL LORDS...................................... 141

CHAPTER 12
ENTER PICASSO 155

CHAPTER 13

IMPERVIOUS 165

CHAPTER 14

THE REMATCH 181

CHAPTER 15

BREAKOUTS AND FIREWORKS 195

CHAPTER 16

OLD FRIENDS...KIND OF 207

CHAPTER 17

ASHES 221

CHAPTER 18

OFFICER JACKSON 231

CHAPTER 19

INFINITY 245

CHAPTER 20

MISSION ONE 257

CHAPTER 21

THE FAMILY TREE 271

CHAPTER 22

SPELLBORN 287

CHAPTER 23

PHONE CALL 303

CHAPTER 24

SINS OF THE FATHER 319

CHAPTER 25

LORDS NO MORE 327

EPILOGUE 343

PROLOGUE

Close your eyes for a moment, and just imagine you have the power to save the world, but you also have the power to conquer it, and very few people could stand in your way. Which decision would you make? Hero or villain? To do the right thing and be boring, or have fun while breaking a few laws here and there? A decision I'll be making soon enough and then, my life will change forever. I just don't know which I'd rather do. To be honest, I can relate to both sides. I just need to find that gray zone. That midway point, between good and bad, you know?

In Atlas City, this decision is always made by people like me. My indecisiveness aside, I'm willing to bet that Atlas City is one of the best places in the world to live. Sure, it has its fair share of crime, but that's mostly in the Ebony District. It's almost impossible for an area that is always so dark, not to have an increase in crime. The rest of Atlas City, though, is full of all the stuff any person could want.

Shops, good food, tons of jobs, people soaring through the skies, all of that. Anybody, and I mean anybody, could be happy here. Regardless of whether you're a person with powers, traditionally referred to as an Icon. Or if you're a Void, I mean a normal person. It's frowned upon to call a person a Void these days. I'm not sure why, though. They are devoid of power, so why not call them Voids? I mean those poor, simple, mundane, and ordinary bastards.

Anyway, good old Atlas City has all you need, and what I needed now, believe it or not, was flowers. Nothing too fancy, but nothing cheap and disrespectful. I was in a little store downtown, one that sold almost everything from medicine to electronics, and as you may have guessed, they also had flowers.

I looked over the rows and rows of flowers organized in front of me, I felt like I scanned each bouquet. I swear it's easier to pick out a new house, than a decent flower arrangement.

I held up one of the bouquets in front of me. Half of the flowers were smashed in, and the other side of the bouquet looked almost dead. I shook my head as I tossed the flowers down, not worrying about where they landed or how they made the display look. How hard is it for a worker to just set out pretty flowers?

"Why don't you just get these?" A voice said to the left of me. It caused me to jump a little, because I didn't see her come up . Then again, why would I? She was, yet again, invisible. I'm talking one hundred percent unseen, light bending around her, you would never know she's there, invisible. "Stop doing that," I hissed at her as I put the flowers down and got myself back together.

I cracked my neck slightly, as she chuckled. She then let out a yawn, and slowly shifted from invisible to her normal self. It was as if some unseen hand was gradually wiping away her invisibility, leaving her for the world to see.

Standing in front of me was Jen, my adopted sister. Dressed the same as me, we both had on dark blue sweat pants, white sneakers, and a gray tee shirt on with *PA* printed on the chest.

We both even had black hair. Jen was shorter than me, though. While she was a little over five and a half feet, I stood a little over six. She also had on a baseball cap. Jen treated a baseball cap like most women treated handbags. Her outfit wasn't complete without one.

She reached for some more flowers to show me. Now, she was holding up some roses. I looked at them and shook my head. "Those are roses. Why would I take roses to a site where so many Icons died?" She nodded and put the roses down. "I guess you're right," she said as she looked over the flowers.

She let out a little sigh and quickly changed her eyes from being locked on the flowers to looking at me. "Not to get in your business, but next time you sneak your girlfriend in the house, try to be a little more discreet." Jen said to me casually. I looked at her as if I had no idea what she was talking about. A look complete with wide eyes and a faint, fake gasp.

"Don't act dumb," she paused as she touched her chin, "well, I suppose you aren't really acting." I snorted as I lifted up a pair of lilies. "Seriously, if dad found out you had a girl in the house he'd freak. Not to mention what he would do if he found out she was a villain. I swear to Atlas, Hunter you simply do stuff just to see how it will turn out."

I shrugged without even looking at her, and continued to focus on my flowers. "Some villains get a hard rap, and Danielle is fun." "I know," Jen said as she walked away from the flowers. "Remember I share a wall with you," she shouted over her shoulder. I made a mental note to try and keep my after- hours activities with Danielle a little quieter for Jen's sake.

Atlas knows I'd hate to hear her and some boy in her room. Or some girl for that matter. Now that I think about it, I have heard her with both in her room before. During the day no less. She doesn't even have the decency to sneak them in at night. I don't know if I should be jealous, proud, or offended. Yeah, proud feels right.

I gathered my lilies and went to the front to pay. They were white stargazer lilies which, according to the tag, and because I know nothing about flowers, were a symbol of sympathy. I placed them on the counter and the man at the register paid me no attention as he reached for them while still looking at his little tv on the counter.

He was an older man. He had dark skin, gray hair, thick glasses and more hair on his arms than I had on my head. "They are still talking about this theory that somebody out there is killing off Icons. You can never trust the news though," he said as he glared at the tv. "Fifteen-" he stopped speaking as he looked up at me. "Oh hey," he said.

I raised a brow. "Uh, hey." He simply looked at me and smiled. It was a creepy smile. Like one of those *hey kid I have some candy so get in my van* smiles. "How much was it again?" I asked him as I reached for my wallet. Side-note, wallets are a bitch to have in sweatpant's pockets. They just never seem to fit right.

He raised his hand up and then pushed the flowers towards me. "No charge," he said. Sure. I thought to myself. *No charge until I got to the door and he shouts stop thief!* "You go to that school, don't you? Purgatory Academy." The man asked me.

I'm guessing the large *PA* on my shirt gave it away. "Yeah." I said as I fumbled with my wallet as I tried to get it to fit back into my pants. "Wow. An Icon, in my store." The way he said the last few words made him sound like one of those over the top valley girls you see in movies. "Not often that I get a hero in here. Your teachers at the school worried about these vanishing Icons, and the ones they have found dead?"

To my knowledge, they hadn't even mentioned it at school. So, I shrugged at him as a voice said out of nowhere, "Icons! Icons in your store . Not just one." The man looked around as he slowly stiffened. I exhaled and looked to my side. Sure enough, Jen was fading into visibility as she drank an orange soda. The man at the counter smiled from ear to ear. As if the Diamond District didn't have dozens of heroes of all sorts zipping around.

He kept looking at Jen with that creepy smile again. Jen didn't help the situation because she could go from visible to invisible, and back again in an instant. This became an apparent thing, only done for show. The man looked at me and I looked at him. According to his name tag, which I was just seeing for the first time, he was named Rufus.

Rufus kind of nodded his head to me, with a smirk on his face, and his brow raised. I knew what he wanted. I just didn't feel like displaying my powers like some animal in a circus.

"Thanks for the flowers, Rufus," I said as I held them up in the air and walked away from the counter.

"Anything for a future hero of this city." Rufus called back. Bold statement. He knew nothing about Jen or me. We could have been rotten to the core for all he knew. That was Atlas City though, people always tended to believe in the best, even if they secretly prepared for the worst.

We left the store and found ourselves walking together down the street. Flower shopping took longer than I had expected. Luckily, classes at Purgatory didn't start until eleven, and since Jen and I were both seventeen and in our final year, we could afford to be late.

So, we had plenty of time. I don't see how Voids, normal people, I mean normal people, our age got up so early to go to school. Some have to be there as early as eight. Not only that but they had to take the bus. The thought of a public bus alone, made me shiver. Years and years of teen germs in one location. I felt the shiver again.

Thankfully I could get around on my own, but if I couldn't, I'd walk before I got on a crowded, germ- infested, dirty bus.

We walked in silence. I kept looking at my flowers in hand, and mentally compared them to the ones I had purchased the year before. Jen was casually drinking her soda and expertly texting on her phone with her free hand. "You know what," I said to her. She didn't reply. She just looked at me as she took a long slurp of her soda. Then she burped. "What?" she finally replied.

"I think I'll get Danielle something nice while we are out." Jen frowned some. "Like a gift? For what?" I smiled at her. "For her stellar performance last night," I said as I nudged her with my body. "Gross," she said as she grimaced. I laughed.

"No, seriously, she has been hinting at wanting a new watch, and Ingram's is right there," I said as I pointed to the store across the street. Jen's eyes all but popped out of her head as her mouth fell open. "Ingram's. Are you crazy? You realize that store only uses diamonds created by Gem, right?" I nodded.

Gem was a female Icon with powers that revolved around diamonds. Like many Icons, Gem had two powers. Her prime power was that she could turn herself into a living diamond, making her highly resistant to damage for a short while. This power seems impressive, but she could only hold the form for as long as she could hold her breath.

Her second power, was that she could touch anything and turn it into a diamond. Diamonds were already rare, but diamonds made by an Icon were even more elusive. Considering only about four Icons in the world had this power, the diamonds created by Gem came with a huge price tag.

Mr. Ingram, just so happened to be Gem's best friend from the old days, so he had a connection.

"Let me guess, you're going to get her the watch from there. She's a villain, can't she just steal a watch or something?" "Yeah, but this way it means more." I said as I nudged her with my elbow and gave her a comically overdone eye wink. Plus, all Jen knew was that Danielle was 'a villain'. She didn't know that she hadn't actually done any villainous deeds yet. She was working on it, but these things take time.

"You coming?" I asked as I began walking to the store. Jen shook her head, sat down on a bench, and continued to use her phone. I gave her the flowers to hold. "I'd rather not see you spend a fortune. That way I can play dumb when dad sees your bank statement."

I hadn't thought about that. It was *my* money though. My parents, well my dad mostly, left me a large inheritance. By large I mean I could retire right now, live out my life, and my kids would still be well off if I left them the rest. I was basically rich.

The down side, was that my dad was a villain, so how he acquired this money was never discussed in detail. It didn't matter in my book. If the heroes couldn't stop him, then as far as I figured, fair is fair and that money was mine.

I opened the store's door, and a freakishly loud chime went off. The guests in Ingram's didn't even look away from what they were doing to see who had just entered. Hell, the workers didn't even look up at me.

"Hello," a small woman said with a smile. She walked from behind the counter and shook my hand. She was pretty. She had long black hair, red lipstick and appeared to have Asian features.

Her dress was a bland- looking gray color, and her tag said her name was, oddly enough, Asia. "First time here?" she asked me. "Is it that obvious?" I replied. Clearly my looking around like a lost child didn't help.

It was hard not to be in awe of this place though. Everything was so, shiny. I don't mean just the diamonds either. The floors were some sort of polished stone, and reflected the light that came from various chandeliers hanging from   above. This same light seemed to bounce off of every piece of jewelry in the store.

"It's okay, what are you looking for?" Asia asked me. "Well Asia, I need to get my girlfriend a watch." I said as I clapped my hands together and rubbed them with a smile. "Nothing too fancy or expensive though." At these words her smile faded. "The most affordable watch we have in our inventory is about two thousand dollars. It's mostly silver, has a few diamonds made by Gem herself, in the face."

I coughed loudly at the price. Apparently, I was too loud because the two- armed guards patrolling the store both looked at me. Both were larger than life to me, and looked like they could easily take out a normal person, no gun required.

I tried to act cool as I shook my head. "Sure. Can I see that one please?" I asked Asia. Her smile returned, and she waved me over to the counter. I stood in front of it and she walked behind it, grabbed some keys, entered a pin number on a keypad, and then unlocked the glass case.

Asia held the watch up. As she had said, it was mostly silver, but in the face those diamonds reflected like stars in the night sky. Was it a nice watch? Without question. Did it look like it was worth two thousand dollars? Not even close.

Asia cleared her throat some as I mulled it over in my mind. "Sir," she said. "Oh, sorry. Just thinking. I'll take it." She smiled and did a little dip. Thinking about her commission from the sale, no doubt.

"Very good choice, sir." "Well she wanted a watch, so here I am." I said again as I fumbled in my pants to get my wallet. Asia had begun moving to ring up the watch then she stopped. "This is a gift?" she asked me. I shook my head. "Yep."

"Would you like a special box for it? I'll wrap it also." "Sure, why not," I said as I finally got my wallet open and searched for my bank card. "Perfect, that's going to be an extra charge of fifty dollars."

"Whoa," I said as I raised my hands up. "For a box and a bow? Nevermind, just leave it in the box it comes in." Asia shrugged and then moved to put the special box she had grabbed back under the counter.

"Wait, wait," I said as I bit my lip. I've already spent that much on the watch, may as well get the damn box too." "Wise move, sir," Asia said as she grabbed the box again. I mean, it *was* a pretty box.

It was a dark blue, with silver sparkles that seemed to be made into the actual box. On the top it had *Ingram's* written in a fancy golden font, and on the inside, was shimmery white fabric. She gently placed the watch inside, making it a point to have the price tag exposed.

I liked this. What was the point of spending so much money if Danielle didn't even know how much it was? As Jen had pointed out, villains steal things, but Danielle hadn't got that far in her career yet, so me spending this much was sure to earn me some special treatment.

Asia began to press some buttons on the register as I tapped my card on the counter top. I glanced at my phone as I heard the loud chime of the door go off behind me again.

Still had plenty of time to make my next stop, and then get to class. Then a sound echoed through the store than sent everybody into a panic. Several rapid gunshots had pierced the silence inside of Ingram's. Asia screamed as she dropped down behind the counter. I turned around quickly and saw the two guards were down. One was grabbing at his leg as blood pooled on the floor. The other guard was crumbled on the floor motionless. Neither guard seemed to have had time to reach their weapons.

Three gunmen were inside Ingram's. Apparently, they were the reason the door chime had gone off. They were all dressed in dark green jumpsuits. All had on brown ski masks and black boots.

To add to their uniform unity, each gunman had an assault rifle in their hands. "Ninety seconds," one gunman shouted out as the other two began smashing cases and grabbing as much jewelry as they could.

"Everybody, right here and get on your knees." the gunman counting down the time said. Nobody moved, and then he released more shots into the air. The customers, and workers behind the counters quickly moved to the area he had pointed the gun to.

The people in the store cried and there were about thirteen of us total in that little area now. I made it a point to stand in front of them as I dropped down to my knees and kept my hands up. I could have stepped in, but I'd rather let the cops sort this out. I figured it would be over soon, and I had someplace to be.

Glass continued to shatter and fall, as the gunmen ravaged the store.

"Forty seconds," he screamed again. Of all days, they had to do this today. I glanced outside through the doors. There was a van parked out front with a man sitting inside it. He was looking around in all directions, and he too, had a mask on.

Despite the gunshots going off. People outside weren't panicking. Sure, they were on the other side of the street and watching, but they weren't running. No, they were waiting for an Icon to arrive. Waiting for a chance to see a caped hero in action. Or for a flamboyant and colorful costume to arrive.

This sort of thing was too low level for the big names, though. By time somebody came, these guys would be long gone. A woman beside me stood up and tried to speak to one of the gunmen. Before she could finish, a shot rang out and she fell to the floor.

Everybody else screamed as her body hit the ground. I took in a deep breath. These three were either very efficient, or so nervous that they had become trigger happy. Either way, I couldn't just watch them kill people. I hated that I had to help, but it seemed like it would be quicker than waiting for the cops. Guess it was up to me.

I dropped my hands, and slowly stood up.

"On the damned ground, kid," the gunman said as he pointed his gun at me. "You want to end up like her?" he said as he jerked his head towards the lifeless woman who was inches from my feet.

"C'mon man, you don't want to do this. Why would you even do this here? In the Diamond District. Isn't this more an Ebony District thing?"

His finger applied slight pressure to the trigger of the gun he held. Then he stopped. I could see his face frown behind the mask. He wasn't looking at me though, he was looking at my shirt. "That's right, connect the dots," I said as I twirled my finger, gesturing for him to hurry up.

"You're one of the freaks?" "I wouldn't call myself a freak," I said to him casually. In all honesty I'd been called worse. "I know the laws though, kid. You can't use your powers until you take the oath. Now sit back down, and shut up. We don't want to hurt anybody else, but we will if we need to." he checked his watch again.

"Time, Jerry," another of the robbers shouted as he stuffed his bag. "No names, you idiot. We gotta go. This kid screwed up my count." "Poor Jerry," I said to him. "Every Icon doesn't follow the laws," I said with a grin.

The gunman, I mean Jerry, looked at me. As he did so, I felt a faint tingle all over my body as I created a large pale blue force field that surrounded myself and the hostages.

I took a deep breath and tried not to panic. Then I looked at Jerry and watched as the room began to turn blue. Jerry backed up some as he saw my eyes glow and out of instinct, fired at the force field. The bullets bounced off in comical fashion, smashing walls and glass inside of Ingram's store.

I released the energy from my eyes in a rocket- like bolt and hit Jerry square in the chest. As he went flying back, the room returned to its normal colors. With the energy gone from my eyes, my vision was no longer blue. To the people behind me, who were cheering now from the safety behind my force field, it likely looked very heroic.

In reality, I was actually aiming for Jerry's gun. Not his chest. Despite what the comics or movies show, it isn't easy aiming beams of concussive force from your eyes.If the beams came from your hands, the more traditional route, then aiming wasn't as difficult. Eyes, though were a different story.

Jerry slumped to the floor. No doubt his chest would be sore and severely bruised when he came to.

There wasn't an official name for what I had just done, but I called it my Impact Blast. The blue beams I shot from my eyes were force- based. So, if I wanted to, with these eye beams, I could punch a hole in a wall of steel with ease, but I couldn't melt or burn things. That's laser or heat vision.

The gunman from the van came running in. Ingram's door chime went off once more. "I hear sirens, we gotta go." The driver slowly saw me, standing inside of a large force field, and one of his partners on the ground.

"Bart, this kid shot Jerry with his eyes!" This gunman, freaking out as he was, seemed to be a fan of name- dropping. "Hi Bart," I said innocently with a wave. I wonder how stupid this guy was. I pointed as I said each name.

"Bart, Jerry, and what's your name again?" I said as I pointed to the name dropper. "Dom," he replied quickly. What an idiot he was.

Bart, who was brandishing a normal hand gun, smoothly shot Dom in the stomach. A single bullet casing fell to the ground and bounced around some. It sounded oddly loud because the room was quiet when the shot happened.

The people behind me gasped as Dom fell to the ground. "He talked too much. I knew he'd be a problem before we even did this job," Bart said as he ran and grabbed Dom's bag of loot. No honor among thieves I suppose. The door to the store chimed again. I glanced to the door, like everybody else, but we didn't see anybody.

I smiled.

The remaining two gunmen moved for the door, and then suddenly, their guns seemingly became became intangible in their hands, falling to the ground and through the floor. They looked at each other and then back to me.

I raised my hands again. "Don't look at me. I didn't do it." And in all honesty, I hadn't. Jen did. I couldn't see her, but she had to be in here somewhere. It was she that had come in the door unseen a moment ago.

Jen wielded two powers and turning things intangible was her go- to joke outside of scaring people while invisible. As long as she could touch it, and it wasn't too large, she could turn it intangible.

The gunman, still holding their bags, ran for their van. The door chime went off once more as they made their escape. Tires screeching, they took off down the street, followed closely by cop cars and a purple blur, which I could only assume was an Icon with superspeed.

I took down the force field from around myself and the other hostages. Jen turned visible as she extended her hand and gave me my flowers back. "I can't leave you alone for a second, can I?

I shrugged. "Wrong place- wrong time." Jen leaned in close to me. "You okay? I saw the force field," she said in a whisper. I shook my head.

Jen, was one of the few people who knew my secret. While my force field was a rare power that made me almost invincible, I was terrified to use it on myself. I didn't like tight spaces and being trapped inside an indestructible bubble was almost worse than having a gun pointed at me.

After being thanked by the hostages and workers of Ingram's, Asia returned to business, as she gave me the total for the watch.

"You still want me to pay for this? I just saved your lives." I said in a low voice to her. Jen cleared her throat. "We just saved your lives." I said. Asia smiled at me. "And we are very thankful, but-" I cut her off as I picked the box up off of the counter and held it close.

"This is mine. We will consider it payment." I said as I looked at Asia. "Cool?" As I asked the question, Asia and everything around her turned to a shade of blue. She looked at my eyes, and gasped some. She had seen what my eyes could do when in this state.

She had genuine fear on her face as she backed up. "Some hero you are," Asia said to me. Jen turned and walked out the store. "I never said I was a hero." I replied, as I gave her a little salute, smiled, and then followed Jen out the store, watch and flowers in hand.

CHAPTER 1

THE BATTLE OF AGES

"**B**efore we go in, I just want to draw attention to the fact that you literally just stopped a robbery, and then turned around and stole from the same store." Jen said, as she leaned against the brick wall before us. "It was more like accepting payment. They would have lost a lot more had I not stepped in." I said as I looked at the lilies in my hand one last time.

Jen had agreed to hold on to the box that contained Danielle's watch. I looked at the brick wall that she was leaning on. No matter how many times I saw it, on this day of the year it always felt different.

It stretched about half a mile in both directions and then wrapped around the block, forming a large square that encased a park. We were at one of the many entrances . Each wall had an entrance, and they all looked the same. The bricks formed an arch of sorts that held two large iron gates in place. Naturally the gates were open now, but at night they were usually closed.

Along with each of the surrounding walls having an entrance, right beside the entrance was a large gold- plated sign. In big letters, displayed under a spotlight it read: *Welcome to Ages Park: A Thank You to The Icons That Madethe Ultimate Sacrifice.*

Ages Park was well known. Not just in Atlas City, but world- wide. It was here that, twelve years ago, a battle took place that has since became known as The Battle of Ages. Jen and I were both five at the time but, like the rest of the world, we knew the stories well.

It was in this battle that many Icons, hero and villains alike, lost their lives to other dimensional foes of extreme power. According to the textbooks of Purgatory Academy, the battle lasted almost six days.

Six days of nonstop destruction, mayhem, and chaos. A large amount of the city was destroyed, but it was here, in the spot now considered a park, where many of the Icons lost their lives in a last stand. A last- ditch effort to save what was left of the city, so our world wouldn't eventually be lost.

We still were not sure how we even won., or if you really considered it a win. The attackers suddenly just left. Maybe they realized we wouldn't give up, and that there was no use in winning a destroyed world. That was a popular theory among some people. All we knew was that the same swirling green portals that brought them to our world had opened up again, and allowed them to just leave.

"You ready?" Jen asked as she placed a hand on my shoulder. "If there really is some person running around killing Icons, I'd rather not be waiting on the street. We all don't have a force field you know," she said as she looked at the city around us.

I took a deep breath and shook my head. At almost the same time, we entered the park. At first glance, it seemed like a normal park. Complete with lush green open areas, man-made ponds, fountains, wooden benches, a dog park, and even cobblestone walkways that created various paths for visitors.

It wasn't until you saw the statues that you could begin to see that Ages Park stood out when compared to almost any other location in Atlas City. For Atlas City, it was a long running tradition to honor a hero with a statue in their likeness, if they did a great deed.

It's almost like how those celebrities use to get those stars with their names in it for being so famous. These statues were made completely out of marble and were identical replicas of the heroes they honored.

As a hero, there was no greater honor that being immortalized with a statue and a plaque giving an account of the deed. Some heroes were lucky to get one or two statues, but then there were the heroes that had more statues than they knew what to do with.

To date the only hero with statues in the double digits was Mr. Impervious. Perhaps the most well- known and one of the most powerful Icons on the planet. He had statues of himself that stretched across the globe.

Jen and I kept walking. We passed a family of four who were posing with a statue and taking pictures. You know how stupid people look when they are taking selfies alone? Now throw a huge marble statue in the mix. You can get the idea of how weird it looked.

We passed more and more statues of the fallen heroes, and I was surprised at the amount of people that were here.

Jen and I come here once a year, every year, and usually don't see such a crowd. For some reason, though, today was different. It made me upset. Sure, some people worshipped Icons, and would want to take pictures with the statue of their favorite, and that was okay. But in Ages Park it was different. These statues were all of dead Icons, and to me, taking a picture with one was disrespectful. Like it almost made a mockery of the sacrifice that was made here.

Finally, I found the spot I was looking for. Near a corner of the park, an area that never seemed to have a visitor, except for me, stood a statue of two Icons holding hands and looking at each other. "I'll wait here," Jen said as she stopped walking with me.

I moved closer to the statue of the duo. On the right was a man, and to his side he was holding the hand of his wife., a cape wearing Icon who was considerably shorter than he was.

Not many knew of their union. It was considered the highest act of betrayal for a villain and a hero to have relations, as a result a villain and a hero that secretly got married had never been documented before.

Despite what the world had lead them to believe, love had won.

The male was the villain known as Blue Rush. He had a rather impressive set of abilities. From the stories I heard, he was the fastest of the Icons to ever live. He even outran Mr. Impervious on several occasions. An act that had never had been repeated.

To compliment his unmatched superspeed, he was able to generate a blue force field, similar to mine, for protection, granting him a high level of durability and allowing him to plow through objects that would kill a normal Icon with his super speed.

His wife, the lady to his side with the cape, was the heroic Icon known as Falldown. She was able to control gravity, giving her the ability to fly and make things either extremely light, or freakishly heavy.

She was a low- level hero, who normally wouldn't even be tasked with going up against a villain such as Blue Rush, but despite their differences, together they had created something special. They had created me.

My parents were among the many who, twelve years ago today, lost their lives in the Battle of Ages. By all accounts, many villains fought the other dimensional beings, but only my father fought alongside the heroes. He had lost his life saving her, and in this very spot, my mother stood by his side and fought until she couldn't anymore.

Despite their heroic demise, people still couldn't see past their origins. In the early years their statues were vandalized. Eventually, we had their plaques removed so that those who didn't know their story wouldn't judge what was left of their legacy.

My mother wasn't much of a hero, and my father was an infamous villain, and their son, the byproduct of some unspoken forbidden law, was just as well known. Many Icons knew of my heritage, and some even judged me for it.

Abomination, mistake, spawn, were some of the names I was called regularly in my youth. Names that, matched with my temper and both parents being gone, resulted in more fights than I could count. I am proud to say that I won nearly all of them, though.

"Well, only a few more days now guys," I said to their statue as I held the lilies. I stood back and looked up at them. Hero or villain, in the end, what had it got them? Disrespect from some of the same people they called friend, and a damn statue in a park that even their peers didn't visit. "I just can't figure out which path to take," I said as I continued to look up to them. The sun reflected off of their chest and into my eyes, causing me to wince

"We gotta get going," Jen said softly as she walked to me. "Hey Mr., and Mrs. M," she said as she looked at their statues. "I guess you're right," I said as I looked down at my feet.

I stepped forward and placed the lilies in a little groove that was between where their feet touched.

I only came here once a year, but for some reason, maybe because I was older, it didn't feel like often enough anymore. Once, I was just too afraid to come inside the park. I didn't want to look at the spot where I had lost them.

Now it seemed different somehow. I vowed to myself to visit more often. Coming here made me feel something inside of myself that I couldn't put a word to. But I liked it, and with the coming days, I would need as many good things to hold onto as I could.

"All set," I said to Jen. I made a motion to move towards the direction we had come. She held her hands up to stop me.

"We are cutting it short as it is," Jen said. "So, suck it up for a few miles, and get us there."

Somehow, I knew this was coming. While Jen knew of my anxiety of cramped spaces, she had no problem putting me in that position when it benefited her.

"We're not far from Purgatory, but if we walked you know how late to class we'd be? Plus, I don't feel like hearing Professor Santos's lecture about how being on time is a major part of the internships."

I didn't respond. She had a point, but I just waited for her to say what I knew was coming. "Flying however-" There it was. "Could get us there just in time."

While I could fly on my own, I was able to fly other people along with me, if I created a force field around myself.

Somehow, likely due to me getting a twisted mix of my parents' powers, I could control the gravity inside of the personal force fields I created. It put a strain on my body and made me hungry like you wouldn't believe but still, I could do it.

Jen extended her hand out and grabbed mine. "Come on bro, put your big boy pants on and get moving," she said as she adjusted her cap on her head and grinned at me. I drew my hand back as if I wanted to hit her with it, and then grabbed her outstretched hand once more.

Instantly, my force field sprang to life. A pale blue circle of swirling energy that surrounded us both. Force fields were rare for Icons, but with my small spaces issues, I would have traded it for normal invulnerability any day of the week. I could have made it smaller, but I could already feel myself beginning to sweat. I allowed it to grow a little larger than normal.

I still hated being inside it, but at least now it wasn't so cramped. "You ready?" I asked her as I gripped her hand tightly. She nodded as she held the box containing Danielle's watch close to her stomach.

"Don't drop that while we're up there." I said to her as I eyed the box. Jen shrugged her shoulders as she looked down at the box, too. "It would just land inside the force field anyway." She spun the box around and looked at the bottom of it. "Looks sturdy too. Only a fifty- fifty chance it would even break. I'm willing to take those odds." She said as she grinned.

I didn't respond.

"I'm just joking." Jen said. "I won't drop the stupid, expensive watch for your villain girlfriend. Now can we get going?"

Nodding, I took a deep breath and in the blink of an eye we exploded into the air, and made our way to the school, leaving a faint blue trail behind us .

CHAPTER 2

PURGATORY ACADEMY

There are few feelings in this world that can compare to flying. Outside of kissing Danielle, to me, nothing else even comes close. In honesty, it's probably my favorite power out of the four I possess.

Flying was freedom. Unmatched, uncontrolled, freedom. I just loved it. From zooming between clouds, to soaring over the city and watching the people below. It was like flying gave me entry to a special world in the sky that only few had access to.

Well, that last part wasn't totally true. Actually, many Icons could fly, in some form or another. Every form just wasn't as *great*. Some Icons had wings like angels that allowed them to fly with moderate speed. While other Icons could hover, but that was it. To a Void, I mean normal person, hovering is great. To an Icon, though, hovering sucked.

Imagine being able to lift yourself off the ground. For a second you feel that elusive power of flying, and then you realize you can only just drift along, maybe a few feet off the ground. Basically, useless. Many an Icon that could hover, usually kept that power to themselves, and hopefully had a better power in their arsenal.

Then you have some Icons that can actually fly, but only at speeds that they could run if they were on the ground. That's not great by any means, but it's a damn bit better than hovering.

Finally, there's supreme flight. That's what I could do. With supreme flight, an Icon could will themselves to fly as quick as they wanted. As long as your body held up, you could just keep going along.

"You okay over there?" I asked as I glanced to Jen. She smiled and gave me a wink up as I expanded my force field a little more. Making it almost the length of a bus. I could tolerate it better now.

Jen loved flying. She always voiced how she wished it was one of her powers, but it just wasn't in her cards. I got lucky. Like Jen, both of my parents were Icons, but one was able to control gravity. Icon powers don't always get passed down, but once in a while, a distorted version of a parent's power was given to their offspring.

Jen on the other hand, had two Icon parents, but neither could do anything close to flying. Her father was the Icon known as Life-Life. He wielded the power of healing. Allowing him to heal others at will, while her mother had powers of the techy variety.

Jen's powers weren't bad, but as in many parts of life, we often want what we can't or didn't have, and for Jen that was flight. Lucky for her, she grew up with a guy who could fly, and didn't mind zooming her around when he was able.

I began to slow down some to just enjoy the moment up here, if only for a second. From here I could see almost all of the city. Atlas City had two districts. The Diamond and Ebony Districts.

The Diamond District, where Jen and I lived, could be seen from here. It was the part of the city that never went dark. From here it looked like a dome of yellow energy pulsated and covered half of the city. Even when it should have been night time, it was still pretty bright out and you could see stars showering across the sky almost non- stop. This district was also home to many of the heroes of Atlas City, and the base location for many of its supergroups.

I shifted my glance from the dome of yellow to the contrasting dark purple dome beside it. This was the Ebony

District, a direct contrast to the Diamond District in almost every way. In the Ebony District, there was eternal darkness. No matter the time of day or night, it was always dark.

Naturally, crime was a little higher in Ebony District, and more villains, including my girlfriend, called it home. Having these two districts created a bonus third district of sorts. We called it the Abyss. A very small area where the two major districts touched each other, and formed a literal gray zone. An area where virtually nobody lived, or would even cross through. It was a place of gloom on the level which even the Ebony District couldn't match.

Now, the clear divide of night and day in Atlas City was the result of two extremely well- known Icons, respectfully named Diamond and Ebony. They, along with their sister Flora, were mythical in nature, and were often referred to as The High Trinity.

They were also said to be the only triplet Icons known to exist. While Diamond and Ebony projected their inner powers of night and day on the city, Flora gave life to it. Trees, grass, and flowers, could all survive in almost any weather because of her.

According to stories, these three were old, I mean very old. Over two hundred years old, if you believed the text books. Because their primary powers were connected directly to the earth, they seemed very long lived. The text also goes on to say that these three were also the younger siblings to Atlas himself, one of the first documented Icons.

Naturally, none of this has been proven, but that's what the books say, and that's what's taught in Purgatory. Even though they are supposed to still be alive today, nobody even knows what Diamond, Ebony, or Flora looked like, or if they even exist. To Icons, they were the equivalent of fairy tales.

"There it is," Jen said as she pointed down. Her words interrupted my thoughts as I gazed upon the city below us.

Yep, there it was. Coming into our view as I began to descend, into the bright dome that was the Diamond District was Purgatory Academy. The world's leading school in Icon development. Icons essentially, went to school like normal people, with minor changes.

For one, as I already mentioned, we didn't get up as early because our classes started at eleven and ended at four. We only went to school from the ages of five to seventeen, and along with basic skills like math or science, we also learned about Icon history, and the powers we each possessed.

Purgatory Academy was *the* school to go to if you were an Icon. There were other schools around the country for Icons, and some were rather good, but not as good as Purgatory. Most people there had to have either, a connection to somebody famous, extreme wealth, or something else that set them apart.

In our case, Jen's dad was our in. Not only was he an Icon, but he belonged to the world's leading supergroup, The Imperial Lords. This alone was enough to gain entry. Even if I wasn't raised by Jen's dad, I'd still likely have ended up in Purgatory.

I still had four powers, and by Icon standards that was unheard of, and on paper, that alone was a signal that I could do great things, if I decided to. That was the sort of thing that Purgatory thrived on and the heads of the school would have been eager to grant me admission, regardless of my heritage.

I decreased my speed as we began our descent . The school was becoming easier to see now as we got closer.

The campus surrounding the center building was huge. It almost looked like one of those college campuses that Voids went to. The campus had four buildings. The main center building where all the primary education took place, the library, a power training facility, and of course, a world- class cafeteria with almost any food you could want.

Each building was connected by adjoining glass walkways and from the sky almost looked like a giant- sized baseball diamond, complete with plenty of grass fields for lounging on between classes, and a water feature made in the shape of the school's initials.

Jen and I landed on the steps to the main building. What stood in front of us, directly in front of the school, was a statue of an Icon that I, for lack of a better word, hated. I could feel my jaw clench just by looking at it.

His name was Flex, and at only nineteen he had set himself apart as one of the leading heroes of the future. He had a damn statue already for Atlas' sake.

His powers were as impressive as the feats had had done to display them. He, like me, could fly at supreme speeds, but that was where our similarities stopped.

He also had growing invulnerability. I say growing, because invulnerability, was one of the few powers that got stronger as an Icon aged. Flex got his powers at age twelve so it had already matured a good bit. Now, at nineteen, virtually no bullet, knife, or fire could harm him, but wasn't immune to all forms of damage.

Finally, he had supreme strength. A power that I wished I had. Don't get me wrong, I'm pretty strong too, and strength was my fourth power, but I only have enhanced strength. Powers usually vary in levels. Enhanced, super, and then the final tier of supreme.

So, while I could lift a car over my head with ease and hurl it about a hundred feet, Flex could catch a falling plane out of the sky, and then hurl it to the moon. See the difference?

With his powerset he was a natural fit for the Imperial Lords, and is slated to be the next hero to take over after Mr. Impervious decides to hang up his cape.

The statue was awarded to Flex, just under a year ago while he saved most of the lives in the school. A plane was actually falling out of the sky, and headed directly for Purgatory Academy.

Several Icons in the school could have come together to save the day, but no. Instead they all looked to Flex. Their heroic mascot. While Flex didn't actually catch the plane, and hurl it to the moon, he did snatch it out of the sky as if it was a falling ball and placed it in a safe area, saving not only the people in the school, but those on the plane as well.

He did all of this on his internship and set himself up for stardom. The world loved Flex, but to me, he was the same old asshat that had picked on me in Purgatory, that eventually led to a showdown between us both that destroyed three classrooms, and put a teacher in the hospital next door that was specially made for Icons.

"You can stand here and glare at this statue of rippling Icon eye candy if you want to," Oh, yeah, Jen had a thing for Flex. "But I'm going to class before the bell rings." she darted off into the building, as I resisted the urge to hit this statue with my Impact Blast.

I walked by the statue, waved 'an offensive hand gesture to it, and headed to the main building. While the campus had some of the best financial backers in the world, and cutting-edge technology, the building itself looked like some old castle.

Complete with the pointy roofs, creepy windows, and everything. If there was ever a building that needed an upgrade, this was it.

While Jen rushed to class, I rushed to my locker to put Danielle's watch away for safekeeping. I grimaced at the amount of papers splattered on the walls. The hallway was covered from top to bottom with posters about the two major events coming up.

One was a concert by a famous artist who was an Atlas City native, who went by the name Young Pyro, and the other was for the end of school year's dance.

Both events I planned to attend. Danielle had said no about coming to the dance with me, but I'm thinking an expensive watch she wanted could maybe change her mind.

I got the books I needed for class, and then slammed the door to my locker. I checked the huge clock in the hallway. "Still got two minutes before the bell rings," I said to myself as I smiled. Naturally, at that moment, the damn bell rings.

"Stupid slow clock," I said as I dashed up the hallway.

It would have been faster to fly to up the hallway, but use of powers was strictly forbidden inside of Purgatory. A rule I utterly broke when I got into a fight with Flex. A fight people still talk about to this day, might I add.

I came to my class door and looked inside. Everybody was listening as if they actually cared what Professor Santos had to say. Jen was sitting in her desk, directly beside my empty one.

She glanced up and stuck her tongue out at me. The girl sitting in front of her looked my way, and rolled her eyes as she removed a pill bottle from her bag. I was already spoken for but still, this girl was extremely cute. No, not cute. Puppies were cute, newborn babies with big cheeks were cute, this girl was gorgeous.

She looked back down to her paper, and then to me again. This time she actually glared at me and for a second, I could see the mist tendrils forming around her fingertips, causing frost to appear around the pen she was holding.

Her name was Zeva Greene. She had a pretty standard power set. Ice manipulation combined with x-ray, and enhanced vision. All of which ranked on a super level. She was also the little sister of Flex, which probably was the reason she couldn't stand me.

Remember that fight I said people still talked about? Yeah, she wasn't a fan of it at all. Well screw her, and her trash talking brother. Even if she did look like a goddess.

Professor Santos continued to speak, oblivious to me lurking at the door. He was an odd- looking man. He was about six feet tall, three hundred pounds, with buzz cut red hair, and some of the palest skin I've ever seen in my life.

Before I could figure out if I wanted to enter the class or just skip it for the day, Professor Santos, while standing in the same spot, spun his entire upper body around to face me. Maybe he wasn't oblivious to my presence after all.

Professor Santos, had elastic powers. Making him able to stretch his body in almost any manner. So, despite, his obese appearance, he was pretty limber.

He motioned his hand for me to come in, and I did so, shutting the door hard behind me. No need to be cautious of the noise now anyway. "Nice of you to join us, Mr. Monroe." I gave him a slight nod. A nod that he responded to with a smug grin that looked forced.

"I was just about to talk to the class about the internships, and their auditions. Considering your," he paused for a moment. "Less than desirable parents, this could be a topic you may want to pay attention to. Perhaps the greater Icon community will stop calling you an abomination, and start seeing you as a hero."

Jen took in a deep breath beside me. I usually had no problem with Professor Santos, but it was widely known that he hated me. Apparently, back in the day, he had a thing for my mother, before my father swept her off her feet, and took her away from him.

Literally, my father ran by when Santos and my mom were on a date and snatched her away from him. What started out as a feud for my parents eventually, became something more. Santos, apparently was still bitter.

"Powers aside, Mr. Monroe, the faculty here at the academy have faith that you will become something great. I, myself, am not so sure." Some of the students in the class laughed.

This seemed to fuel Santos and made him laugh under his breath. "Now, let's discuss your auditions. Listen closely, because everything you've learned up to this point has prepared you. Will you walk, fly, superspeed, or teleport down the path of greatness?"

Professor Santos looked at Zeva as he said this. Zeva came from what was called *pure-stock*. Meaning every single member of her family had powers. Not a single void on the family tree. "Or will you go on to become infamous," he said as he looked at me.

I could have avoided his gaze, but what would be the fun in that? I looked back at him, smiled, and then put my head on my desk. Professor Santos huffed, and then stopped looking in my direction.

I exhaled. The disturbing part was that I had still had no idea which path I was going to choose when this was all over. On the bright side, I still had some time. I just had to tolerate Santos a little longer. A few more days and this would be over.

I'll be on my internship, and headed for my destiny. One way, or another.

43

CHAPTER 3

MY TEACHER'S AN ASSHOLE

Professor Santos paused for a second and took a few sips of his morning coffee. I could have used some coffee myself. I wasn't tired, but I could still feel the cold chill that Zeva was giving off, and warm coffee would take a little of the edge off.

I leaned up in my chair. "Do you mind? It's freezing in here." I whispered to her. She acted like she didn't hear me, as she popped a pill in her mouth. She took those damn vitamins once every hour or so. She was incredibly fit, so whatever they were, they were working. Maybe I should get myself some of those.

Even though she didn't respond to my request, I could feel the area we sat in get a little warmer as her powers calmed down.

As I sat here behind her I realized fully that, Zeva Greene really had no reason not to like me. Okay, her brother and I got in a fight. So, what?. Things like that happened. I secretly thought she didn't like me not only because of my clash with her brother, but because many people said I, the younger and less experienced Icon, had won the fight.

His invulnerability wasn't mature enough to completely ignore my Impact Blast back then. Still may not be able to now for all I know. At the time, Flex was the top dog at the school. His powers were to be envied, and never rivaled in comparison. His natural abilities combined with his family tree made the entire Icon community love him, and losing to me, the one people considered a half- villain bastard of all the people, had tarnished his golden boy persona.

I will give him credit when it's due, though. Flex is one of the few natural forces that my force field has a hard time standing against. During the fight, his supreme strength fueled punches did puncture my field. Not by a lot, but still it was enough to make me worry.

A crack in the only form of defense standing between you, and an Icon strong enough to punch a hole in a mountain would worry anybody. I continued to look at Zeva as she sat there, paying me no attention. She had short black hair, strong cheek bones, olive- colored skin, and that curvy, athletic figure.

She was no stranger to the gym and it showed. Even though she was in the same academy uniform as Jen and I, she filled it out very well. I made a mental note that I had to get me some of those vitamins. No maybes about it.

"Thanks," I whispered to her again. Still no reply.

Zeva's ice ability, like many people with elemental powers, was tied to her emotions. It was pretty cool actually, no pun intended. In a good fight, if she put her heart into it, her abilities would get an extra boost if she was emotional enough. That could turn the battle her way because, according to whispers around school, her ice abilities were average at best.

"Tomorrow morning, I expect you all to be on time." Professor Santos said. I was paying so much attention to Zeva, that I hadn't realized he had begun walking around the room, and was standing beside my desk.

He looked around the room and then down to me sitting in my chair. "Be. On. Time!" I twisted my face up at him and for a second, the room suddenly shifted to blue.

It was only a second but judging from how Professor Santos raised his eyebrows, and moved away from my desk, he saw my eyes change for an instant.

"When you arrive tomorrow, instead of coming here, you will head over to the training facility building and wait for your name to be called. Once your name is called, your moment to shine will be upon you."

I glanced at Jen who seemed to be sketching on a sheet of paper that was intended for notes. Seeing as her father, a working Icon in a well- known supergroup had raised us, we knew pretty well how the process went. Her dad, Marcus or Mr. Reid as I called him, had been talking about the audition process for the better part of the last month.

Along with that, he was trying to help Jen and I find what was called a True Name. Almost all Icons are born Voids. Many don't get their powers until years later, and as such we have the names we were born with.

We go by that name for most of our lives, until the internship comes along. At some point in that two year's stretch we have to pick the name we will go by when we decide to go hero or villain. That's our True Name. Ryan Greene, went on to become Flex. Marcus Reid, went on to become Life-Line.

Jen was leaning towards the name Houdini, but I'm not sure if she stuck with it. I had no idea what I wanted to be called, but Mr. Reid told me it would come to me when the time was right.

Professor Santos continued to talk, despite some of the class not even paying attention anymore. "This single moment will impact your internships. We will have a few reps of some supergroups onsite in person, while many others will be watching via live feed. After every student who is eligible has auditioned, the supergroup heads will decide if they want you or not. This selection process will take a few hours."

Professor Santos, paused as he looked to his desk. His walking had taken him a good distance from it. His arm stretched out to about nine feet and grabbed the coffee mug on his desk. His neck then followed, stretching to the same length. He sipped his coffee, and then returned to his normal shape.

This was his only power, and I personally thought elastic powers were gross. They just looked weird to me. Like every time they were used, the Icon looked like they were taffy being pulled. On the flip side, while pretty useless, it did give you a decent amount of resistance to physical damage.

Heat- or ice- based powers could take you down in a second, but done right, bullets could hit Santos and then bounce back as if being fired from a sling shot. Not sure why he decided to go the civilian route, but here he was. Hate him as I may, he had an ability that could be good no matter which side you chose.

So even if I did decide to use my Impact Blast on him, an urge that I had on a regular basis, it would do no damage at all. Not to mention it would get me kicked out of school. Destroy a few classrooms, Mr. Reid could talk that away. Attacking a teacher, not so much. Plus, I'd look like an idiot, if my own power was bounced back at me.

"After selected," Professor Santos continued, "you will pack your bags, and the next day or so you will start your two-year internship with the group that selects you. These two years will allow you to use your powers in real life instances, and not just for destruction."

As he said the words *destruction*, he stretched it out some and clearly was looking at me. I could hear a few kids in the class choke laughter under their breath. "After these two years, your education will be complete." He clapped his hands together as if he was removing dirt from them. "You will venture out into the world and become either a hero, or villain."

To my surprise, Zeva raised her hand. The entire class was so silent you could hear a hero's cape flap across the city. "Yes, Zeva?" Santos said in a tone that was way nicer than any he had used for me.

"Do you know of any families that have both heroes and villains?" Santos and myself both seemed to grimace at the same time. It was a damn weird question to ask. I glanced at Jen who shrugged and then went back to her sketching. Professor Santos clear his throat as he rubbed his chin.

Zeva continued "I think it would be pretty messed up if a hero brother had to take down their villain family member." Professor Santos nodded somewhat.

"I suppose it has happened here or there. It would be crazy to say it hasn't but if it has, it is very rare. I can't think of any instances myself, though. Usually when an Icon is raised by hero or villain, those ideals and beliefs are set in their being." Santos shrugged. "Then again some people are just destined to be what they are."

Santos glanced in my direction. "Mr. Monroe is living proof that some things, just happen." Then he looked at Zeva again. "Just as your family is a shining example of purestock heroes." He turned to walk away as Zeva smiled at him and then adjusted herself in her chair. I couldn't help but stare at her. Why would she ask that? As if she was trying to get me singled out by Santos. The favorite student versus the hated one.

It was time to tug the cape, as they say. I raised my hand. I couldn't help it. Professor Santos looked at me, sighed and then flicked his hand towards me. "Yes, Mr. Monroe?" I cleared my throat. "What if you didn't want to be a villain or hero? What if you decided to be, oh I don't know, an underpaid, overweight, bitter teacher instead?"

A few people in the class drew in a breath. Zeva turned in her seat and looked at me in disgust as her pencil became completely frosted over, and snapped in her hand. "Nice," Jen said to the side as she smiled and keep right on sketching without looking up.

Professor Santos, now a little red in the face, walked to his desk and slowly sat down. He took a few breaths in before he said anything. "Take a look around class. Some of the people next to you will go on to do great things, while others will surely go into the family business and either become low rate heroes, or even villains. Fancy powers aren't enough to actually cut it in the real world. You need drive and sadly, some just don't have it."

"A low rate hero, that still didn't want you," I said under my breath but it was loud enough for the people up front, including Professor Santos, to hear. "Also, a low rate hero that gave her life in the Battle of Ages, while you were sitting here sharpening pencils, grading tests, and adjusting your waistband."

Jen stuck her fist out to me, which I bumped in kind with my own fist. I could see the anger oozing from the face of Professor Santos. He reflexively cracked his knuckles as his nostrils flared.

He told us to read something, but I wasn't paying attention. I packed up my books and raised my hand once more. He didn't even say my name he just looked at me. It took him a few seconds to respond, as if he didn't know if he wanted to acknowledge me. "What?" Professor Santos finally said.

"I need to go the bathroom," I said as I stood with my things. "You're taking your books to the bathroom?" he asked. "Reading material," I replied back to him. He shook his head. "Go," he said to me as he looked down to his desk, and began looking over some papers.

His attitude was nothing new, but on today of all days, the day of the Battle of Ages anniversary I couldn't deal with it. My Impact Blast couldn't hurt him, but I could create a force field around his head and close it in until his skull imploded if I wanted to. Figured it be better if I just left early.

I leaned over to Jen and whispered in her ear, "see you later sucker, enjoy class." I walked to the door and as I opened it I shot Jen a grin across my shoulder. She didn't let the words out, but I could tell what she silently mouthed.

I hate you.

I gave her a thumb's up and left the class.

CHAPTER 4

HOME SWEET HOME

Okay, so my excuse to get out of class wasn't a complete lie. I did actually go to the bathroom, and reading materials were needed. Ten minutes later I was done, and considerably lighter. Now I had the rest of the day before me.

I pulled out my phone and gave Danielle a call. She picked up only after a few rings. "Hey handsome," was her reply. Her voice made me smile instantly. It was soft, and she always had a way of making it sound very sexy. "Hey you," I replied back. "I'm out of class for the day, and have some time to kill before I head home. Want me to come over?"

Please say yes. Please say yes. I thought to myself. I could feel my eyes darting from side to side as I walked through the halls and waited for her answer. A muffled sound came back to me in reply. "Hello," I said back once more as I grabbed my backpack from my locker and stuffed her watch inside. "Sorry boo, I dropped my phone. I'd love for you to come by but I'm out with some friends looking for a bank."

I could feel my face grimace, as I slung my backpack over my shoulder. "I assume you don't mean you're looking for a bank for traditional purposes." I said with a slight laugh. "You'd be right," Danielle replied back to me. "Who's with you?" I asked. There was a slight pause as she cleared her throat.

"It's me, Ron, and Angelica," she quickly replied back. I burst out laughing as I pushed the door open and trotted down the front steps of Purgatory.

Ron and Angelica were two Icons who had chosen to go down the villain side of the street after their internship. To be honest, Ron didn't even finish his internship. He had a power that was as pointless as the ones Angelica had. Ron went by the name Aerosol and could, at will, blow a pink cloud- like mist from his mouth. Said mist could either make a large group of people extremely happy or severely sad. The mist he created did, however have a remarkable radius.

Still, it sounds like a horrible power, because it is. Despite that, he was the powerhouse between the two. Angelica happened to have two powers, but both were horrible. She could hover a massive two feet off of the ground, and talk to birds. Birds. It would have been better if she could talk to all animals, or even control them. That would have been cool, but no, she could only talk to birds.

"Don't laugh," she said as her voice dropped to a whisper. "It's all I could find on short notice." As I continued to laugh I could hear her exhale on the other end. "You couldn't find another person with a better powerset to help you? This would be your first official, major act as a villain. Don't blow it because of the help."

"Well, the strongest Icon I know is my boyfriend and he's too much of an upstanding citizen to rob a bank," she hissed back to me.

"Ew, burn!" I heard a voice call out in the background with a laugh. "Shut up," Danielle said. "Wait, was that Ron? Do I need to-" "No, you don't need to do anything," she said as she cut me off. "Good. Tell him to watch his mouth before he gets a blast between the eyes, that mist- spitting asshole." "Hunter said hi guys." Danielle said to her friends with her.

"No, I didn't," I said in the phone as I raised my voice some. "Hey guys give me a minute. Okay they aren't near me now," she said in a low whisper. "You think I don't know their powers suck? I do. They were all I could find on short notice. I figured I could use them as bait at least. Ron could do his thing, I'll give Angelica a gun, and then I can grab the goods, and get away alone if need be. I mean, if they make it we will split it, but otherwise I'm planning on returning home, solo."

I felt my chest stick out as I smiled. This did make sense. Danielle's powers were borderline impressive and they could allow for a good getaway. Danielle had darkness powers that worked on what was commonly referred to as a Two-Fold. A Two-Fold, is pretty much having a power that, under the right conditions, can have an extra attribute or boost to the current attribute. In Danielle's case, she could create dark blast of energy from her hands, very similar to my eye beams but not as strong, normally.

I say normally because, while her blasts are weak, they can become stronger if she uses them at night. Luckily for her, she happens to live in the Ebony District, where darkness is eternal. Her second ability, my personal favorite, allowed her to turn into a living, corporeal mist shadow. In that form she can hover, move through solid objects, and not be harmed. She could only stay in this form for a few minutes, but still it was supremely cool.

"Look babe, I have to run. We are just checking things out tonight, but you can come over tomorrow, after you're done. Sound good?"

"Yes ma'am," I replied back. "We're the same age, you ass. I hate when you do that," she said over a laugh. "Talk to you later." I replied back one last time and the phone went silent.

I shoved my cell in my pocket and looked around. I hadn't realized that I was still standing on the campus grounds.

I really had nothing to do now that Danielle was too busy with her underpowered friends. I could go catch a movie, but nothing was out that I really wanted to see. I could just head on home and relax. Make myself a sandwich of epic proportions, and watch some movies there.

Since time was on my side I decided to walk because it was so nice out. Not only that but flying too much makes me hungry. Many people believe that Icons with super speed are the only ones that burn enough calories to want to eat their body weight in food, but trying holding yourself up in the air as you move around at the speed of sound. In my mind it's like doing a million pullups. Either way, doing it too long makes you very hungry and very tired.

I cut through the grass on the field and headed to the streets. Each tree I walked by either turned and watched me as I passed or stretched its branches towards me to touch me. The flowers were even worse. They weren't as rooted as the trees and every now and again they will jump from the ground and walk along with you.

This was Flora at work. While her sibling's Ebony and Diamond control light and darkness, Flora as her name suggested, gave almost all plant life in Atlas City the ability to be sentient. This was fine, but they were just so damn nice.

These trees were tame compared to some others. Hell, the trees on Strome Ave, actually whistle music as people walk by and if you go to the park on Brentmoor, and walk barefoot, the grass will literally massage your feet as you walk through it.

This was one of the hardest things for visitors to Atlas City to get used to, but once you did it was pretty cool. Even the plants in the Ebony District were nice, and they lived in darkness year- round.

Several news vans were unloading equipment on the streets as I continued home. Because this was the anniversary of the Battle of Ages, reporters would be scattered through the city to broadcast various stories about events that happen all those years ago. Did they ever mention my mother or father on those broadcasts? Rarely.

On the few times I had heard mention of my folks, it was usually not in the best of ways. I didn't let it bother me, though. Some people reported what they wanted to, how they wanted to. I did make a mental note of the ones who spoke ill of them . Just in case I decide to go the villain route like pops, I'll have a list of people I will go visit first.

Eventually I made it to my house. The walk took more out of me than I expected and according to the damp shirt sticking to my back, and the faint hint of musk coming from my armpits, I needed a shower. As I looked at the house, I felt like I was going to need a new pair of underwear, too.

The home I grew up in with the Reid's was fine. It looked normal, like it always did. Two stories, tan paint, blue shutters, blue door, massive porch, and green grass that didn't grow so it didn't have to be cut. Actually, no grass in Atlas City was cut. The grass was alive remember, so that was basically murder to most people.

Back to the house. It even came with a built- on two- car garage. The downside, and what caused me to almost need a fresh pair of underwear were the cars parked in the garage. Both of Jen's parents were home. But why?

I looked at my phone once more. It was only five minutes to twelve. Why were they home so early? Mr. Reid was a full-time hero. He usually didn't get home until late. Karen Reid was the breadwinner, since being a hero didn't pay. Another reason villains have more fun. She was the lead engineer for some space tech company called Nimcor.

She was an Icon who decided to go the way of just getting a job. Her powers weren't usually needed for hero work anyway. She was able to fix, understand, and build, all things tech. Because of this, she demanded a salary double what usually was paid for the role. She pulled in six figures a year for only working part time hours. Yet still, she wasn't due home until around four.

Well, I could always just leave, right? It's not like anybody had seen me yet. As if on cue, that was when the door leading from the garage to the house opened. I don't know if it was the shock, but I couldn't remember the door opening that fast before in all my years here. It was like it wanted me to get caught. Coming through the door was Mrs. Reid.

She was a nice woman, and she looked like she was in her early thirties even though she was almost fifty. She had long black hair, a pointy nose, freckles and wore glasses. She always joked that she was destined to work with computers, because she already looked like a nerd.

She saw me standing there clutching my backpack and tilted her head somewhat. "Hey Hunter. Short day?" she said as she moved to her silver BMW and grabbed some bags out of the back seat and put them on the ground.

"See you inside, dear," she said as she slammed the door shut and moved to the trunk. From how she was tossing stuff around and grunting, she was clearly looking for something, so I headed on into the house. Maybe I could get inside and up to my room without being questioned.

As usual, I had no such luck. I felt my brow raise as I walked toward the house and entered through the same door that Mrs. Reid had used moments ago.

"So, let me get this straight." I heard the booming voice of Mr. Reid through the house as I got inside. "He insulted your sister, and called her a baseball cap- wearing smartass? To which you replied by hitting him?" I made it to the kitchen and saw two people.

Sitting on a chair, with a scrape on his head and a black eye was Jen's little brother, Junior. He had his head propped up in his hand and was looking down at his red shoes, avoiding the man standing above him.

The man stood about six feet tall, had a stern jaw, and a brown buzz cut. His outfit was gray and covered his body from head to toe, and he had a green cape on. Naturally this was Mr. Reid, aka Life-Line. "The funny part about it," Mr. Reid said as his left hand began to glow in the same color green as his cape. "That is an accurate description of your sister, and wasn't worth getting in a fight over."

He raised his glowing hand to his son and moved it near his face. Instantly, as if time sped up, the scrape healed, and so did the black eye. Mr. Reid wasn't a powerhouse, but he was one of the most popular Icons in the city.

For the longest time, he didn't even know he was an Icon, until he was about thirteen, and his friend cut himself. From the stories he told us, the massive cut on his buddy's hand was bleeding so badly, that his friend fainted from the sight of it.

Mr. Reid then went to cover his friend's hand to slow the blood, but just then his hand began to glow, and in seconds, the cut healed.

He later found out that he was able to heal others. An extremely rare ability for Icons. As a result, he was scouted by almost all of the major Icons of that day and age, but he decided to go with the most famous group around, when his time came.

Even though Life-Line was powerful, some things he simply couldn't heal on others. Shot by a bullet, he can heal that. Head chopped off, on the other hand, there was no coming back from. He found that out the hard way, when a team member was killed two years ago.

He turned and looked at me. "What are you doing home so early?" He looked at the clock on the stove and then back to me. Junior sat up and glance at me. "Oh. I." I let out a sigh. "Honestly, Santos was coming down on me hard today. That and the anniversary of the battle just weighed down on me so I left."

Sometimes, honesty really was the best policy. Mr. Reid twisted his mouth as he shook his head. "Yeah, that Santos always was a dick." He said with a smile. Junior laughed out loud. "Don't get too happy, you're still grounded for fighting," Mr. Reid said sternly. Junior's smile faded away as fast as his wounds had moments ago.

"Throw your ice pack away and go help your mother unload all that techy crap she loves to bring home from work."

Mr. Reid said casually as he rubbed his son's head. Junior looked at the icepack still in his hand.

It was clenched tightly in his fist. He opened his hand and the ice pack began to float in the air. Quickly it zoomed across the room, to the trash can, which in response opened its lid and then shut as the ice pack landed inside.

Mrs. Reid walked in. and dropped a bag of rocks on the table. "Junior, come with me I need your help," she said to him casually. Mr. Reid smiled, "Didn't I tell you she would?" Junior removed one of the rocks from the bag as I sat down at the kitchen table and removed a cookie from a center dish.

"Go ahead and transform it. I'm working on a device that, in theory can mimic powers similar to yours and Icons like Gem. Junior shrugged and held onto the rock. It went from rust and dirty, to gold and shiny in an instant. He now held a rock in his hand of solid gold.

Like many, Junior had two abilities in his powerset. His prime power was telekinesis on a supreme scale. He could move anything of any size as long as his body could hold up to the pressure. In this case he was lucky.

Some Icons could only move things with their mind if they could lift it with their own hands too. His secondary power was that he could turn anything inorganic to gold. It seems cool, but the power isn't as uncommon as one would think. So, by default, gold didn't have as much value as it once did, but still could fetch a pretty penny.

Mrs. Reid smiled and walked off through the kitchen, stopped to give Mr. Reid a kiss on the cheek and left the room, as her heels clicked through the house. Junior, and his bag of rocks followed.

"Those two will be in her lab for a while." Mr. Reid said as he sat down at the table with me and ate a cookie. "You're home pretty early, too." I said two him as I downed my fourth cookie. "Yeah, but only for a little bit. I had to pick Junior up, and wanted to grab some food before the transport takes me back to base."

He chomped on his cookie some more as crumbs fell on his costume. "You know I hate the food there. It's that meatless meat that they use. Meatless meat! It's worse than turkey bacon. Don't even get me started on that," he said as he made a face and continued to eat the cookie.

"Well, I better be off," Mr. Reid said as he grabbed a bag from the counter and headed to the door. Just then Mrs. Reid came back into the kitchen. She had her shoes off now, so I couldn't hear her coming.

"Marcus, they just reported on the news that another dead Icon was found," she said as she raised her brow and put her hand on her hip. "Anything we should worry about?" I looked at him and he avoided every eye in the room. "Honey, the

Lords are looking into it." "Well the Imperial Lords, mighty as they might be, don't run this house, so if there is something your family should know, secret or not, promise me you will tell us. For Atlas' sake Hunter and Jennifer are out her walking around like everything is fine."

Mrs. Reid was breathing heavy now as she used her last breath to finish her statement. Mr. Reid let the door knob go, and moved to place his arm around his wife. "You guys will always be my first priority." He kissed her on the forehead, and walked past me, then stopped.

"Hunter." I turned to him with my fifth cookie in my mouth. "First, easy on the cookies." I shook my head as I continued to chew. Mrs. Reid turned and walked out of the kitchen. Mr. Reid lowered his voice. "When you and Jen are out, keep your eyes open. If you see anything off, and I mean anything, make those eyes blue. You got me?"

"I got it." I said as I straightened up in my chair. Whatever was going on must have been serious for him to pretty much give me the go ahead to use my powers if need be. For an Icon of his status to tell another Icon who hasn't taken his vows yet that, said a lot.

He patted me on the shoulder. "Good man," and then left through the door, letting it slam behind him and leaving me alone with nothing but cookies to keep me occupied.

CHAPTER 5

THE PONY SHOW

Jen and I arrived to Purgatory on time the next day, believe it or not. Naturally she was ready to show her powers off. She did it all the time and now she had a legit excuse. Myself, I was in no hurry to do my thing.

I didn't know what I wanted to do, but I knew I didn't want to be late to see the others who were going to perform alongside me. I had no intentions of showing off, but I damn sure wasn't going to be shown up, and unless they had been keeping it a secret, nobody else in the school had four powers. So, in theory, I had nothing to worry about, but there were some Icons in the school who, although they only had one or two powers, they were impressive powers.

We were among some of the first students to find seats, Jen and I. What was to come was only for people who were old enough to participate, but most of the school still turned out to watch the older Icons, and it was a great excuse for teachers and students alike to get out of class early.

The auditions took place in the campus' power training building and this building had everything. I looked around and then heard the sound of a bag rattling. I instantly looked at Jen. She was eating a bag of chips and leaned back on the bleachers we were sitting on and propped her feet up. "Well, this should be an interesting morning." she said as she tossed a chip in her mouth. She crunched on it loudly, and rubbed her stomach before plunging her hand back in the bag.

"I just hope I go last, or at least close to the end." I said casually. "That way I can know how thick to lay it on." Jen pulled another plate- size chip from her bag, ate it, and then wiped her crumb- filled hands on her blue Purgatory sweats. "What do you mean?" she asked me as she chewed.

"I can see how well the other people do and gauge it. If everybody sucks, I don't need to put on a show and flash all of my powers." "Yeah whatever, you just don't want to flex your force field?" Jen said to me. I sighed. "Please don't say that word."

"What? Force Field?" She asked. I casually replied, "No, Flex." Jen laughed as I rolled my eyes and smiled. "It has nothing to do with that, though. I just don't like being told what to do, like I'm some dog in a show." Jen simply eyed me.

"Maybe I'll just say screw it and destroy the place. Or freak some people out and have some fun with it." Jen shook her head. "I vote no. Was hard enough for dad to fix the last mess you made. Damage done in here will likely be three times worse and more expensive." I gave her a wave of my hand. "I can afford to cover damages."

"Just do your part, and then come sit back down beside me. For once, go with the flow. And don't throw your money in my face, rich boy." Jen said as she snorted. "Fine." I said as I looked the entire building over.

The facility was broken into various different stations. For example, let's say you had strength- based powers. If you had super strength, you went to the station that had this larger than life platform connected to a machine that came from the ceiling. Once your hands were placed in the proper spot, the machine began to press down on you, measuring your strength as you pushed back against it. At some point I would make it there. Flex, actually had broken the machine when he went up against it.

This put him in an elite class that, outside of a select few, most didn't fall into. Then there was the test for people with speed- based powers. The entire facility was outlined by a large circular track to test their speed.

There were areas designed to test elemental powers and had roaring waters, rock debris, and raging fires. Floating rings that were suspended in the air for the flyers, a targeting range for people with projectile abilities, and a projectile range for people with defense style powers. The list went on.

In total there were about fifty different stations set up and covered all four floors of the building. Each station was manned by a Purgatory representative, and had cameras sending live video to all the supergroup heads that couldn't make it here today.

In the area above it all, was a private viewing station where some high- profile Icons came to see the talent. First hand and in person. It was the equivalent of a scout coming to see a sports star play. I looked up at the viewing station. It sat in the middle of the building and for all purposes looked like a ball that had been sliced in half. Naturally, the bottom was flat and the roof was dome shaped. How else would a ball cut in half look?

This domed- shaped roof was surrounded by glass on the sides, so the viewers could see anything going on in the building at all times. No matter the floor or station, it could be seen from here. Jen continued to eat the last of her chips and adjusted her hat as more and more people came into the building.

Our section, the area restricted only for people participating for the day, had slowly begun to get crowded, too. While Jen and I were relaxed, many others weren't. Some students seemed twitchy, a few were biting their nails, while others had sweat rolling off of them as if perspiration was their prime power.

Finally, in the next ten minutes or so, the place was packed tighter than a hero in a phone booth. Jen and I were sitting close now as we had to make more room for people who came in after us. In unison, various projector screens were lowered and began counting down all around us.

"Showtime," Jen said as she sucked the chip remainders from her fingers. "Good luck when you go," she said. I snorted. "Thanks. You, too." I replied as I extended my fist to her. She bumped it back and grinned.

After the large screens around the inside stopped counting down, they all were displaying an open area on the ground floor. In an instant a large man made his way to where the cameras were aimed.

As he floated casually to the center, several students booed as he landed on the ground. He promptly ignored the booing of the crowd and casually waved his hand in all directions. A silent *I don't care about you or your booing* gesture.

Principal Griles, was a large black man, with curly hair, a round nose, and glasses that were so large that they had to be a few decades old.

He wore a hideous brown suit, with an equally ugly tie. He couldn't fly, only hover, and it was his normal means of transportation. I found that funny because he was so large. Let me explain, had he actually walked around he would have likely been slimmer. Not by much but smaller but calories burned, are calories burned.

While his hovering ability was laughable, his secondary power had its uses. Principal Griles was effectively a human lie detector. He could literally tell when a person wasn't being truthful to him.

Is it a pointless power? To a degree, but as a Principal of a school, it had made him a disciplinary legend, and served him well. Teachers respected him, and students hated him. By that logic, he was likely doing his job well. Griles and I had bumped heads several times, but none like when the fight between Flex and I took place. I thought he was going to try and kill me that day, he was so angry.

He looked around and held up a wireless microphone to his mouth. Per usual there was no fancy speech, no introduction, or anything else that some people in normal schools had. There was no need for it. We all knew why we were here, and if the booing crowd didn't give it away, many people didn't like Principal Griles, and he likely disliked each of us just as much if not more.

"Members of Up, Up, and Away, and The Imperial Lords will be onsite watching today. First up is Kasey Morrison,"

Griles said as he read his first name from his sheet of paper. "Please report to your assigned station."

A slender blond girl had stood up a few people over from us and made her way to where she had to go. Like all of us, she had been given her testing location last week when the sheet went out to students giving details about their stations.

Downside of having multiple powers was that you have to visit each station, before you could be finished. When Kasey would start her demo, a second name would be called shortly thereafter. There were so many screens that up to nine people could do their demo at the same time, as long as they had different powers, and didn't need the same station.

"Did you know an Imperial Lord would be here?" I asked Jen. She shook her head casually as she yawned. "Pops, didn't mention it to me," she shrugged. "Maybe it was a last- minute thing."

"Maybe so," I said as I glanced up to the half- globe viewing area. Up there, looking down below on us like we were kids at a playground, was a member of the Imperial Lords, and Up, Up, and Away, I just couldn't see them. I knew a good amount of the Imperial Lords already because of Mr. Reid, but all I knew about the latter was that they only allowed people in who could fly.

Flight was a requirement. The clapping around me brought me out of my mind. I looked around and found Jen kneeling over with laughter. "What happen," I asked. "Seriously?" Jen asked while she still laughed. "Kasey passed out. Nerves got her, I guess."

I looked up at a screen and saw Kasey slowly getting to her feet. She shook her head some as her peers kept clapping to cheer her on. "Let's hope she can get the job done this time," Jen said, as she watched Kasey on the screen.

"Hunter Monroe," Principal Griles called out over the microphone. An eerie silence fell over the crowd. I looked at Jen and then back to where Griles stood. I could see on the screen that even Kasey had paused to look up at the screen near her to see me go to where I needed to be.

"Usually they save the big names for last," Jen said as I stood up. "Yeah but usually they don't call the big names' *abomination* to their face, so I don't fit the mold," I said as I casually made my way to the floor.

I looked up to the private viewing box, and was surprised to see that several silhouettes were in the window looking down on me. Clearly the spawn of a hero and villain was known even to the upper level supergroups.

Even though the silence had faded, I knew several dozen cameras were on me. Across the world at various superbases, Icons were watching me to see the show I would put on. To see how the infamous half- villain, half- hero spawn would perform. I took a deep breath and decided to go all out and make it a display they wouldn't soon forget. Could I have followed the rules and gone to each little station they had set up for me? Sure, I could have, but that would be dull.

I'd rather play in that gray zone again. I cracked my neck and looked over my shoulder to where Jen was sitting and watching. I winked at her and grinned, as I felt that smooth tingle as power flooded my body. Her eyes got wide and she shook her head from side to side.

I allowed my view of the inside of the building to turn blue, as energy began to illuminate my eyes. As I began to rise in the air, with a smile on my face from ear to ear, I looked down on the crowd. They had no idea how much fun I was about to have.

CHAPTER 6

FLEXING MY POWERS

So, what to do first? I was so excited that I almost rubbed my hands together and grinned like they did on cartoons. I had four stations that were assigned to me, all revolving around my powers. What I needed to do was find a way to show all I could do, without having to bring my force field up, or if I did bring it up, finding a way to make it larger instead of small would be ideal.

Flying was done first. As I rose higher in the air, I could still hear names being called, yet so many of the cameras in the building were set on me. Many of the projector screens were following me as I flew, with my eyes leaving a faint trail of blue in my wake. The wind as I zoomed around caused my hair to blow and I could feel my lips getting dry.

I stopped quickly in the air, and earned a gasped reaction from the crowd. I reached inside the pockets of my sweats and pulled out some Chapstick. To the people looking from below, no doubt this seemed cool. I'm sure they assumed that I was so unbothered by the demo, that I had time to casually apply lip protector. In reality, I just really hated chapped lips. I don't know about other flyers, but it drove me crazy.

I put my Chapstick back into my pockets and gave my hands a shake to loosen them up, as I smiled and darted in the air towards the floating circles designed for the flyers to move through. In a few moments I had flown through the circles several times front to back so fast that they were now playing it in slow motion on the screens.

I didn't collide with a single one of the floating circles. I flew from them then stopped in the air and looked at them. As I looked them over, I looked down below and saw a stretch of water. This was the area designed for people with swimming, or water manipulation based powers. The people who could breathe under water, or turn into water, stuff like that. The area had two people in it, swimming. Perfect. Just perfect.

I aimed my eyes at each of the floating circles and concentrated. My aim wasn't the best, but the circles were so close together that luck was on my side. I released the blue energy from my eyes and let out two swift Impact Blasts. More gasps came from the audience of teachers and students.

"What in Atlas's name is he doing?" Griles said over his microphone. My blast powered through the floating rings and caused them to crumble, sending chunks of whatever the rings were made of to come falling down. As the debris picked up speed, it was headed directly onto the two people in the water below, and as of yet, no other person had made any attempts to save them. Perfect.

"A little more," I said to myself under my breath. The chunks continued to fall and just when they were only a few feet from the people in the water, I moved my hands. My pale blue force field sprung to life around the two random idiots in the water who didn't even try to move to get to safety.

They looked around wildly as they found themselves trapped inside ball- shaped orbs of energy. One of them, a young girl with pale skin and red hair, actually slammed her fist on the force field. Before she could continue her pointless assault, the debris crashed down on them. When the smoke cleared and debris had stopped falling, they were still safely trapped in my force field.

I moved my hand around again and the force field flickered away. I'm glad the display was over fast. While it was easy to surround myself in a force field, but it was a strain to keep it up around others, especially when I wasn't nearby .

"Monroe, come down here this instant," I heard the screaming voice of Principal Griles. I wagged my finger to him and shook my head. Instead, I ran down my list out loud as my two victims got out of the pool. "So that's flight, eye blast, and force field," I said to myself. "Oh strength," I said as I snapped my fingers. I looked around. What could I use instead of going to the strength station. Then it hit me.

There were several rings still floating in the air. May as well keep it all right here. I flew over to one of the rings and with a small Impact Blast, I let my beams fly from my eye and clip the top of the circle. The entire large, stone circle began to fall but it was falling in one piece this time.

These stone circles were a little bit of a wonder. They literally appeared to just be floating in the sky off on their own power. Nothing was visibly connecting them to the roof of the building, or any other attached structure, but as soon as they were damaged, they would fall.

As the stone circle fell to the ground, I gave it a second to increase distance from me, and then began to fly towards it. I picked up my speed as the circle began to fall faster. In the next seconds I was flying past the circle. The ground below me was coming up fast and I was cutting it close. I positioned myself under the falling circle and raised my hands up. As it touched my hands I could feel my arms bend.

An Icon like Flex or Mr. Impervious, could catch this with ease, hell even Lady Omega could do this easily, and while she had immense strength, she only had one arm. I myself was having a harder time. I was holding the circle up, but its weight was still pushing me down. I glanced over my shoulder at the ground, and the people on it were still approaching.

I could feel myself gritting my teeth, and pushing myself to fly up as the stone circle finally began to slow down. About fifteen feet in the air from the ground, I finally had control of the circle and gently placed it on the ground as I slowly descended.

Once the stone was on the ground, I allowed for the room to turn back to normal as I removed the energy from my eyes. Then, I took a fancy bow, and put both of my hands in the air. Much of the crowd actually clapped. Not a single teacher seemed amused by my stunt, and several students actually walked by me and glared. Two of them being the students that had been in the water. "Hey, I knew what I was doing," I said to them as they passed.

I turned around and looked up to see that, somehow, all of the floating stones I had just destroyed, were replaced by copies of the previous stones that were there. It was as if I hadn't destroyed anything. Hell, had not the rubble been scattered on the ground, it would have looked as if nothing even happened.

A firm hand was suddenly placed on my shoulder. "Go. Sit. Down," Principal Griles said as he spoke through gritted teeth. Sweat was visible on his forehead and his eyes were bulging. "You okay?" I asked. "You look like you are about to have a heart attack." His grip on my shoulder tightened as he began to breath hard.

I jerked my shoulder away from him. I didn't think Griles had super strength, but for a moment it sure felt like it. I went and found my seat beside Jen again. As I sat down, I looked up to where the special viewing area was. The silhouettes from the Icons watching were gone now.

I wonder if they were impressed with my abilities. I figured they were either so impressed that they were discussing who would get me, or so outraged, that they were hatching a plan to have me contained. Had I gone too far? I looked around the area. Everybody lived, and the debris was getting cleaned up now. Nope, not too far at all. Not a drop of blood was shed in the process, either.

"You know you could have just went to the stations like everybody else, but no. Hunter has to stand out." Jen said as she rolled her eyes. "I just wanted to be memorable." I replied with a smile. "You almost killed John and Heather."

I grimaced. "Killed who?" Jen exhaled. "The two students in the water." "Oh, you mean dumb student one, and dumb student two?" I let out a laugh at my own pet names I had created. "They didn't even try to move. Do you really want Icons like that out there saving the world?" Think about that." I said as I wagged a finger.

"You're an idiot," Jen said, but I couldn't take her seriously because she was holding in a laugh. "I thought Griles was going to explode when you shot the circles." I waved a hand. "He'll live." Jen glanced up into the sky as she looked at where the Icon judges were.

"I wonder what they thought of your little display. Matter of fact, I wonder what all of the supergroupswatching thought." I shrugged. "I'm not sure," I replied. "If anything, they know the abomination is a force to be reckoned with," I said as I extended a fist to her. She shook her head. "Nope. I'm not helping you stroke your own ego." We both laughed at her words.

A few moments went by and more students were called. One girl, who was easily over six feet tall, and had muscles like a statue and could actually become into any creature she wanted. Any creature, past, present, or future, she could turn into. One second she was a bear, the next she was a unicorn, and then to finish, she turned herself into a dinosaur. A real-life dinosaur. I didn't know her name, but man, did she have a cool power. How had I been here so long and not have known about her?

Very few powers impressed me, but her's did . In a real-life situations, I don't know how much she would contribute, but that didn't take away from the awesomeness of her power set. "Damn when is Griles going to call me?" Jen said as she balled her fist in the air.

I slapped her on the back. "Don't worry about it, everybody knows they save the best for last." "Shut up," she quickly replied. "In other news," I continued, "you coming with me to the Young Pyro concert? I saw the flyers in the hall. It's in Downtown Atlas City. It's either tomorrow or the day after. I forget, but I'll find out before it happens. They are going to shut the street down, it's going to be loaded with food, drinks, and mayhem." I could feel the smile on my face as I gave her the details.

"So, you still have this man crush on Young Pyro, huh," Jen said. She made air quotes with her fingers when she said the words *man crush*. "You should just come out of the closet already. It's accepted now. "I don't have a man crush on him, I just respect him." "Sure," Jen replied.

It was true, though I did respect him. More than I did most Icons. Young Pyro was almost a trend setter. He had fire-powers on a supreme scale. He could control it, create it, and was resistant to it. He was even a member of The Imperial Lords for a short moment, until he just quit.

According to the many magazine articles written about him, he decided to do what he loved and being a hero wasn't that. He had a passion for music. Rap music, mainly. So, he followed that career. In the next two years he became both the first Icon to following a music career, and one of the most well-known rappers in the world.

Despite his ability to be a great Icon, his lyrical ability as a rapper was even more impressive. "I just like how he didn't do what was expected of him. He followed the beat of his own drum so to speak, and it worked out just fine for him." I waited for Jen to reply. I glanced at her, and she wasn't even listening. She was talking to some blond sitting beside her.

"Jen. Jen." she turned to me. "Are you listening?" Her eyes darted from side to side. "Sure. Young Pyro concert. Trend setter. Drums. I got it." I shook my head. "So, you coming or not.? It's free because it's his homecoming special so it will be recorded." I said.

Jen shook her head. "I'm down." "Good," I said as I stood up. "Wait where are you going?" she asked. "I'm leaving." She stood up in protest. "You haven't seen me go yet." I turned my face up to her. "Seen you go?" I responded. "I was raised in the same house as you. I've been seeing you use, and abuse, your powers for years." She moved her mouth to respond but I cut her off. "Years!" I said once more.

"Plus, you are being entertained anyway," I added as I pointed my thumb to the blond girl who was now watching the current students on the screens. "Just make sure you figure out who we are assigned to before you come home." She shook her head. As if we both didn't know we would be with The Imperial Lords.

"Where are you going," Jen asked as I grabbed my backpack. "I'm going to The Ebony District," I replied. "Oh, to give the villain her gift," Jen responded. "Yep. To which she will be so happy with that she will throw herself at me." I smirked. "I have this all mapped out."

Jen grimaced. "Don't be too late getting home. We have to pack our stuff for the morning." she added as she sat down. "Yes mom," I said over my shoulder as I began to descend the bleachers and head out of the training building.

CHAPTER 7

EBONY DISTRICT

First, let me say that I personally hate The Ebony District. Not because of the increase in crime, that didn't bother me. It wasn't even the eternal darkness. It was mostly the fact that there was always somebody, either Icon or Void, looking for a point to prove. Everybody wanted to be a tough guy. I hated it, and to avoid drawing attention to myself, I figured it was best to change clothes before I made my way to the darker side of Atlas City.

I usually kept a spare pair of jeans and an extra shirt in my locker at Purgatory. Most students just had a spare pair of the standard sweats and shirt given out by the school, but I didn't always do what most kids at Purgatory did.

You never knew when you would spill some food, or have some sort of chemical from class splash against you. In either case, you'd want out of those clothes as soon as possible. Despite what movies and comics would have you believe, a random chemical on you doesn't make you an Icon, it makes you sick, is what it does.

With my casual blue jeans, and white shirt on, I didn't stand out as much as an Icon from school. To give myself the added look of a person from The Ebony District, I swung by a store on my way and grabbed a black leather jacket. At only one hundred bucks it was a bargain, and after almost dropping that much on a watch, I wanted to keep myself on a budget for the next few weeks. That's how the rich go broke, spending with no regard. I can thank Mr. Reid for drilling that lesson in my head whenever we talked about my *inheritance* from my father.

As I walked down the street I saw several Icons fly at almost top speed in the same direction I was going. I couldn't tell who they were, but they were all dressed in the same color of blue. That much I could make out. They must have been in the same supergroup. Not only that, but they were clearly headed to Ebony District. As usual, something must have been going on there.

I didn't do much, but I knew enough to keep my head down and nose clean if I had to be in Ebony. I didn't run from fights, but I didn't go looking for them either. Not usually. More and more as I walked down the street, the ever shine of the Diamond District, slowly began to fade, and was replaced by a darkness that enveloped me with each of my footsteps.

Everything around me was changing the closer I got to The Ebony District. The expensive, flashy cars that were common in my District, were suddenly replaced by older, worn out vehicles. The buildings were gradually changing from skyscrapers of tomorrow, to semi run- down buildings, covered with graffiti, and with boarded up windows. The only thing that remained the same as I walked were the trees.

On this road in particular, there were small trees planted along the side. Nothing that would grow to a significant height, just smaller trees for aesthetics, to make the area look appealing. While trees in Diamond District looked like these, they acted differently. In mdistrict, the trees would stretch as if to touch you. People were nicer there, so the trees were more open. However, in The Ebony District, as I casually walked by these trees I extended my arm as a sign of my nonaggressive nature, and the trees all leaned back out of my arm's reach.

It was as if they didn't want to be touched. I wasn't sure what they were used to in this District, but they avoided my hand like the plague. "Fine," I grumbled as I finally made it fully into the darkness.

I turned and looked behind me one last time. I could see the shine of Diamond District from here. It looked about ten feet away. I took a breath and snuggly grabbed the straps of my backpack and headed to Danielle's place.

I wanted to just fly there, but even that could attract attention from the wrong people. Especially if you were flying alone. That's why those Icons from before were in a group and dressed alike. To show all who saw them that they were together. An attack on one of them was an attack on all of them.

It was smart, and sometimes the strength in numbers approach was needed. Other times Ebony was one of the best places to be. Some of the best dates Danielle and I have ever had were here in this very district.

In time, I found myself close to her apartment. I was glad because the stench of smoke and car fumes seemed to flood the air around here nonstop. "Finally," I said to myself as her building came into view. I don't know why but it felt like it had taken me forever to get here. Likely because I was so anxious to see her.

Her building was one of the nicer buildings in Ebony. It stood eight stories high, which was basically a skyscraper by Ebony standards. It was also a newer building composed of brick, and had all the bells and whistles that you normally didn't get in Ebony. It wasn't often you saw new, high- end buildings, here but a wealthy developer from Diamond District, was undergoing what the papers called a *visual reconstruction effort.*

Essentially, he was investing money to make certain parts of Ebony desirable, in hopes to turn a profit in time.

According to Diamond District standards, the rent in the building was pretty low. For Ebony standards, the rent was unreal, and somehow Danielle was able to pay it. I had offered to just pay the rent for her but she insisted that she could do it herself.

What I admired about this building was that, because of how pricey it was, there was almost no random people hanging around, which was the case in most of Ebony. So, when I saw the old red pickup parked in front of the building with five guys hanging around it, smoking something that smelled awful, I was more than a bit surprised.

I tried my best to act casual. I didn't want any trouble, for their sakes, not mine. Their music from the truck was blasting, and most of them were just sitting on a part of the truck. No purpose in life, was my first thought. Who randomly hangs out and just plays music loud, while smoking? No doubt they thought they were cool, but they all seemed like a waste of space.

Now, don't get me wrong, I can respect the villain life as much as a person could. My father was one, and so was my girlfriend, but these five idiots didn't seem like villains. Villains had goals, these five just had time to kill.

Of all the places to park, of course they were directly in front of the walkway to the door. As soon as the surprise of seeing me and my gift is over, I'm going to ask Danielle if she wants to go do something. There is no way, I can stay here and deal with these assholes and their music.

I gave them a good, solid glare as I walked by. I couldn't help it. "What you looking at partner?" One of them asked in slang. It actually came out as *patna*, instead of *partner.* Apparently, my glare lasted too long. "I'm talking to you," he said again as he slid down off the hood of the truck. He was average height, but had a solid build.

His facial hair was the same color of black as the hair that was visible under his cap. He took a step towards me, and as if on cue, his friends seemed to fall into formation as well. See what I mean? One look, and now it was suddenly five versus one. "We're good man." I said as I move to head into the building.

"Don't turn your back on me," he said a little louder over the music. I stopped and as I turned around, the area in front of me shifted to blue. "I said we're good. Unless you don't want us to be good." With my last words, I slowly rose in the air a good six feet.

They knew I could do more than just hover now, as they backed up while looking at me. The leader raised his hands. "Nah, homie. We good." I descended back down to the ground, as my surroundings changed from blue to normal again. A few of the goons were whispering among themselves as the leader just looked at me.

I stuck my hand in my pocket, reaching for my spare key to her apartment. As I grabbed the knob to the entrance one of the thugs asked his friend a question. "Damn man, how long he gonna be up there with that Danielle chick. I'm hungry." My posture stiffened even more, as I could feel my eyes grow wide with the words one of the goons just said. "I don't know, but I'm going to get me a big ass burger when this is all over. He's been up there half an hour; how much longer could he be?" Another goon said as I could hear him take an inhale of whatever they were smoking.

I could feel myself shake a little. After a few deep breaths as I walked inside, I told myself there could have been other girls called Danielle in this building. It didn't have to be my Danielle. Plus, she was smart. She wouldn't be up there with another guy. For one, she loved me, she wouldn't do that. Secondly, she knew I was coming over today. Didn't she?

Panic hit me like a super strength punch to the stomach. She thought I was still at school. I wasn't expected to be out for a few more hours. I had told her demos were today, and like everybody else, she had said I'd likely go last because of my powerset.

Without even knowing if my concerns were valid, I could feel myself breathing harder now as my casual walk became a sprint down the hall. As I ran, soft music was playing in the hall over unseen speakers, and I had to step over several people sitting on the white stone benches in the hallway. There were potted trees spread through the hall, but they were fake so they didn't move as I ran buy.

I slammed my finger on the button to call the elevator. The bell went off, but the elevator seemed to be moving too slow. I jammed my finger several more times on the button. The doors opened and I almost ran into a tall man in a long black overcoat as he tried to get off at the same time I was coming inside. "Sorry. Sorry." I said to him.

He didn't reply. He simply looked at me. He was dressed in all black and had a white mask on his face. A mask that had no features, just a faintly formed mouth and holes for the eyes.

"That was unexpected, indeed," he said as he looked me over once more. Dude was creepy. Without looking away from him, I once more I slammed my finger on the button with a six on it to go to her floor. As the doors shut, the man in black took a step forward slowly as if he wanted to get back on, but then he stopped moving. Damn Ebony District weirdos.

I was on a mission now, and didn't have time for extra stops along the way. As the elevator rose, there was silence.

Only the sound of my heavy breathing could be heard. The door finally opened and I literally flew down the hall.

I didn't want to be heard running at full speed to the door. In a second I was hovering in front of a door with the number six hundred and twenty on it. I looked at the door numbers. It was special. She had picked this number, because it was the date we started dating. June twentieth.

I put my ear to the door. I couldn't hear anything. No sounds of passion, nobody talking. Maybe this was all in my head and I had nothing to worry about. Still, I didn't knock. I slowly put my key into the door. Lucky for me she had given me a key of my own. I rarely came over unannounced, so it was never me surprising her. After figuratively paying two grand for a watch, I thought a surprise was in order. Now look at me, so afraid of what I may find that I didn't even have the balls to turn the doorknob.

Then, I heard a sound that made my insides boil. A man's laughter. A man was inside of her apartment. Damn being gentle. I didn't even turn the knob now. Instead I accessed my strength and with a swift open hand push, the door flew open, leaving it on the hinges, but the locking mechanism was destroyed from the force of my push.

The fear I had felt as I made my way here was personified as I looked at them both. She was sitting on her counter in her kitchen. He long black hair was in a tight bun, and not flowing down like usual. She had on a shirt that showed every curve she had up top, and some blue sweatpants. Blue sweatpants, that were mine. I had given her those.

She had her arms wrapped around his neck. Some guy who was taller than me, with curly black hair, a strong jaw, and oddly enough he had on a black leather jacket as well. I knew him, from somewhere. I just couldn't make it out.

They were so close in their embrace that a slight breeze would have pushed them together and made their lips touch. "Hunter," she gasped as I made my entrance. She quickly dropped her arms. "Babe, it's not what it looks like," she said to me as she slid down from the counter.

"It's not?" the guy said as he looked at her in confusion. His voice was deep. Deeper than mine, and for some reason I instantly felt angered by this. "What are you," I interrupted her as she tried to speak. "Doing here? What am I doing here?" My voice came back in a crackle. "How about what are you doing here?. With this guy?" I said as I pointed to the guy who was in her embrace only moments ago.

He had leaned on her counter now with his arms folded. As if me, her boyfriend, being here was messing up his time with her. "We were just talking about the job. You remember you told me to find better help." She was stuttering now. A clear sign of her guilt if ever there was one.

"So, you had to have your arms around him for the last thirty minutes?" They both looked at me confused. "Your friends downstairs told me." He shook his head some but didn't say anything. "Just calm down," she said as she tried to grab my hand but I jerked it away from her. I could barely stand now. My knees felt like pudding, and I could feel the betrayal and sadness build up in me.

It had no place to go, but finally found an exit in my eyes as I could feel the tears coming down my face. I hated myself for this. I didn't want to cry. I wanted to be furious. "Really. You're going to cry now? Caught your lady doing, what they all do, so you're gonna cry?" He laughed.

There it was. I had found the fury I was looking for. I took my backpack off and removed the watch box from it. I summoned my strength and crushed the box between my hands, destroying the watch and tossing it to the ground. Along with the backpack that she had given me. I didn't want it anymore.

He stood from the counter now and looked at me. It happened so fast, that it felt natural. I ran towards this asshole, and balled my fist up as I did. I couldn't figure out his face, but I was certain he was an Icon. So, he had powers of some sort. "Hunter, no!" Danielle screamed as she tried to stop me.

Her pleas were no concern to me. I knew she wasn't going to get her deposit back after I was done with this guy though.

I extended my fist, and delivered a punch to his stomach that sent him flying to the wall.

To my shock, he actually went through the wall, leaving a man- sized hole in it and he fell to the street below. This caught me by surprise. I didn't know if he could survive that sort of fall, and I quickly looked through the hole and saw him getting up off the ground.

So, he was durable. Okay then, so he could take whatever I dished out. "Perfect," I said under my breath. "In case you didn't figure it out," I said to Danielle as I floated out of the hole in her apartment, "We're done."

She didn't reply, and the fact that she didn't hurt even more. Her new guy was surrounded by his little goon squad now and looking up at me. He wanted this it seemed. So, I descended down to them and allowed my vision to turn blue.

I couldn't remember who he was, but as my feet touched the ground I didn't care. They all were going to feel my pain. To flex my power even more, I manifested a large force field around me. So large that as it came to life it touched their truck several feet from me.

"Kick his ass, Erase." one of his friends said. Then realization mixed with panic washed over me. I had finally remembered where I knew him from. His name was Eric Rasenburg, but to the public he was the Icon known as E-Rase. He had two powers.

The first was that he could make his body dense, allowing him to take a good amount of punishment, but he wasn't by any means invulnerable. This explained why he was able to survive that fall, and my punch. His second power could have been his claim to fame, had he had goals above petty street crimes. It was short lived, but it was very rare, and the reason for his true name. E-Rase, could render an Icon powerless for three minutes.

Doesn't sound like much, but look at a boxing match, and notice how tired they are after three minutes of defending themselves. As he walked towards me, I felt sick to my stomach. My force field began to fade against my will, and the area in front of me was slowly turning back to normal and not blue. He balled his fist, and so did his friends. "Get ready for the longest three minutes of your life chump." With those few words said, he smirked as if Christmas had come early, and he drew his fist back.

CHAPTER 8

LOBO

I've never been one to run from a fight. I've been called plenty of slanderous names in my time, and I wasn't about to add chicken, punk, coward, or any of the like to it. So as my powers faded I tried to come up with a plan in those few precious moments before the first punch landed. I will say this though, there are very few feelings in the world like knowing you're about to get your ass severely beaten.

Had I run, I could have at least wasted half of that three minutes. I could have just fought back. It was one of me, and five of them. The odds were not in my favor already, not to mention I just can't fight. Not even enough to take Eric one on one if I had to. There was just never any point in learning.

When you had enhanced strength, energy eyes that could punch through steel, and a force field that made you almost invulnerable, learning the proper technique on how to throw a punch, or how to block one for that matter, just never came up. Now I was wishing it had.

With no surprise at all, his punch found its mark. Square in the center of my face. I could hear the icky sound his fist made as he withdrew it from my now broken nose. My nose didn't hurt as much, as the actual force of his fist hitting my face.

It was as if he had hit a button that had access to all the blood I had in my body, and now the blood wouldn't stop. I had never had my nose broken before, but I'm sure it was now. Blood was everywhere, mainly on my face and in my mouth, and now my nose was feeling like it had begun to swell.

My first reaction, was to try to ignore the pain but I couldn't. As his buddies laughed at my injury, I grabbed my nose, leaving the rest of my body unprotected. A swift punch came to my stomach, which caused me to drop to my knees.

The next thing I knew, some hands were grabbing my shoulder, and I was slung, head first, into the side of their red truck. At least my blood blended in with the paint job. I fell to the ground, and didn't move.

I wanted to, though. I wanted to get up and kick this guy's ass just on the principle alone, then his friends would be next.

Between the pain in my face and head, and the spinning of the area in front of me, I wasn't going to be kicking anybody's ass. I thought to myself, how much of the three minutes could be left. Surely it was almost over.

Another thought that came to me was Danielle. In my eyes, she was a heartless bitch right about now. A heartless bitch who had the nerve to cheat on me in a pair of my own sweatpants. I made a mental note to get those back once this was over.

I was still surprised she didn't even come and try to sort this out. Anything she said, I would have considered a lie, but at least she could have tried. "Hey E, you wanna take it easy on the kid?" I heard one of his flunkies say. Kid? I was only a few years younger than Eric was.

I couldn't see E-Rase, but judging from the panic in his friend's voice, whatever he had seen wasn't good. I slowly found the strength to move my body, but before I could, a kick came and connected with my back. I made a funny noise as the air was kicked from me. A sound similar to a gasp. No, it was a scream. No, it was more like if a gasp and a scream had a baby. That was the sound I made.

"Roll his ass over," I heard E-Rase say. As several hands found me I was rolled over with more force than needed. I was sprawled on the ground, looking up at my attackers. I tried to create a force field and nothing happen. Longest three minutes of my life indeed.

"Not so tough now are you, Hunter?" I wanted to show surprise on my face. It was a natural reaction, but I was in too much pain. "You think I don't know who you are?" Eric said as he leaned over and looked at me. "Mr. bi-g time Icon, with his fancy four powers. You think that makes your better than those like me. The so- called low levels, with powers people don't care about. Think you can flex your powers and awe people. Scare people?"

"Damn E, jealous much?" a friend of his said as he laughed. Eric looked up at his buddies and the laughing stopped suddenly. I wasn't sure if his friends were Icons or not, but I was willing to bet they weren't.

He looked back down at me and to insult me more, he spat on me. It was oddly warm, and I could feel it roll down my face. I wanted to pull away, but couldn't move. I knew it was on my face, but there was so much blood and pain now, that it honestly didn't matter. I coughed and forced a smile. He wasn't going to see truly how bad it felt.

"You done yet?" I said as I winced in pain. My entire midsection felt like it was on fire. "How long you think we got?" Eric asked. "Maybe about a minute," a gruff voice replied.

I could feel my eyes widen. A minute? Seriously? An entire sixty seconds of this was left. "Give me the knuckles." Eric said as he snapped his fingers. A brown arm extended from the corner of my vision and was holding a pair of shiny brass knuckles. Not the traditional style either. These pair had enhanced grooves on the edge. Likely to provide maximum pain delivery to the person on the receiving end of the punch.

That, of course being me. Eric put the knuckles on his hand and flexed a fist. "You know," I said through heavy breaths, "whatever you did to Danielle," Eric smirked. "Oh, and she loved every minute of it too, chump." My heart skipped a beat and broke a little more as he said this. I know he was just taunting me but it hurt. "Don't dare assume this was the first time." Eric said as he dropped down and raised his fist.

My vision got blurry. His words hurt me more than any punch could. I felt sadness on a level that I never knew I could before. "Well, I hope you enjoyed it," I said. "Because once this is over, I'm kicking all of your asses, and then I'm going to do to your mom, what you did to Danielle. Over, and over, and over again." His eyes widened and then narrowed followed by the corners of his mouth pointing downward.

I winced as I spoke. "I'm not even going to pay her either. That's for lesser men who have to pay for it. Me, I never have, and never will." "Damn," one of his friends said from behind me. Eric's head jerked up and looked to the source of the word. I smiled on the inside.

It was a well- known story in The Ebony District, that Eric's mother, like many women, supported her habit by selling herself. It was these methods that turned Eric to the villainous side of living. He did almost any job he could for money to support her and himself. I didn't know if these stories were even real but I knew I had to say something, and going off of his reaction, it wasn't far from the truth.

"Okay," he said as he tossed the knuckles from his hand. I was confused for a moment. He stood up and walked to the truck. I used this moment to get up and as soon as I had one foot planted on the ground, another foot was placed on my back and forced me back down. "Yo, E," I heard another of his boys sound out.

Next, I hear the sound of a door on the truck opening and closing. He stood over me with a silver gun in his hand. A gun! This idiot had a gun. Clearly, his mother and her lady of the night ways was his hot button. I could hear the sound of people running behind me.

It appeared that his friends didn't expect this turn of events, and had no intentions of being witnesses. As the sound of their running feet grew faint, the wind around us began to pick up. Odd.

I took a deep breath and began to wonder if he was going to kill me. "Don't get scared now, asshole," Eric said. "I'm not going to kill you, but I promise, this will leave a mark," he said as he aimed the gun at my leg. Even though Mr. Reid could heal me, I'm sure it would still hurt like hell afterwards.

I wanted to scrambled to my feet and run. I tried my force field again. Tight spaces be damned, that's better than getting shot. It flickered into existence for a second and then faded away. His powers were almost gone over me, a few more seconds, and I should have my abilities back. I'd be hurt, but I'd still be bullet free.

The flicker of my force field wasn't missed by Eric and his finger wrapped around the trigger of his gun. I cursed Danielle in my head. This was all her fault. I was seconds away from being shot, and she was up there in her comfy apartment doing nothing.

Suddenly the wind picked up even more. Violently so. Eric had to frown his face just to see. Then I heard several sounds. As the wind wrapped around us, A blur of something hit Eric square in the chest, and sent him into the air for about five feet. As he came crashing down, another gust of wind caught him again and this time sent him flying into the wall.

"Lobo," I heard Eric gasp as he scrambled on the ground. I didn't waste any time as I used the truck to pull myself up completely. Eric was slouched on the ground near the wall he had just hit, as a man stood looming over him.

The Icon in question, my savior, was a tall, black man. He was bald, but sported a well tamed black beard. He wasn't a large man by any means but he clearly had defined muscles. They were practically stretching his black tee shirt to its limits. He had on green cargo pants, and a large pair of military boots.

Eric was right. It was Lobo. Atlas as my witness it was Lobo in the flesh. Lobo was an Icon that was half myth, half legend, and according to stories, was all badass. His powers revolved around air manipulation. Which is technically, one power, but had a variety of uses.

Some said he was in his late twenties to early thirties, and was once a heavy hitter for a super team outside of Atlas City, but he had decided to do his own thing and travel some, with the end of his travels bringing him here to Atlas City.

"What was it you told him?" Lobo said as he walked towards Eric. He had a smooth calm voice as he spoke. Lobo smiled. "I remember," he said as he snapped his fingers. "Don't get scared now, asshole," He flicked his hand in an upward motion and the wind around us came alive again, and lifted Eric off the ground then began to swirl around him. Eric's hands reached for his neck as the air was pulled from his lungs.

This is why Eric, despite his rare power, was considered a low- tier Icon. He could erase a person's power, but after that he had to wait a little while before he could do it again. It was as if his powers had a recharge time. Funny how powers are so different. Some Icons can use their abilities non- stop, while others had limitations, and drawbacks.

The miniature cyclone swirling around Eric stopped moving, and rushed back down to Lobo, who then rocketed in the air, grabbed Eric by his jacket, and then slung him down to the ground. I was starting to see that not only was Lobo strong, but he was smart. He had to have known about Eric's dense skin, and that's why he sucked the air out of his lungs. It made him weak and susceptible to the following damage.

Lobo landed on the ground. His boots made loud, ominous clicks as he walked and stood over Eric. I was just now able to move with complete strength again, and my bleeding nose had slowed down some. Lobo flicked his hand once more, and swirling winds surrounded the body of Eric.

He gasped again as the air was pulled from him. Lobo continued to move his hands slightly as if he was turning a dial, and then, just like that, Eric passed out. Even in pain, I did take joy in seeing his body go limp.

It would have been even better if I was the source of his passing out, but beggars can't be choosers. Especially when said beggar was just getting his as kicked and was moments away from being shot. Lobo stopped moving his hands and the winds faded away. He reminded me of a conductor, and the winds were his orchestra.

"Perfect," he said as he scanned the ground around us.

"Thanks," I said to him, but he ignored me and continued to look around. He stopped scanning the area as he walked and picked up the fallen gun Eric had moments ago. I glared at the gun as he held it.

Lob looked down at the gun in his hand for a second and then shook his head. Next, he spun his right finger in a circle as small funnel of air appeared in front of him. He tossed the gun into it, and the funnel shot into the air, sending the gun to who knows were.

"You okay, kid?" he asked me. I nodded my head. To nervous and embarrassed to answer. "I watched for a little while. Probably should have stepped in sooner. Sorry about that. But you should have your powers back now. If you want, wait for him to come to, and kick his ass. That's what I would do," Lobo said as he looked at Eric breathing slowly on the ground.

I looked up towards the area where Danielle's apartment was. I felt a strong gust of wind blow around me. "I think I'm just going to head home, with the sliver of pride I have left." I forced out a laugh, but as I looked back down, Lobo was gone.

Where had he gone so fast? I looked around the street, but I was alone, standing there in the darkness. I looked down at my hands and shirt, both were covered in my own blood. My body was sore, my head was pounding, and I could barely walk.

Eric made a noise on the ground. I didn't want to hang around to fight him again. His powers may have recharged by them. What I did do was deliver a stomp to his face. His nose didn't break like I wanted but it still felt good.

"Wait until Jen hears about me meeting Lobo. She's going to freak," I said to myself, as I grabbed my sore stomach and slowly rose in the air to fly home.

CHAPTER 9

THE TALK

Flying above the Ebony District was a personal favorite pastime of mine. Granted, I'd rather do it in clothes not covered in blood, and a body that was so sore that it hurt to breathe, but still I loved it. I didn't do it often because I wanted to keep a low profile, but after the evening I had just had, I figured some fun was in order. It was naturally harder to see because of the eternal darkness, but once up here the view was amazing.

I hovered in the sky for a few moments. Even the buildings were way below me now, yet I was still low enough to be inside the dark dome that was placing the district in never ending twilight. Had I flown up and higher I would have escaped the dome and would have been back in the normal surrounds of my world.

As I sat here in the gloom floating, I loved looking down on the district below. While Diamond District's eternal daylight was great, and the shooting stars in its bubble created by Diamond's powers were beautiful to watch, it didn't create what I was seeing now in Ebony.

The cars moving below all looked like little balls of light, slowly going along their way to unknown destinations. It was peaceful to watch, and I needed peace now. It helped me clear my mind of the flashing images of seeing Danielle with Eric. It helped me almost reflect.

As I hovered there in the air, bruised and bloody, I realized that maybe this wasn't the worst thing that could have happened. Sure, my heart was broken, and sure I almost got shot but I still had a life to live. I still had a family that loved me, I was considered powerful by normal standards, had a shit ton of money in the bank, and a bright future in front of me regardless which path I chose.

Then that sinking feeling came back to me again. One of the big reasons I was having such a hard time on my decision for the future. I could be great as a hero or a villain. The world would either respect my name or fear it, but what about my family? What about Mr. Reid? He had raised me. Raised me to do the right thing, but he also raised me to follow my heart. How would he react if I became a villain? A man so perfect. What would he think of me?

Not only that, how would he react if one day he or his team were to come after me? Even if I didn't stay in Atlas City, they could be sent for me, because of their renown as being one of the top supergroups in the world. Would Jen stand in their way, or would she come with them? Even worse, if Mr. Impervious came. Could I stand up against arguably the most resilient Icon alive?

I let out a sigh, and for the next ten minutes I just watched the cars and building lights below me. No matter how trashed Ebony was on the ground, from up here it was always beautiful. It was peace trapped in a district of chaos.

"Well, fun time's over, and I feel like shit," I said to myself. I spun around in the air once more and continued to head home. Crossing over from the Ebony District to the Diamond District, was the same experience as sitting in a dark room, only to have a person randomly turn the lights on.

If done too fast, it would leave you stunned for a few moments as you adjusted to the new world of day around you, so once I saw the edges of Ebony in view, I began to slow my flight speed and kind of drifted into the daylight. The shock was still there but not as fast, and not as bad.

My phone went off. I looked at it and realized it was Danielle, again. I held it in my hand and just looked at it, heart pounding in my chest. She had called around six times now. I wanted so many things. I wanted to scream at her, to ask her why, to just hear her voice. I knew I shouldn't have, but against my better judgement I answered the phone as I landed on the ground in the Diamond District.

"Yes," I said sternly as I answered the phone and began walking home. I was too upset and too pissed to even appear casual so I didn't even bother. Jen should have been home now or on her way there. At least I hope she was. I needed to vent to somebody. "Hunter!" her voice came back to me. She sounded surprised. "I didn't expect you to answer, and had already prepared my message to leave you." I cleared my throat. Her voice was strained and she sounded crackly as if she may had been crying.

"Would you prefer I hung up instead?" I hissed as the words were thrown out of my mouth. "No, I just," she stopped talking and there was silence for a few moments, that seemed like minutes. "I love you, Hunter. I just want to talk," I rolled my eyes and could feel my hand tighten on the phone. " Oh, shut up," I replied. "I do. You know I do."

"You didn't love me while you were screwing Eric, though did you?" "Screwing Eric? What are you talking about?" she asked. "We never slept together. I wouldn't do that you. If you would just listen. It's not what it seems." "Well, that's not what he said," I replied. "You're going to trust him over me?" she genuinely sounded hurt over this.

I wanted to scream at her how she was a villain and that she couldn't be trusted, but that sounded like something a hero would say, and I didn't want to sound that way. "You know what? It doesn't even matter anymore. I'm done with this and I'm done with you," and then I hung up. Before I could even get the phone back in my jeans it rang again, and this time I may have answered too fast.

She didn't even allow me to say anything, and went right back into her response to me hanging up. "Look I know what it looked like, because he was here and I had my arms around him, but I promise I was just flirting with him to get him and his guys to help me with the job. I needed more muscle and a wild card. That would have been E-Rase."

I didn't say anything, and in my silence my breathing sounded heavier than I had ever heard it. "Hello?" she asked. "I'm here, but I don't believe you. You say you love me, but you didn't say or do anything to try and defuse the situation. Even while I was outside getting my ass kicked you did nothing. I was almost shot," she gasped at those words.

"Yeah, that asshole almost shot me, but don't worry, I'm working on a plan for him. He will get what is due to him in time. I just don't want to talk right now. My internship starts tomorrow, and I need a clear head so please, just let me be." There was silence on the phone and with it, I could hear her keeping her sobs at bay.

"Okay," she said in a weak voice. Either she was an actress of extreme talent or she was really hurting inside. Either way, I was being fueled by anger and didn't care how she felt. The more she sounded hurt, the more bitter towards her I wanted to be. I had no doubt that I would return the pain to E-Rase, but this was the most I could do to Danielle to let her feel something like I had.

"Well, good luck tomorrow," she said as her voice finally came to. "Uh huh." I replied back coldly. "Text me when you're free. Give em hell and I love you," she said. "Thanks," I replied and then swiftly hung up.

"I love you, too," I said to myself as I put my phone away.

I walked up to the house only to find Mr. Reid sitting on the porch. "Damn," I said under my breath as he stood up when he saw me coming. I was trying to get in unseen. The original plan was to fly directly to my window, or Jen's window and enter the house that way. I could change clothes and at least clean up some before the rest of the family saw me.

"Hey." I said as I waved my hand casually. "Oh, shut up boy," he said as he walked down the steps. I felt my brow raise. "Come on," he said as he motioned me towards the garage. I didn't move.

Mr. Reid stopped, looked at me, and then motioned again for me to follow. "What's going on," I asked as we entered the garage and the door shut behind us. "Seriously?" he said as he rolled up the sleeves to the dress shirt he had on. "Did they kick your ass so much that you can't remember it? Sit down," he said to me as he pulled a chair out from one of the desk in the garage.

"Jen hasn't made it home yet, and I sent Karen and Junior to get dinner so we have a little time, but not much." His hand began to glow green as he moved closer to me. I felt relief as I saw this. I knew what was coming next, and I was ready for it. He placed one hand over my face and I felt a cool and tingly sensation as what was broken became whole again. As cuts closed and blood stopped flowing. It was a relief. Oddly, it reminded me of the feeling when you have a stuffy nose, that suddenly opens up.

Next, he clasped his hands together and allowed a larger green cone of energy to radiate around my midsection, and my breathing went from painful to normal again. Mr. Reid shook his head and his hands returned to normal. "Second day in a row I have had to heal my boys. It's a sad day in the Reid house when Jen is the responsible one."

He tossed some clothes to me. "Change and give me the bloody clothes. I'll get them washed before Karen sees them." I didn't ask questions and quickly removed my bloodstained shirts and dirty pants. I replaced them with another pair of jeans and a red shirt that had a comic style picture of Mr. Reid on it as Life Line.

He folded the clothes and placed them in a bag. "Now, go wash your face. You still look like somebody broke your nose," he went to move for the house but stopped. "And for Atlas' sake don't use a white cloth. Get one of the darker ones. Easier for the blood not to be seen," he said.

Clearly, hiding blood from his family, wasn't a foreign concept to Mr. Reid. I wondered how often he went through this process before he came home. As he walked away I stood from the chair and called to him.

"Wait," I said. "How did you know I needed all this?" "I was out on patrol and got word from a void snitch, I mean informant, in Ebony District. He said he saw my boy getting his ass handed to him by some punks, but then some Icon saved you. I figured you were there to see your girlfriend." As he said these words my eyes got wide.

He rolled his eyes a little as he exhaled. "Yes, I know about the villain girlfriend, but you have to make your own way in life. I can't tell you what to do, even if I don't agree with it." he raised a finger. "Don't get me wrong, I don't encourage it, but I won't damn you for it either. You're still my boy."

He adjusted his pants some and smirked. "While I never actually dated one, I'd be lying if I said I never found a villain attractive or messed around with one in my younger days." I couldn't believe what I was hearing. Maybe we weren't so different after all.

Still smirking, he shrugged as he began to walk to the house, followed by me. "Either way, my guy told me, so I flew home, lied to my wife and kid, something I try not to do often, and sent them away so I could help you out of a pinch and let you save face." "Thanks." I said to him. "Just get some rest as soon as possible after dinner," he said as he opened the door.

I didn't say anything. I was waiting to see where he was going with this. "Looks like you and Jen are to report to The Imperial Lords' base tomorrow," he said with a smile. I balled a fist and thrust it in the air. Jen and I had made the cut.

"Was it just us selected?" Mr. Reid shook his head as he loaded the washer with my clothes and detergent. He then looked at all of the selections on the machine. He randomly hit some buttons until water came out.

"No. Flex's little sister will be joining you, too." I let out a sigh. Zeva was coming too. She hated me, but it was no surprise that she was along for the ride.

I heard a door shut outside. Mr. Reid leaned over the kitchen sink and looked through the window. "That's Karen and Junior, go clean your face, and act like nothing happened. Say anything, and I'll make sure you get your ass kicked tomorrow as an intro to the team." He said this, not with a smile, but with a smirk. Was he serious? I didn't know, but didn't ask either. I rushed upstairs to remove the blood from my face, and packed for my first day as an Imperial Lord intern.

CHAPTER 10

R.M.F.C

"Jen! Hunter! Get your asses in gear., a voice screamed through the house causing me to jerk out of my drool making slumber. I looked around. Confused a little as I removed the sleep from my eyes. I glanced at my clock to see that it was seven in the morning.

I groaned as I fell back and let my head hit the pillow. It was blissful. There is just something about a pillow that had molded to the shape of your head for several hours that just made you not want to get up from it. I refused to move. I knew we had to leave early, but did it have to be *this* early.

This was another reason I doubted the life of a hero. They got up early all the time. Their time wasn't even theirs. No, their time belonged to the people they saved. Robberies, bombings, kidnappings and things of the sort don't happen on a schedule. Villains on the other hand did what they wanted, when they wanted. No alarm was going to wake villains like Jupiter's Fury or Double Down up at seven in the morning.

My internal debate was suddenly interrupted by shock. A single drop of something cold and liquid touched me on my neck, causing me to flinch and open my eyes. I took in a small breath. "Who put you up to this?" I asked without even moving my head. The response I received was a slight snicker.

Hovering about a foot over my face was water. Easily a gallon worth of water was sloshing around on its own, as if the water itself could fly. "Mom told me to make sure you two were up," Junior said. I turned my head and saw him standing there in his pajamas with his hand stretched out. He was using his telekinesis to keep all of the water afloat in the air. Beside him, on the floor was a red bucket.

"Okay, I'm getting up. Can you move this already?" "I could, but I don't know if I want to. I have a job to do. Mom's orders." he said as he laughed. "Fine," I replied. In a second a blue force field came into existence and was surrounding the water, not me. "Okay, so now what?" I said, as I moved the force field out of the way and sat up in the bed.

"Push war?" Junior replied with a smile. "Push war," I said as I stood up. Push Wars was our own personal game we would play. While Junior had a powerful form of telekinesis, I could control my force fields as if they were just an extension of my being. Usually, Junior would lift something with his ability, and then I would enclose it in a force field.

The *Push War* would then start. Junior would push the object towards me, while I would push the force field towards him. Whomever got their object to the other person won. We were both fairly good at this game, but I usually won if I was well rested, but over the last few times, Junior was proving stronger than he had been .

I placed my feet, and so did he, as we prepared to face off in a battle of force, but before we could, Mrs. Reid walked pass the door, smacked Junior in the back of the head, and shot me a glare. "I sent you to wake them up, not to play around," she said to Junior. "Sorry mom," he replied as he rubbed the back of his head.

"You got it?" I asked him. He shook his head, and I retracted the force field away. At the same moment the floating water quickly went from hovering in the air, to moving towards the bucket and finding a home there. I walked over to him and extended my fist. "She just saved your ass, kid. I was about to win."

He laughed as the bucket hovered off the ground. "Whatever. This is to be continued," he replied back as he bumped my fist and walked out the room screaming, "Oh, Jennifer."

I scratched the back of my head, yawned and then inhaled the smells of food being cooked down stairs. Bacon. The universal, good with, and on, everything, food. I had to hurry up and get ready before it was all gone. Jen may had been slim, but she could put bacon away like it was a third power.

I grabbed my two bags and placed them by the door. I already had my clothes ready from last night so I could skip the *what am I going to wear* panic. My phone buzzed again. I grabbed it off the charger and realised it was Danielle again. She had sent me a good luck message. I held the phone in my hand, trying to figure out if I should reply or not.

I decided to stick to my guns, and let her squirm a bit. I wasn't against sending her a message back, but I didn't want to at the moment. Instead, I ran to my bathroom, used it, and then took a quick shower. Once out and dry, I threw on my white casual sneakers, a pair of blue denim, and my favorite green plaid shirt. Quickly, I rolled up the sleeves and tamed my hair, then I was good to go.

I grabbed my bags and looked at my room one more time. "Hurry up. I'm not saving you any if I don't have to," I heard Jen say as she walked down the hall and headed to the stairs. She too, had two bags with her, tand as usual a ballcap was on her head. "I'm coming." I called back to her.

I did a final once over in my head to make sure I had the major stuff. I felt like I did, but in normal fashion, a day or two from now, I'll realize I forgot something and need to either come back for it, or purchase a replacement. I flicked off the light and headed down the stairs.

Jen, true to her nature, ravaged the food. Lucky for me, it was expected and Mrs. Reid had set a plate aside for Junior and I. She had coffee, and Mr. Reid was off at the base, so we would be seeing him pretty soon. See what I mean? Off at the base already. Heroes had early mornings.

"Well, it's about that time," Mrs. Reid said as she took a final sip of her coffee and stood up. She had on a pair of gray sweats, and a white shirt from her college days that had her alma mater's logo on it. I stood from the table followed by Jen and we both put our plates in the sink and grabbed out bags.

We said our goodbyes to Junior as he began to wash the dishes. He was always the dishwasher because of his powers. With telekinesis he could do it in a fraction of the time it took anybody else. Even now as I adjusted the bag on my back, three plates were in the air being washed by a sponge that moved on its own, while as the same time the coffee mug was dunking itself into the foamy water.

Mrs. Reid opened the door for us as we walked out. It was a little before eight now, so we had to go wait in the yard for our ride. As usual, it was daylight out and brighter than it would be twelve hours from now. Mrs. Reid looked up in the sky several moments. No doubt she was looking for our ride.

I didn't know how other supergroups worked, but being one of the leading groups, gave you a large amount of funding, and as such fancy things like being picked up by a personal transport of some sort was no big deal. "You two nervous?" Mrs. Reid asked casually while still searching the skies above us.

"Nah," Jen replied. "What's the worst that could happen? Dad will be there every step of the way, and it's not like they are going to give us a major crisis as our first assignment. Unless they go crazy and tell us to hunt down this killer that's on the loose." Mrs. Reid grimaced as she shook her head. "Sometimes I wonder if we went wrong with you," Mrs. Reid said with a smile as she looked at Jen.

"Went wrong?" Jen replied. "Between Junior, myself, and boy wonder here," she pointed at me. "I'd say you guys did soso. ." Mrs. Reid nodded and, under her breath mumbled "I'm changing the locks as soon as you're out of sight."

We all shared a laugh at this but Jen, much as I hate to admit it, had a point. Over the next two years of our internship, we would prove our worth and eventually be involved on some major stuff. Our first few assignments however, were sure to be small time grunt work. Stuff that was likely dull and a vast waste of our time and abilities. Paying our dues is how Mr. Reid phrased it. "I'm just ready to get it over with," I added. "The first year at least anyway." Mrs. Reid eyed me, and nodded her head to agree.

"No matter how it goes, or what you two decide for your futures, I love you both. Marcus and I couldn't have asked for better kids." She paused for a moment. I could see her swallow before she cleared her throat some. "Your mom would be proud of you Hunter." she said to me with glossy eyes.

I couldn't help but feel like all of this was for me, and Jen was just added in to divert it. It was a safe bet that she was going the hero way, but with my villain blood flowing through me, I was still up in the air, and my adopted family could likely tell. Either way, I was happy to have them.

My mother, and the Reids all went back. They had all been close most of their lives up until the very end. They even sat with each other in their days at Purgatory. When my parents died in the Battle of Ages, the Reids didn't hesitate to become my guardians, and for that I will always love them as if they were my parents. That's also why my indecision was so troubling.

"Thanks," I finally replied to her. I wanted to say more, but just then we all felt a sudden rush of air around us. For a second I felt like Lobo was back. It was unrealistic, but would have been cool. Then Jen would have gotten a chance to meet him. When I told her about him she had pelted me with over a dozen questions, and I eventually had to tell her to stop being a groupie for the guy.

In this case, the wind issue was from our ride. We all looked up as the empty sky above us, suddenly flickered and our transport came into view. It was larger than I expected. Dark gray in color, and easily a hundred feet in length. Large wings stuck out from the sides, and nearly one complete side of the transport itself was a large rectangular glass.

On the side was a large number four painted in yellow, and the outline of a door had a faint neon glow. The transport finally landed a few feet from us, and the large door beside the number four opened. "Well, this is it," Mrs. Reid said as she hugged us one last time. "Be careful." As she said this she sounded like she was about to cry. "We will, I said." Jen and I both stood back and took a photo of the transport after we returned the hug back to Mrs. Reid.

It seems lame, but for us this was still a big deal. As we showed each other the photos we captured, we walked onto the platform and headed inside the transport. To my surprise, Zeva was sitting on the inside and was already strapped in. She looked up, put a few pills in her mouth, gave a slight wave of her finger to us, and then turned away.

I was shocked she even acknowledged either of us. I was also not expecting her to be here already. For some reason, I thought she would have had her own transport there. Guess I was wrong. She had on some black shoes, black jeans, and a cream- colored sleeveless shirt. Her arms were toned, and she looked like she would have been a fit to wield super strength.

As I sat down I looked around the transport. It was full of lights, and panels that did who knows what. Our seats were almost like the bucket seats in racecars, and was perhaps the most comfortable chair I had ever had the pleasure of putting my butt in. Where we were, in the middle, was all business. Monitors, switches, and buttons covered most surfaces, yet the back of the transport looked more like a lounge. Complete with bolted down tables, chairs, and even a couch that was facing the large glass that I saw from outside.

In the front was a lone seat positioned in front of more buttons than I could count, and three large touchscreens. It was something, I just didn't know what. I couldn't see it too well but it didn't look human. The head was a square shape, and the arms appeared to be two rods connected to wires that were mounted on a center.

The arms moved with ease, as buttons were pressed, and the large door quickly closed. There was silence for a moment. The square head turned and touched some monitors. I looked at Jen and frowned. Zeva looked to us both. She sighed, as she picked up on our confusion. "It's an RMFC," she said as if she didn't want to answer the question that we hadn't even asked yet.

"A what?" I replied. "A Robot Manned Flight Craft," she said as she moved her hands around in the air. "That's what this is, and that it, the robot, mans it. Get the picture?" "You trying to sound like a bitch or does it come naturally for you?" Jen asked as she laid back in her seat.

I felt my eyes bulge a little as I looked from Jen and then back to Zeva who was glaring at her. It suddenly got very cold inside of the transport. "You would think with your father being *in* the Imperial Lords that he would have told you some of these things. Flex told me." Zeva said as she undid her straps and went to sit in the lounge.

"I guess some of us are going to be more prepared than others on this internship. But then again, some of us are here for more than family ties." "Meaning?" Jen asked as she sat up in her chair. "Because last time I checked your family was the one with the high and mighty purestock."

I had mixed emotions about what was about to go down. Clearly these two were about to go at it, and a part of me wanted to see how it would turn out. Then I realized that two Icons fighting in a flying transport was not in anybody's best interest. Especially when one could freeze things, and the other could make them intangible.

"How about we all just calm down and enjoy the ride. It's too early for a cat fight anyway." "Whatever," Jen said as she laid back once more and closed her eyes. "Wake me when we get there, princess." Zeva, thankfully, didn't say anything snarky in return.

I pulled my phone out and saw I had yet another text from Danielle. I didn't even open it this time. I knew if I kept giving in, I would eventually forgive her for what she did. She knew it too and was why she was so persistent.

I got up from my chair to go sit on the couch in the lounge. I twirled my phone in my hand as I seriously considered just texting her back. Zeva, surprisingly, moved from her lounge chair, and sat beside me on the couch. "Nice view, huh," she said as she was looking out the large window at clouds around us. The shift in the air from her sitting down blew a sweet fragrance my way. She smelled amazing. "Sure is," I said as I looked at her.

I was certain we were admiring two completely different views. While she was looking out at the world below us, I had taken notice of her figure in those black jeans, and her almost perfectly toned frame in that sleeveless shirt. Her hair bounced effortlessly as the transport moved, and as I admired her, as if on cue, my phone went off as another text message came through.

I was sure it was Danielle, and I didn't even look at the phone. The alert, did make me feel bad a little. Here I was gawking at Zeva, sister of my nemesis for lack of a better word, while ignoring my girlfriend. Ex- girlfriend. Whatever she was.

"We should be there in no time. These damn transports move faster than any plane ever could." As Zeva said this she licked her lips some and put her face in her hand. That slight movement sent her fragrance to me again. As fast as I felt bad, I suddenly didn't anymore. Hell, Danielle had her chance to do right by whatever we had and she didn't so tough shit.

"So, what does it feel like?" Zeva asked as she looked at me. "What does what feel like?" I responded. "Being part villain. Being able to do whatever you want. You have a freedom many of us can only dream off." I didn't respond. Instead I just looked at her.

I was confused as to what she was doing. At first, I thought she was making fun of my parents. Plenty of people did. Then, as I didn't answer, she never took her eyes from me. She really wanted an answer. Why did she want to know what it felt like to be half villain? I began to think this was her roundabout way of flirting with me. "It doesn't feel like anything," I finally said.

She nodded as she slipped yet another vitamin between her perfect lips. "You ever think you take too many of those?" I asked. She shook her head. "They keep the demons away. Keep me level headed, and keep me fit," she replied. "I've had to take them forever. My brother loses his shit if I don't."

I nodded and smiled. "When you come from a family of purestock like you do, it's probably best to keep the demons away." She didn't respond to this verbally. Instead she just took in a deep breath and let her head and shoulders dip some. She clearly had something on her mind, but I didn't really know how to ask her about it. Maybe I should make the first move.

Sister to my nemesis or not, she was stunning. She smelled like heaven and looked like an angel. Then suddenly, as I was looking at her, I saw an image of Danielle in my head, and it made me flinch a little.

"Approaching Imperial Lords' base," a robotic voice echoed inside of the transport. "Soon as I drift off, we are ready to land," Jen said. "Shut up and come see this," I replied to her as I turned from Zeva.

Jen unbuckled from her seat and walked over to the couch Zeva and I shared. "Excuse me," Jen said as she clearly bumped into Zeva on purpose and sat beside me. Thankfully I was in the middle of both of them, so no more petty interactions could occur.

"Wow." Jen said as she let her mouth drop open. "I know," I replied as I looked out of the window too. "I'm guessing you two have never seen the base before," Zeva replied. Her casual attitude led me to believe she had been here before at least once with Flex. Jen and I didn't respond to her question. We were too busy taking it all in.

As we moved through the clouds, we could see the base slowly coming into view. Clearly the funding they had was going to good use for more than just luxury transports. The

Imperial Lords base looked like something out of a fantasy movie.

For starters, there was the location. Located on the edge of Atlas City, the base was partially on land, and then partially in the water. The portion of the base that was on land was circular in the middle, but had tall spires around it composed of steel and glass, that touched the skies. In the back was what looked like it could have been a large tunnel, also made of glass, so it was completely see through, that lead into the water and, to my best guess, to the second part of the base which was found under water,

I didn't see it at first, but surrounding the base itself was a large energy barrier that rippled or pulsed every now and again. Had it not been for this ripple, I wouldn't have noticed it even being there. "Is that a force field?" I asked as I turned from the view to Zeva. She nodded her head.

"Being one of the leading supergroups in the world, comes with enemies. They have to be prepared. It will open for us when we get close enough to land."

Before I could respond, a loud alarm began to go off inside of the transport. I looked to the RMFC as its robotic arms began to press different buttons. "Zeva stood up and so did I. The alarm continued to wail. "What's going on?" Jen asked as she stood beside me. "I'm not sure," Zeva said.

My first reaction was that the transport was going down. Then the robotic voice echoed in the transport once more. "Enemy projectiles are engaged. Prepare for impact. Prepare for impact." My eyes widen, and just then I glanced out of the window and saw something. Several somethings, fly by the transport.

They weren't humans, but they did have a humanoid shape, and as they moved red trails streaked behind them from what looked like jetpacks. The transport shook as a loud explosion happened. "Critical hit detected. Shields at fifty percent," The robotic voice was all around us.

Zeva and Jen seemed to be on the same page now as fear consumed them. "Who in Atlas would be attacking us?" Jen said as the ship was hit again. "Shields at thirty percent." "The Lords have enemies, it could be anybody," Zeva responded.

"Call your brother," I said to Zeva. I couldn't believe the words were coming out of my mouth, but Flex could catch this transport as easy as a person catching a falling football. She frantically pulled out her phone. "It's not working."

Not working? How could her phone not be working? It wasn't like we were in an area that could block the signal. We were in sky after all. I looked at my phone and so did Jen.

My phone was out too. It was on but it seemed to be locked. The transport shook one final time and everything went black inside. "Shield power depleted," the robotic voice said. "If we get hit again, we are going down," Jen said with panic in her voice.

I had never seen her this way. She was breathing so fast that I could barely understand her words. My mind raced for a second. "Stay in here," I said as I pressed a button beside the door we used to board the craft. With ease, and a hum, the transport door opened.

"Be prepared to turn yourself and Zeva intangible if you need to," I said to Jen. She shook her head quickly, as she continued to breath heavy. I turned to Zeva. "Keep trying to reach Flex." "What are-" Jen went to speak, but her words faded away because before she could finish, I jumped out of the transport, and out into the open sky.

CHAPTER 11

IMPERIAL LORDS

For a second, I let myself fall through the sky, and then I used my power, and took control. My descent stopped and I was hovering in the sky now. The transport is still moving, but three of those things are flying behind it. I couldn't make out what they were, but they were still shooting at our transport, with beams of red energy. Luckily, they were missing more than they were hitting.

It was funny. They had better aim, when the ship had shields protecting it. While I was inside of the transport, their attacks seem precise, and now they were barely getting close. Was it a diversion to draw me out? That didn't make sense at all, considering they were paying me no attention.

I could see the red trails they were emitting from their jetpacks as they moved in the open sky around me. I didn't have much time to do whatever it was I intended to do. I knew Jen and Zeva could keep the transport up in the air and on course for a little while. If I remember correctly, they both did good in our flight simulation class. I however didn't have to take the class, because I myself could naturally fly. Still, if one of those things found its mark, the transport would crash.

I felt energy crackle within me as I created a larger than normal force field, so that I could still have some room to breathe. As the pale blue field expanded, I stopped it once the field was about the size of a minivan.

I shook my arms for a second. Pro tip, it's always good to loosen up before you go into a fight. Then with a force so strong that it created a booming sound, I flew. There was only three of them, so I set my sights on the one closest to the ship. Oddly, he hadn't shot at the ship in a few seconds.

As I got close to it, I could see that it wasn't a person at all. It wasn't even a humanoid creature. It was, a robot, or android. I have a hard time remembering which is which. With a square-shaped head, no facial features, and long legs and arms, the robot reminded me a lot of the one that was the pilot of the RMFC.

The major difference between the two was that this one flying alongside me in the air, had a portion of its back that allowed for it to fly. As I got closer, it raised its hand up and fired a pulse of red energy. This pulse was headed directly for the transport, and we were so close the blast couldn't miss. I zoomed ahead of the android, or robot, as fast as a I could, but I still wouldn't get to the transport in time.

I stretched my hand out, and created a thin, force field in the air. The blast from the android collided with my force field and exploded. The transport was safe, but to my surprise, my force field had a minor crack in it. A crack! Not only could I see it, but I could feel it.

My force fields are an extension of myself, so when they are damaged I can tell. Much like if somebody cut my hand. Even if I wasn't looking, I'd still be able to feel it. This told me that whatever these guys were, they packed a serious punch. Not too much can damage my force fields.

I looked over at the android beside me, and moved closer to him while at the same time shifting the size of the field around me. I could have just shrunk the force field, but then I'd be trapped in a tiny space, and the thought of that alone was enough to make me want to heave. Instead, I caused one side of my force field to retract, while making the other side large.

Once I was beside the android and had very little force field between us, I formed a fist and punched it in the back. Thankfully, whatever they were made of wasn't able to stand up to my super strength. Had they been diamond- plated or titanium, I may not had been strong enough to do damage to anything other than my hand.

As I pulled my fist back and readjusted in my force field, the first android fell, and now there were only two left. I could see the transport, circling in the air now. "What in Atlas's name are they doing?" I said to myself. Why didn't they just land?

Just then, a beam of red energy hit my force field and caused me to flinch and fall through the sky. I was fine, but my force field took a beating. I caught myself in the air, and flew back towards my attacker. Before I could get close enough another blast hit me from a different side that once more swatted me away like I was a pest.

These guys were starting to piss me off. The sky around me turned a familiar shade of blue, that had nothing to do with it being a sky. "Let's see how you like it, asshole," I said under my breath as I flew towards one of the androids, releasing bolt after bolt of my Impact Blast. My aim wasn't the best, but at least one of them had to hit the damn thing.

Or so I thought. To my shock, the android dodged them all and fired back several times at me. Many of his blasts missed, while others collided with my new Impact Blasts midair .

To the people below we likely looked like the makings of a great science fiction movie where the flying enemies fired lasers at each other. I zoomed around a cloud and stretched my hand open, creating and closing a force field around one of the android, robot, things.

As it fought the inside of my shield I could feel my energy draining. I was getting tired. As I closed my fist, the force field grew tight around the android. His partner turned its attention from me to help his friend.

I smiled as he flew in the direction of his trapped comrade. I unleashed a volley of blasts his way, and one found its mark directly in the spot where a butt would have been, had this been a human. The android exploded in the air as debris fell. The explosion caused my flying to be thrown off some as the waves of force echoed back through the sky.

I was confused as to how nobody from below in the Imperial Lords base had come to see what all the blasts, and explosions were. We were in the air, yes, but still we were also practically on their doorstep. I tried not to think about that, and instead focused on my task. This was almost over.

"One more," I said as I continued to close the force field around the last remaining android. He began to fire inside the force field and two things happened at once. Just when it fired, I removed the force field and punched it in its back causing its means of flight to fade and thus it fell to the ground below.

Despite this, that single shot the android got off had found its mark. The bolt of red energy had hit the ship, and now it was falling through the sky. "Think, think," I said to myself. I flew towards the transport and found myself in the front of it. I put my hands on it and pushed with every ounce of power I had, and the transport may as well had laughed at me and my efforts.

It continued to fall as if I wasn't even there. I wasn't strong enough. "Okay, new plan." I said as I moved in the air around the falling transport. From where we were, the transport was going to fall directly on land, and hit the Imperial Lords' base. No not the base, the force field. This was good. I could get the others out and just let the force field do its job. Easy enough, I thought to myself as I smiled.

I prepared myself to fly inside to grab Jen and Zeva, but just at the moment, the large dome- shaped force field around the base faded away as if it was turned off. "No," I screamed out loud. This is what I get for smiling and thinking for once, just once, something would have been easy. "Okay, so a new plan, for the new plan," I said as I watched the transport fall.

I wasn't strong enough to push it back or catch it in the sky. Its natural force of motion was against me, but what if I just redirected it. I flew around the other side of the transport and once more placed my hands on it and pushed. I could see Jen and Zeva inside looking at me eyes wide.

This time I pushed it to the side, and to my amazement, the damn thing moved. In less than a minute I had spun the transport around in the air and aimed it towards the water below.

I could feel the little energy I had fading away. I was using all of my powers in unison and the effects were draining. I was going to need a king size feast when all this was over.

I flew inside of the transport to find a heavy breathing Zeva watching monitors while Jen was sitting on top of the RMFC and controlling the transport. "That was impressive, but please tell me you have a plan," Jen said. "I lost control minutes ago and have no idea what to do." she screamed out as we continued to fall towards the ocean below us.

"Get up," I screamed at her. I grabbed Zeva by the hand as Jen got close to me. "You know we can't fly right?" Zeva shouted as we went to the open door. "Trust me," I yelled back over the wind that circled around us.

As we all held hands, I lead the way as we jumped out of the transport. As soon as we were out, I created a force field. Once my field was up, I let their hands go and they sort of floated beside me.

I wanted to watch and make sure that the transport actually made it to the ocean as I had planned but I was too tired, and felt myself slowly descending to the ground near the Imperial Lords' base. Oddly enough, once we landed on the ground, the force field protecting the base returned to normal.

I fell to the ground on my knees, breathing hard as the last bit of energy and my force field faded away. I laid on my back, spread eagled on the grass and felt the gentle massage all over my body. "Thank you, Flora," I said through broken breaths as the grass continued to massage me. "Nicely done," a voice said from behind me.

I sat up and looked around me. The girls were already on their feet, but they hadn't expended the energy I had. A man was walking towards us and clapping his hands. He had strong cheekbones, a pointed chin, and greasy black hair. His uniform was a navy blue, microfiber suit that covered him from head to toe.

Once he finally got close to us, he stopped clapping and bowed slightly towards us. "I'm the Mechanic." Nobody said anything. I was pretty sure everyone knew who he was because of our ties to the Imperial Lords,

The Mechanic was a less popular member of the Imperial Lords, and he had an ability similar to Mrs. Reid's, in a lesser fashion. The Mechanic could build, and understand all things tech, but on the flip side, once something was built he could control it with his mind.

As I ran through his powerset in my head, I felt my face stiffen as my breathing increased. "I was worried there for a second, but you figured it out," he said quickly. He spoke very fast, as if he were racing with himself to see just how fast he could go. "Figured out what?" Jen asked. "How to get here safely while preventing casualties." He looked up at me and beamed. Well, moreso him than you two. His reputation is well-earned." The Mechanic looked me up and down. "You really do have four powers. It's fascinating."

Another voice came from above, "And he shows them off every chance he gets." Jen and Zeva looked up, but I didn't. I knew that voice all too well. As he landed Jen screamed to see him. Standing over six feet tall, with muscles that could be easily seen through his shirt, as loose as it was, was Zeva's older brother, Flex. Everything about him looked perfect, his hair his teeth, even his damn skin was flawless.

er six feet tall, with muscles that could be easily seen through his loose shirt was Zeva's older brother, Flex. Everything about him looked perfect. His hair, his teeth, even his damn skin was flawless.

He had on some green sweatpants and sneakers. Clearly a casual day for him. He looked at the girls behind me and smiled somewhat. Flex walked by me and, despite all of the open space, he bumped into me with his shoulder a little too hard. The blow, appeared accidental, but shot pain through my entire right side and caused me to grit my teeth. His strength made even a shoulder bump feel like a truck just hit me.

It took all of my control not to grab at the pain with my hand. "My bad," he said with a laugh.

Jen, unable to control herself, ran and gave him a hug. He gently patted her on the back with one hand, and then embraced his sister. "Hey Z," he said to her as he let her go. Then he held her face in his hands and looked her over. He even quickly placed his hand on her forehead. Did he think she was sick or something?

"When was the last time you took your pills?" "I'm fine," Zeva said. She had always carried on like they were vitamins, but he said pills. Like they were more for a specific issue, not just support. "I got your room all set, you're going to love it. It's like five feet from the main gym."

A woman suddenly walked up and stood beside Flex and cleared her throat. He instantly went from big brother mode and back to Imperial Lord again. She was a dark- skinned woman with long black hair, and dressed in all white. "Nice to meet the new interns. Welcome to the Imperial Lords," she said as she shook all of our hands. Her voice was soft, and her figure was very slim.

I recognized her as the Icon called Detach. She could split herself into four copies and each copy had the same powers as the original, which was that she had enhanced reflexes, but only while around Voids and only for a certain amount of time. Not the best power to have, but certainly not the worst. She mostly handled the day to day operations of the Imperial Lords, and thus served as a vital and high- ranking role.

"So, you two knew he was going to give us that little test that could have killed us." I asked. "No. We didn't," Detach said as she glared at him. The Mechanic avoided her eyes and whistled slightly. "He gets out of hand from time to time with his little, inventions. Sadly, most of the tech here he either created or he is the only person able to understand it."

I nodded slowly. "I see." I said as I stepped forward and sent a punch directly to The Mechanic's face. Guess some of my energy had returned after all. He fell to the ground instantly and grabbed his jaw. "You almost got us killed, asshole." My eyes turned blue as I looked down on him. "Easy. Easy," Flex said as he put his hand on my shoulder and applied more pressure than was called for. I threw his hand off of me as quick as it landed. "Don't touch me Ken doll."

"Stop it. Both of you." Detach said. "Flex, help him up and take him to my office." Flex narrowed his eyes at me, and then did as he was told. With ease, he lifted the man to his feet and lead him to the entrance of the base. "Girls, follow Flex inside and wait for me there. I need to have a talk with Hunter." Zeva and Jen glanced at each other. I stood silent, trying to figure out just what was going on here.

"What about our bags and stuff that were in the Transport?" Zeva asked. Detach smiled. "They will be delivered to your rooms. The Mechanic controlled the transport so it landed safely in the landing bay." Zeva nodded her head and trotted off to catch her brother. Jen looked at me for a moment as if I was in trouble, then walked off behind Zeva.

"Jennifer," Detach called out over her shoulder. I smiled to myself. No doubt Jen was cursing in her head. She hated being called Jennifer. The only people who got a pass were her parents, and even they said it rarely. "Your father should be inside. Tell him to swing by my office in an hour." Jen gave a thumb's up as she walked in. Detach seemed so, nice. Her soft tone, her smile, even her eyes. They seemed almost motherly. Comforting.

"Okay so here's the deal, you little bastard," she said as she glared at me. So much for motherly and comforting. "I know your backstory, and I, personally, don't give a shit. I don't care who your mother was, who your father was, who raised you or what the world sees you as. When you step foot in that building you're an Imperial Lord member for the next two years. You're part of a team, this team, because somebody saw something in you. Saw that you had the potential to be a hero." I scoffed. "Fine, but strike another member like that again, and I'll recommend for Impervious to kick you out. If you have a problem, you bring it to me, or Impervious himself. Got it?"

I didn't respond. "Do I need to repeat myself?" she asked. I swallowed slightly, and shook my head. "Good," she said as she returned to her nicer self. "Now, follow me inside for the tour, and welcome to The Imperial Lords." She turned and walked away. Leaving me, and my sliver of pride, standing there alone.

153

CHAPTER 12

ENTER PICASSO

I followed Detach into the inner workings of the base. Her strong words only a moment ago seemed like something the person holding the door for me would never say. Had I not actually heard her say the words, I would think she didn't have it in her to be so, direct.

She even did a slight fancy bow, as she held the door open for me to walk in. Jen and Zeva were standing on the inside chatting. Apparently, dealing with a near death experience, even one that wasn't real, with each other had brought the two closer together. For some reason, that made me a little jealous. I didn't say anything, but part of me was upset that Jen had become friends so easy with Zeva, and the other part of me secretly wished it was me. I was newly single, and couldn't think of anybody else that I'd rather get close to than Zeva.

Her brother may have been a dick, but Zeva was still amazingly attractive, and smelled like something I could inhale for hours on end. I kept my feelings for her in check, though. It was entirely possible what I was feeling was a rebound effect from my breakup with Danielle.

"Okay, people, this tour will be short and sweet. I'm giving you the basics," Detach said. "This is the visitor's entrance." I looked around, the entrance was nice. It gave me the feeling of stepping inside a fancy bank.

Plenty of lighting, a shiny decorated floor, a few elevators on each side, and there was even soft music playing around us. All it was missing was a directory mounted on the wall. The focal point of the entry way however, were the statues. As we walked in there were several golden statues standing over fifteen feet tall, that didn't even come close to touching the ceiling.

As I walked closer to the statues, Jen and Zeva seemed to have noticed them too. Detach was still talking. Saying something about how the members have a different way to enter the base. I doubted any of us were listening at this point because we were in such awe of the statues.

"Every newbie in the base, drifts here to the statues," Detach said as she stood behind us. "Some even call it the Heroes Hall, but that's not an official name." She stood silent, as she too looked at the statues. There were nine of them. Four on each side, and one statue in the middle.

Each of them had more detail than any statue I had seen before. Facial features, clothing, and even the hair looked as if they were merely people dipped in gold, and left on display. "These are the original members of the Imperial Lords." Detach said as she placed a hand on her hip. "See anybody that looks familiar?"

Zeva answered quickly. "Is this, Mr. Impervious?" she asked as she point to the statue furthest to the left. Detach nodded. "Yep. That's him." she answered with a smile. "He looks so, young." I said as I took in the statue. I knew Impervious had been an Icon since he was younger, but his statue made him look like he was no older than we were, and he was a full- fledged member?

"How did he become a member at such a young age?" Jen asked. "I never knew he was this young. I just thought he was born old, like Morgan Freeman." I said before Detach could answer. She laughed. "Impervious, or Davis as he was called by his first name back then, joined the Lords so young because at the time, his brother was one of the most," Detach paused and looked at me for some reason. "well- known Icons in the city. They offered him membership because of this. He was in his early twenties."

From the looks on their faces Jen and Zeva were just hearing this news for the first time too. I never knew Impervious had a brother, and it seems like he used his connections to bully his way into what would lead to his greatness. "Sadly, the rest of the Lords died shortly after their statues were made. They went on a mission that was kept secret, and never returned." She wiped at her eyes and pointed at another statue. "Including my father, Slowpoke."

I could feel my eyes grow wide, and we all looked at her. "Wait," Jen said as she held her hands up, but finished her question. "Your dad was Slowpoke?" Detach nodded her head and smiled.

"That's right. Being an Imperial Lord runs in the family for me, too." Slowpoke was an Icon with a well- documented power set. It was assumed that he had super speed, but in reality, he had the reverse. He had the ability to create time bubbles. Time bubbles could grow to a decent size, similar to force fields, and then effectively slow down time inside of them for everything inside except for the caster. So, to people looking at him, it seemed like superspeed.

The cool thing about what Slowpoke did, was that it also gave him an edge in many situations, according to documented text. Because he wasn't actually moving fast, he had time to do so much once the time bubble was in effect. For example, he could create a bubble, and then workout for two hours inside the time bubble, but in reality, only two seconds passed. It was a very complex power, both to use and to understand.

So, that's a bland example but you get the point. "After the founding members never returned, Davis took the name Impervious, and began to reform the Imperial Lords over the next several years. As you know, the rest is history. He went on to do many great deeds. None greater than ending the war we now know as the Battle of Ages."

Detach was a founding member's daughter. She, like me, had lost a parent to the life of being a hero. Hell, she didn't even get closure because the founding members never returned. How could she live with not knowing what happened?

She turned from the statue and smiled at us, with her eyes slightly red. "Now let's move, along shall we?" What followed was a rag tag tour of the place. The level that was on land, was mostly a tourist attraction. This was for people who wanted to see inside one of the most well- known hero bases in the world. It was even complete with gift shops, diners, game rooms, an autograph and picture booth, and perhaps the most advanced security you would ever see outside of a spy movie.

The lower levels, where it went underwater was where we would be spending the bulk of our time. As she lead us below, we were given details on areas we weren't allowed to access. Imperial Lord members were never to be disturbed on their downtime, so unless Zeva wanted to see Flex, or if Jen and I wanted to see her dad, we had no reason to go to a Lord's personal chambers. This was not a major issue for Jen and I, though. Life-Line usually spent his nights at home with the family so he was rarely even in his area.

As the hour went by, we were shown the medical bay and how to access it, just in case something happened and Mr. Reid wasn't around to heal us. We saw several cafeterias, even more game rooms, lounges, libraries, training areas, costume repair shops, a viewing deck to see the ocean around us, and even where The Mechanic did his stuff.

It truly was an amazing base, that felt almost like an underground mansion. We finally stopped in the middle of a hall and Detach clapped her hands. "Well, this has been fun, but this is where I leave you with Prism."

We all looked at each other and then looked around. Jen lifted her hat and fixed her hair. "Um, who?" she said as she placed her hat back down. Detach held a finger up and smiled. She looked into the air and loudly said, "Prism."

A person flickered into being. Literally flickered as if he was a blinking television. "Yes, ma'am." Zeva jumped back at the random appearance of the man. He was an old white man with a head full of gray hair. He had on shiny black shoes, gray pants, a white shirt, black blazer, and snow- white gloves. For all purposes he looked like a butler.

"Everyone, this is Prism." The man did a slight bow. "Teleporting Icon?" I asked. "No sir, I am a hologram," Prism said as he flickered a little more. "Hologram?" I repeated. Prism turned to Detach and made a face to her, in which she laughed at. "Yes, a hologram." Detach replied. "Prism is our automated assistant for the entire base. He can be accessed anytime, and at any location in the base. He can be in several places at once too. Think of him as a search engine for the base."

I stepped forward and looked at him in the face. He looked so, real. Had it not been for the flickering, I would not have known he wasn't human. Jen walked up beside me and moved her hand through the hologram. Prism screamed, causing Jen and I to flinch. The he burst out laughing, and so did Detach.

"Sorry, young Lord's," Prism said. "I am only joking. I feel no pain." To solidify this point, Detach moved her hand through Prism back and forth. Just at that moment, another woman walked up to us, that looked exactly like Detach. "Prime," the woman said. "Life-Line is in your office."

Detach, or Prime, as she was just called, nodded. "I felt him talking to you. Thanks for coming to me to let me know." she said as the other woman smiled, and then suddenly, the woman identical to her, turned into a gaseous form and faded into Detach. We looked at her with confusion on our faces. I had guessed this was one of her clones, but seeing them join like that was a little gross.

"As I'm sure you have guessed, that was one of my clones. When I use my ability to create them, we are linked. Anything they see, feel, or experience, is sent back to me. For some reason they all decided to call me Prime. Now, I have a meeting to attend." she turned to Prism.

"Prism, show them to their sleeping areas." Prism nodded and then, another version of him flickered into existence. Now there were two of them standing in front of us. "Oh, Hunter." Detach called from down the hall. I looked at her with my brow raised.

"Don't forget our talk okay?" I rolled my eyes some and then nodded. "What talk?" Jen asked as Zeva looked on." I'll tell you later." I replied. "We just got here and you're having talks already?" Zeva added in as she shook her head.

"Follow me, Young Lords," both of the Prism holograms said in unison. One walked away in the same direction as Detach up the hall followed by Jen and Zeva. I stood there as I watched Zeva walk away. I enjoyed the view, until they were no longer in sight. "You finished? Did you see enough? Or shall I ask her to come back and then walk away again?" Prism said with a smirk on his face.

I wouldn't have expected a hologram to be such a smartass. He really was life- like. "No, I'm fine." "Good," he replied.

"Now follow me, young Lord." He slowly walked up the hall. "We have to get you to your room and settled in before dinner."

His words, were music to my ears. I had been fighting hunger for the last hour and was still running on empty after saving us from a crashing transport that wasn't even really crashing. I couldn't wait for dinner.

As I followed Prism around a corner, a young man was looking down at a notepad, and walked directly through Prism and right into me. We both stumbled some as he dropped his pad.

"Sorry. I didn't see you," he said as he stumbled over his words and dropped down to pick his pad up. "That happens when you walk, looking down." I replied as I saw his pad for the first time.

It had a picture drawn on it. It was of a woman with her hair in a bun. She had a full round face, and lips to match. I didn't know who she was, but the picture he was drawing had looked like a real photo. Walking skills aside, he had talent. "No. No. No," he said as he shook his head.

I stepped back from him. "You okay?" "Yes. No. Yes," he finally said. "I'm fine. Fine." My eyes narrowed. "Lord Walter, this is," Prism stopped talking and looked at me. "Oh. Hunter," I said as I extended my hand.

As he looked from his sketch pad to my hand he seemed conflicted. He looked up to me finally and said nothing. It was weird. He had black curly hair, a keen nose, and a cleft in his chin. Despite his awkwardness he was dressed well. He had on brown designer boots, some blue pants, and a black hoodie under a brown overcoat.

"I," he stammered. "Don't shake hands." His eyes darted away from me, as if he was ashamed of what he just said. He quickly added, "I don't mind touching things though. Or being touched. Just not hands. I don't touch hands. Never hands." I raised my hands up to halt him from speaking.

"Okay, no hands, got it." I looked at him as a second passed, then it hit me. The sketchpad, his awkwardness, and his name. It all fit. "Are you Picasso?" I asked. He looked away from me and took a step back. "By Atlas, it is you!" I looked at Prism who gave a slight nod in my direction.

"Holy shit! You're Picasso."

CHAPTER 13

IMPERVIOUS

"**P**lease, don't shout," he said as he stepped back from me some. "Shout?" I repeated. "Yes, young Lord. Shouting is what we call what you are currently doing." Prism added. I looked from Prism, and then back to Walter, chest moving back and forth as I continued to breath as if I was running.

"I'll see that he gets to his room," Walter said to Prism. Prism nodded and then shot me a glance, as he flickered out of existence. We stood alone in the hall now. With neither of us talking for that moment it seemed quiet on a creepy level. I could only hear the humming of computers, and the air circulating in the hall.

He took a deep breath and stepped back from me a bit more. "Yes, I am," he froze. "I'm Picasso," he finally finished.

I clapped my hands together. "I knew it." I hated how I felt right now. I don't like to get star struck by Icons, and I usually don't. I tended to leave that sort of thing to Jen. Picasso, himself, wasn't even really that famous, but the rumors of what his powers were, was.

"Let's get you to your room, before dinner. Father will want us there on time, especially if you are to take your oath tonight." He held his sketch pad close and then turned around and walked up the hall. "You mean Impervious, right?" I said as I jogged to catch up with him. He didn't reply. "Had I not known the stories, I wouldn't believe he was your dad, you guys look nothing alike." I said as I finally caught up to him.

"Picasso." A man walking up the hall said as he waved in our direction. Picasso paused, as the person got closer to us. He was an Asian youth around my age or a little older. I was taller than he was, but only a little. I took in his appearance.

His spiky black hair, strong cheek bones, and very pale skin. "Who's this,?" he said as he nodded to me. Standing next to Picasso, the man looked very, casual. While Picasso was dressed like a model from a magazine, this guy simply had on some gray jeans, a dark red shirt, and some white shoes. An outfit that I myself likely had the same clothes to put together. So, points for his style, or lack thereof

"He's one of the interns." Picasso said as he stepped back so as not to be between us both. "Oh. Internship. I just finished mine last year," he said as he stuck his hand out to me. "Kevin Lee, but you can call me Power Prince."

Immediately, I recognized the name. I shook his hand and in return received a minor shock. I say minor but I could hear the pop as we touched. I looked at my hand as he pulled away. "Hunter Monroe." I said as I shoved my hand in my pocket and pulled out my cell. I looked at it, and the battery was at fifty percent. Then I gave it to Kevin.

"You mind?" I asked. He smiled, took my phone, held it for all of three seconds and then gave it back to me. I looked at the phone again and it read that the battery had one hundred percent. I shook my head. "You really are a living battery?" I replied. He opened his arms and did a bow. "One of my many talents."

Power Prince had a power portfolio of one ability that focused on energy generation. He was actually able to generate energy on a supreme scale. He could power a city as easily as he charged my phone if he wanted to. He also could channel his energy, which when manifested had a pink appearance, into his hands, allowing him to use it to enhance his strikes and to propel himself into the air. It was more like, super jumping, and less like flying.

"Kevin joined us last year after his internship with The Conduits." Picasso said as he flipped to a fresh page in his sketch pad. The Conduits were a supergroup from a neighboring city. Lower level indeed and with supreme energy powers like Kevin's he would have been an easy choice for The Imperial Lords.

"Nice meeting you," Kevin said as he waved again and walked around us. "I have a date with a tv series that I'm binge watching." He continued up the hall, and then turned around to face us once more. "Oh, and don't let Picasso freak you out, he takes some getting used to, but he's an okay guy."

We watched him walk a few more feet and then go into a room on the same hall. "I always assumed Power Prince would be taller," I jokingly said, but Picasso didn't laugh. Not even a smirk, instead he picked up the conversation as if we didn't just meet Kevin.

"To your statement about our looks, no, we don't look alike at all," he responded casually. "I knew who you were long before you introduced yourself to me, by the way," he said as he glanced at me and then continued to walk. "You're almost as famous as Flex is." I stopped walking.

"You think the pretty boy has more fame than me? I'm offended," I said as I fake gasped and clenched my chest. Still, no grin or any sign of humor being received. "No. It's just that Flex, is famous. You are just widely insulted and as a result, have become infamous." I grimaced.

"I was just joking," I said as I smacked him on the back. "I don't care about being as famous as anybody. My fame has done nothing for me, but kept me in the public eye when I didn't want to be."

He said nothing but nodded and continued to walk up the hall. "You have to loosen up a bit," I said as I looked at him. His jaw visibly clenched but still no additional reaction followed. "So, what's your deal?" I asked.

"Excuse me?" he replied. "Well I have always heard that you never leave the base." "I have no reason to. We have everything here that I need." I exhaled as we finally came to a door. "Remember what I said about loosening up a little?" he nodded. "You may want to do that sooner, rather than later. You're giving off a serial killer vibe." His eyes widened.

"Yeah. Creepy, follow you down a dark alley, stab you, serial killer vibe. Not to mention, with your powers you could be running this place when your dad retired." He looked at me with a blank stare.

"I prefer to simply sketch. Time is slow, and that is how I spend it." He turned to walk away. "Wait," I said. He looked at me. "Look," I stammered some. I didn't know exactly how to ask him to show me his ability. It was just so rare that I had to see it, though. Having energy powers was common for Icons, so while seeing Kevin's ability was cool, it was more of a quick way to charge my phone. Hell, even I had an energy based power with my Impact Blast, but what Picasso could do was, out of this world like and I had to see it. Had to.

"Could you draw me something?." He took a deep breath and then looked down to his feet. "I suppose so, what would you like?" I thought about it for a moment, then my stomach growled. "A slice of pizza." I replied finally. "You will ruin your dinner." Picasso quickly said back. I shook my head.

"You have to learn this about me Picasso. In my book pizza is eternal. Anytime, is a time for pizza." He bit his lip and then slowly nodded in agreement. He raised one hand, and extended his index finger, which now had a glowing tip.

"Holy shit." I said as I watched the finger glow. It was so intense. As if a tiny sun was somehow trapped inside of it. He slowly moved his finger and as he did a line was created in the air. He drew a triangle, and then drew several circles inside the triangle.

Instantly the glowing triangle he drew in the air, turned into a slice of pizza. "Hurry," he said. I quickly stuck my hands out and grabbed it. It was pizza. Real live, warm, cheesy, pepperoni pizza. I looked at the slice in my hand and then back to him. Even the smells were unreal. The aroma from the slice made my mouth water and my stomach all but screamed.

In a few large bites the pizza was gone, and was in fact the best pizza I had ever tasted. "So, anything?" I asked as I licked my fingers. His brow raised. "Anything," I repeated. "Anything you draw, with your fingers becomes real. If what my school says is true, you're the only reality warper ever documented."

He avoided my gaze. I could feel myself going full fanboy, but I couldn't help it.

"By definition, you are literally one of the most powerful Icons alive. Not to mention who your dad is. Which, well hell you're like Icon royalty." He said nothing, but his finger began to fade back to normal.

"It's almost like magic." I finally said just to end the silence. "Magic isn't real." he replied quickly. I could feel my eyes roll. "I know magic isn't real, I'm just saying. Like that is how amazing your powers are. You, nevermind, forget it." I placed my hand on the doorknob to my room. "How long before dinner?" I asked.

Picasso had already started walking away from where we were. "Half an hour," he said without looking back. "Prism will escort you there." "Hey wait," I shouted down the hall. He stopped walking. "Thanks for, you know, showing me. It took your serial killer vibe down a little. Now we just have to get you to actually want to leave the base."

He nodded his head and then continued up the hall.

I entered my room to find that, surprisingly, it was an identical replica of my room back home. "How in," I stopped mid- sentence. My bags were already on the bed. I didn't know if I should have been confused, or comforted. It was weird, because I wasn't sure how they even knew what my room at home looked like to copy, yet at the same time, I was enjoying being in a familiar setting.

I wondered if Jen and Zeva found replica rooms, too. I sat down on the bed, and checked my phone. I hadn't heard from Danielle in a while. Maybe she finally got the hint that I didn't want to talk. Was I missing her without even realizing it? Why else would I check the phone for a message from her?

I figured it was better to put my clothes away, Prism would be coming to get me soon. It was then that I realised that something was different about my replica room.

Every detail was perfect, even my attached bathroom was there. The major difference, was there were no windows. My room and bathroom back home had windows. Shitty views, but still I had windows. This room didn't. Maybe they thought a window to the ocean would take away from the replica rooms' appeal.

My hand touched the wall where my window would have been. "Young Lord," I heard a voice say from behind me as I jumped. I turned around quickly with my eyes glowing blue. Prism laughed. "Really? Did you forget I wasn't real?" The room turned to its normal colors.

"I know, but damn, announce yourself next time. Like from outside the door. What if I was doing something private with myself?" "Private with, yourself?" Prism repeated back to me. I shook my head. "Never mind."

Prism looked at me with his holographic face passive. "Shall we go?" he said as he turned, and walked through my door. When I opened it, he was standing on the other side waiting for me. "This way, young Lord."

I followed him and in a time shorter than it took for Picasso to show me my room, we were greeted by the smells of savory foods, and chatter. Despite having the slice of pizza earlier, my stomach was still growling like crazy. I had used my powers too much for one slice to tame the beast of my belly.

Prism stopped walking as we entered the room. I could hear people but I couldn't see anything. I looked at Prism. "Just up there," he said as his flickering form pointed to a set of four floating steps.

I placed my foot down on the first step slowly. It didn't move. I didn't know how it was staying afloat, or how it was able to support my weight, but it was. As I walked up the steps I could see a great hall before me full of people.

It was a scene almost like out of a movie. The walls all around the great hall had purple glowing lights cast on them while the main lights were turned down low. Different areas of the great hall were separated by walls of glass wrapped in a steel frame. One room had a few dozen tables, and several tables of food spread out. This was the room I wanted to enter first.

Another room had people dancing inside, and the final room had nothing at all going on . In the main room there were around a hundred people that were casually talking to each other and drinking. A waiter even walked around with food on trays for people to grab as they pleased.

"Hunter," I heard a voice calling to me from inside the crowd. In a second, Mr. Reid showed up and was eating a mini hotdog, dressed in his Icon uniform. He stood beside me and placed his hand on my shoulder. Thankfully it wasn't the sore one that Flex bumped me in. "This is all for you three. The interns," I nodded my head as he took a bite of his hotdog again.

"Who are all these people though?" I asked with a grimace. I didn't mind people, but I hated tight spaces, and so many people here made me get that cramped spaces feeling. "Various assholes and important types," Mr. Reid said. "Mainly people who donate money to the Lords."

"Several faces you will know though, as you walk around." he looked down at me. "Detach told me about your, incident when you arrived." I snorted. "Incident? I punched him. Nothing more, nothing less."

Mr. Reid shook his head. "Yeah, I know but you can't go around punching people. You bring it to me or one of the Lords. I already have spoken to The Mechanic." I looked at him as he finished his hotdog.

"You did?" He nodded as he grabbed a mini burger from a waiter walking by. "I told him if he puts my kids in jeopardy again, I'll use my powers and drain the life from him." "Damn. Can you really do that?" I asked him. He laughed slightly. "Nope. He doesn't know that though. He got the point."

"Thanks," I said. "Just no more hitting." Mr. Reid repeated. "This place is awesome, isn't it," I heard Jen say as she, once again became visible in front of us. I looked around expecting Zeva to be with her, but spotted her with Flex talking to some people across the room.

"Whoa. No cap?" I asked as I looked at Jen's hair being exposed. She glared at Mr. Reid. "No. I was instructed to leave it behind." He cleared his throat. "Make sure you guys eat before you take your oath," and he quickly made his way through the crowd.

"Your room look like the one from home, too?" she asked me. "Yeah. Weird, isn't it?" I said as I lead the way to the food room. Once inside the food area, Jen looked around as she decided what she wanted to put on her plate.

The fact that she had a plate was funny to me. "Amateur," I said to her as I just began grabbing food and piling it in my mouth. Several rolls, chicken legs, slices of roast, three cookies, one slice of cake, and a small portion of broccoli later and I was finally feeling full again. I wiped my hands clean and finally noticed several people, including Jen, watching me in amazement.

I shrugged. "What, I was hungry." "Yeah but you weren't raised in a barn. Mom would go ape shit if she had witnessed you scarf all that down using just your hands." Jen said as she wrapped a few cookies in a napkin and put them in her pocket.

I quickly grabbed a napkin and did the same thing. It's always good to have snacks for later. As I selected my cookies, the chatter in the great hall suddenly stopped, and was replaced by clapping.

Jen and I turned to look through the glass wall of the room and saw what all the fuss was about. Mr. Impervious had finally made it to the dinner. Jen and I slowly made it out of the room full of food and to the main area again.

He could have been dressed in his uniform like the other members of the Imperial Lords, but instead he had on a navy-blue suit that, seeing as how it looked perfect on him, had to have been tailored. His white shirt that he wore with it had the top three buttons undone, so it exposed his salt and pepper-haired chest to the world.

Jen and I made our way to the edge of the crowd as he walked towards us. He stopped here and there to shake people's hands, to casually wave, and to even take pictures with those bold enough to ask.

We both knew of Mr. Impervious, but neither of us had ever seen him before this close. He was an Icon that few could compare to in popularity or power. While in his late fifties he still had the body of a college athlete. Perhaps the only person with a better physical build in the whole room was Flex. In reverse, Impervious was about the only person that could match pure strength with Flex.

He finally made it to Jen and I. He looked at us, well moreso me than Jen. He was about the same height as I was. His face and head were cowered with salt and pepper hair and even his teeth seemed to be impervious to outside damage. They were perfect in every way.

There were rumors that he wanted to retire and pass the torch, but seeing him in person now, he looked like he could go on kicking ass well into his eighties. "You two are the interns, right?" he said as he extended his hand to me.

Camera flashed around us as I shook his hand. "Life-Line's kids." he said as he shook Jens hand. "Yes sir." she replied back. He looked at me once more and had an unusual look on his face. Like he wanted to say something but didn't know the right words. The camera finally stopped flashing and the people around us went back to their fun.

"You look, a lot like him." he finally said to me. Jen looked to me with a frown on her face. "Like who?" I asked. "Your father." I felt myself swallow a lump in my throat. This was unexpected. I didn't realize Impervious knew my dad. "You fought my father?" I asked slowly.

Mr. Impervious grinned and shook his head. "No. We raced before though. Before he chose the life that he did. The stories are true. He, to this day, has been the only Icon with speed greater than mine."

It was weird. He spoke of my dad as if they were old friends. Maybe they were in school together or grew up together. The Reids knew so much about my mom, but my dad's life was always a footnote in my upbringing. Maybe Impervious could change that.

"Davis," Flex said as he approached us with Zeva beside him. While Flex was dressed from head to toe in his traditional red and blue uniform, Zeva still had on the same clothes from when we arrived. Clearly Jen and I weren't the only ones who didn't have time to change.

"This is Z. I mean Zeva." Mr. Impervious shook Zeva's hand. "Nice to finally meet you. Flex brags about you more than himself." Zeva smiled and I could feel my heart skip. Had I been this attracted to her in school and just suppressed it because of Danielle, or was this still a rebound attraction?

"Well since we are all here, let's handle the oath. After that, you will be teamed up for your assignments so we can unleash a new group of heroes on the world." He clapped his hands together and grinned at us all. Turning to the crowd, Impervious raised his hand, and the entire room fell silent. All I could hear was the AC system now.

Jen and I bumped fists. "Here we go," I said to her as my heart began to race. It was our time now, and despite not knowing if I wanted to be a hero or villain, I was ready.

CHAPTER 14

THE REMATCH

As the room remained silent, Impervious lead the three of us to the only empty room in the great hall. Several people followed us, as they sipped drinks, ate food, or quickly whispered to each other. It felt off putting knowing they were all there for me. Or for us, I should say.

I saw Detach among them as I walked by, and Mr. Reid was among the crowd still, too. He took a bite out of a miniature burger that he held between his fingertips, and gave a slight wink to us. Even The Mechanic and, not surprisingly, several other Imperial Lords were there. Power Prince among them. Seems his television date was cut short.

It wasn't just Icons of note, though. Several high- ranking officials, various teachers from the academy, and community leaders were among us. There were plenty of supergroups doing the same thing tonight I was sure, but none of them were The Imperial Lords, and none were led by the world's most popular hero. None were helmed by the man who ended The Battle of Ages.

I was already wealthy, but seeing all the well- paid people here to watch me take an oath, made me feel like I should have charged a fee. Especially with them gawking at me like they were now, as if I was on display. I wonder if Jen and Zeva were feeling the same way that I was right now.

Impervious walked into the room, and placed a small circular black dot on his throat. "Testing, testing," he said as he spoke. To my surprise, his voice was not only heard through the room, but through the entire great hall itself. I saw The Mechanic give him a nod and a thumb's up. This must have been another of his inventions.

I had the mixed urge to either punch him again or to apologize for hitting him. I knew apologizing was the best thing to do, but I felt like if I approached him, the punch would be delivered instead of an apology. So, I left it alone, and tried to avoid him.

When the three of us finally made it into the room, Jen went in first. Zeva stood at the door talking to Flex who was holding both of her shoulders and talking quickly, all while shaking his head. It looked like he was a coach telling his star player how to win the game for them. Zeva shook her head, loosened her shoulders some and then walked into the room occupied by Mr. Impervious, and Jen.

All that was left was me. Flex turned and looked at me. I still disliked the asshole, but I was trying to keep Mr. Reid's and Detach's advice in my head. So instead of making eye contact with Flex, or using a variety of insults for him inside my head, I just casually tried to walk by him. "Excuse me," I said as I turned some to slide by.

He didn't move. "You sure you want to do this?" I didn't say anything, because I had no idea what he was talking about. The room was still silent as people behind me, and the others in the room looked at Flex and I talking. Of all the faces I could see, Jen was the only one who looked nervous. She knew not only of the past between Flex and I, but she was the only one who knew why we truly got in a fight. I never even told Mr. and Mrs. Reid. He had insulted my parents. He had said things that no child should hear, or ever forgive, and here we were again. Face to face.

I was sure, the rest of people assumed he, an older and experienced member of the Imperial Lords was giving me advice. "I know people think you're tough shit, with your four powers, but I don't trust you. Not at all. I'm sure you'll end up like your father. A waste of talent on the wrong side of what's right, and when you do, trust and believe, I'll personally bring you down." He looked over his shoulder and then back to me.

I said nothing. I kept hearing Mr. Reid's voice in my head. I pushed all of what I was feeling inside down, and simply shook my head. "Thanks for the advice Ken doll," I said with a smile as I patted his shoulder. "Now, if you're done being a dick, I have to go stand beside your sister and try to block out how delicious she smells while I take my oath."

I nudged by him and let myself bump into him as I did so. A point was made to put some force into it. I didn't have his strength, but I still was able to exert myself. He bumped into the frame of the door as I nudged him, and several gasps came from the crowd around us.

"Just ignore him," Jen said as I stood between her and Zeva. "Trying to," I replied back without looking at her. All three of us were standing in front of Mr. Impervious now. He stood with his hands behind his back and beamed at us. I glanced at Zeva and could see sweat on her brow. Wow, she really was nervous. The room went cold, as the sweat on her brow froze. Zeva gasped a little and removed her pills from her pocket and placed two in her mouth. The chill in the room faded almost instantly.

I was starting to question more and more just what those pills were, and made a mental note to look into it. They may have been pills for fitness, or something a little stronger. When she said keep the demons away, maybe she meant they put her at ease. I felt my head jerk slightly as the thought that Zeva was on mood altering drugs came to me. Now, I definitely wanted to know more about them.

" Your oath," Impervious began, "Will be the spark that will light your path as you grow as an Icon. Once you speak the words you are to live by them." I could feel my face contort some. He was already laying it on thick. The oath was basically pointless if you became a villain. "Regardless of which path you take, keep the oath in mind. It is possible, that one, two or all three of you, could become villains."

As he said this, the crowd began to speak gently, and I was positive I heard the word *spawn* and *abomination*. I thought it was all in my head, until Impervious spoke. "Silence." He said forcefully. I could have been imagining it, but it felt as if the walls rattled. "If I hear those words again, you will have to deal with me for insulting an Imperial Lord." "Wow," Jen said as she smiled.

"As I was saying," Impervious continued. "While villainy is a possibility, it is also a choice. You can choose to be great. To have statues all over the world, to save lives, and even have your own line of merchandise when you decide your True Name, if you so see fit, but first it all starts, with the oath. So, repeat after me."

He cleared his throat and as he did so, we all took a knee, and looked down to the floor. We almost looked like those people who were becoming knights on the old tv shows set in medieval times.

"I am an Icon. I was born a Void, but now I have power." We repeated this back to him and the crowd. "With my power, I am set free. Free to protect the world, even though I have the power to conquer it. I will save, even if I have the power to hurt."

I glanced up, as I repeated the second portion to see Mr. Reid mouthing the quote as we went along. Impervious continued. "I will give freedom, even though I have the power to enslave. I will become their light of hope during their darkest hour. The choice is mine, and mine alone. I am an Icon and this is my oath."

It wasn't the best oath I had ever heard of, not even close. What it was, was old. Old enough to date back to Atlas himself, so we continued to say it. You weren't *supposed* to use your power publicly unless you had taken the oath. It was almost the only thing heroes and villains agreed on.

He touched us all on the shoulder one, by one, and we stood up. "Now, the decision is yours." Impervious said as the people outside clapped. They clapped for a long time, until he raised his hand and silence fell again. He walked slowly by us and looked almost like a drill instructor. "In time you will figure out your True Name and what path you want to take. But for now, you will be given your first assignments of your internship."

As he said these words, several other people walked forward and stood behind Mr. Impervious. Flex, Life-Line, Detach, Picasso, Power Prince and a female with a glowing aura. It was Solar Goddess. I didn't realize she was here. Which is funny considering she has a constant glowing aura around her.

Solar Goddess could channel sunlight to form a continual aura of power around her. While her aura was active she could create constructs out of her light energy. She wasn't a heavy hitter at all, but it was long whispered that her family and Impervious went way back, and she was accepted into the Lords, as a personal favor. She also rarely came out in public. If she ever lost control of her aura, it could blind those near her. Or, at least that was what rumors would have you believe.

Each of them all stood beside Mr. Impervious. "You will be in teams of two, to help with the process. Jen will be teamed with my son, Picasso, since he is close to your age. You two will be looking into some leads that will help in the case of the dead Icons appearing across Atlas City. You have likely seen reports on the news about it." Impervious paused to glance at Detach quickly. It was almost done in super speed, and some likely missed the action.

"Despite our efforts to keep reports and word of mouth contained about the deaths, the issue continues to grow. You will report findings directly to Life-Line and myself."

Jen nodded slightly to Picasso who, in turn, gave a wave to Jen and then quickly put his hand down.

"And Zeva and Hunter will be teamed together." Impervious said. Flex looked at Impervious and then back to me. I, in return, smiled and stepped a foot closer to Zeva. "They will be looking into what has been reported as gang activity in the Diamond District. Seems various Icons have been doing minor acts of vandalism, just to show off their powers. You'll look into it and put an end to it." "Impervious, if I may." Flex said. Almost every eye shifted to him.

"I think it would be better if Z, I mean Zeva, was to work with Picasso." Impervious turned to him. "And why is that, Flex?" Flex avoided the question. "It doesn't have to be Picasso. I'm only a little over two years older than Z. She can team with me. I'm surely a better influence."

"Careful," Mr. Impervious said. His eyes narrowed on Flex, who put his hands up. "I'm just saying siblings should probably stick together. Last thing we want is him rubbing off on her and sending her down the wrong path like his father. It's not his fault, he just has bad stock. We all know it." "Flex," Mr. Reid shouted as he turned to face him.

I could see Power Price and Solar Goddess casually take a few steps away from Flex. Murmurs went around the crowd. Even Zeva was looking at her brother with her face turned in disgust. "I just want to keep an eye on her," Flex continued. Mr. Impervious was visibly red in the face. "Leave. We will discuss this later." I looked from Impervious and then back to Flex. "Whatever," He said as he turned and walked out.

In seconds he was through the crowd and walking up the great hall alone. I could still feel myself breathing hard. "That's it?" I said out loud. "Pretty boy says whatever he wants and he just gets sent to his room like he's five?"

Mr. Reid went to speak, but as he did the entire room went blue as I felt that familiar charge as energy flowed through me. I saw the look in everyone's face around me. "Hunter," Jen said as she reached for me, but it was too late. I was already in the air. I let my Impact Blast fly, and destroyed one of the glass walls in the room. People began to scream and disperse as glass shattered around them, and rained down from above. In seconds a force field wrapped around Flex as he was walking.

I landed in front of him. So angry that I could feel myself shaking. "This shit ends now. You don't have to like me and your sister working together, but you will respect my parents. No matter who they were." The force field closed in tight around him. I figured I only had seconds before the Lords came to break us up, so I halted them.

I stretched my hand out and created one of the largest force fields I ever had, as it separated Flex and I from the rest of people in the hall. It was a futile attempt. As Flex continued to struggle with my force field, Picasso lit his finger and drew the shape of a door, which in return, turned into a door that was smack in the middle of my force field. The Imperial Lords rushed out.

Flex, then screamed and in a burst of strength he began to repeatedly punch the force field. It cracked severely, but it didn't give. The gravity of this hit me hard. Flex was stronger than I thought, and clearly stronger than our last fight.

As he drew back far to punch once more, I removed the force field causing him to stumble. As he lost balance, I sent a punch to his face as hard as I could. He moved all of two inches as pain flooded my hand. He smirked and delivered a punch to my chest.

In comic fashion, my eyes bulged as I was sent flying backwards. I caught myself midair as I hovered. Detach, standing beside Impervious and the rest of the Lords looked on, as she summoned her clones to her aid. Several large puffs of gaseous mist floated from her and transformed into her doubles. They all took a step toward us at the same time, but Impervious halted them and shook his head. I felt confused.

He was allowing us to fight. The door created by Picasso was long gone now, leaving other members of the gathering still stuck behind my force field. Flex capitalized on my hesitation as I watched the Lords. He was next to me in an instant, and grabbed me by the neck. We flew higher into the air, and as we did so, his grip tightened. I couldn't breathe, and my punches at his hand were not strong enough to even tickle Flex, let alone stop him. Before Flex could do anything else to me, I looked down at his blue face, and released as much of my Impact Blast as possible.

He screamed as he fell to the ground below. I, too, fell but started flying before I hit. He wasn't so lucky. Invulnerable as he was, my Impact Blast still caused him pain like it did when we were in school. He was back to his feet quickly, though.

He wiped blood from his face with back of his hand." You little shit," he said to me as he hovered in the air. Before he could move, I formed a force field around him once more, and slammed it on the ground over and over. "Are we going to just stand here and do nothing?" I heard a voice scream from the side.

It was Zeva, and before I knew it, I could see my own breath blowing from my mouth. She was in panic, and because of this her powers were more prominent. Still, nobody answered her question. I continued to eye Flex. My plan was to keep him away and off his feet. If he got his hands on me and was able to display that strength he had become famous for, I was dead.

Down side, I was using a lot of power just keeping up with him. The eye blast had been at almost full power, so had my punch and force fields and he was still in the game. The force field around him faded and he slowly stood to his feet.

I could feel my throat getting dry from breathing so hard. "This isn't close to over," Flex said. I felt like he was taunting me, and gathered as much energy as I could to focus it on my next Impact Blast. This was it. Either this was going to put him down, or drain me. One of us was about to be in a world of pain. So much energy was in my eyes that they felt painful as if my head was going to explode from the pent- up energy.

I released the energy directly at Flex. The light from my blast was so strong that the walls around us flickered with shadows of the   Blast. As I released the blast I heard a thunderous sound. Then I saw a blur, and instantly Impervious was standing in front of Flex. My Impact Blast hit him in the chest, full on. My blast was strong enough to destroy a mountain, and it didn't even phase Impervious.

When the light faded from my attack, Impervious still stood tall. His shirt was mostly destroyed, but he didn't even have a scratch on him. I may as well have been hitting him with a wet string. As he looked at Flex and I, he truly was, imposing for a man his age. Such raw power trapped inside of one human shell. Likely still stronger than Flex, and totally impervious to any and everything. How could one defeat an Icon such as he?

Well, they didn't. He was like a force of nature. You didn't stop it, you just let it do what it did and hoped you were around when it was over.

Camera lights flashed all around. "Great. This cluster fuck will be online and viral in no time," Impervious said. "Prism, shut it down." he yelled. Instantly the lights went out and several Prism Holograms appeared and began directing people out.

Jen ran to me and helped me off the ground. I was so tired, that it was hard to stand. The rest of the Imperial Lords, even Mr. Reid looked at me with scowls, and Zeva didn't look at me at all. She was too busy helping Flex. "Everyone to their rooms. I will deal with you both in the morning." With those words, Impervious moved in super speed, and was gonna in the blink of an eye and gust of wind. Then in another burst of speed, he was back. "Hunter, don't unpack your bags just yet." Then he was gone again. I looked at Mr. Reid as I walked by him, and he simply shook his head, then turned away.

CHAPTER 15

BREAKOUTS AND FIREWORKS

On the way to my room, Prism took pity on how awful I looked and directed me to one of the smaller cafeterias so I could put some food in my stomach. Even though I had eaten at the dinner, I had depleted a large amount of energy fighting Flex.

That was another thing the comics and television shows got wrong, all the time, about having powers. If you used them at full power nonstop then you would defeat yourself much faster than your foe would. Let movies and comic books tell it, you could put on a superpowered show for over an hour and only be slightly out of breath when it was over.

It was all bullshit, though. Even in fights like The Battle of Ages, many Icons had to carefully decide when to conserve power, and when to unleash it. Something I hadn't mastered just yet. "Young Lord, I must say that was quite impressive." Prism said as he walked, or floated, down the hall with me.

"Flex is a formidable Icon with considerable training. Surviving with him is no easy feat," he added. I absent mindedly rubbed my neck where Flex had his iron grip only not long ago. "He's no pushover, I'll give him that. The most I could do was to keep him at a distance or contained," I said as I reached for the knob to my door. "He may be a dick, but he is an asset to the Lords."

Prism flickered a little bit before he commented. "Asset or not, he was out of line for his comments. Off with you, tomorrow is a new day." Prism said as he did a slight bow, and then flickered away. I stood alone on the empty hall for a second and considered just leaving. I didn't want them to have the satisfaction of trying to kick me out, but Impervious told me not to unpack my bags, so what else could the outcome be?

"Dude!" I heard a voice come from up the hall. I looked and was surprised to see Kevin running towards me. Funny how we kept having conversations in the hall. "That was insane." He said as he punched my shoulder. I felt a brief charge flow over me from his hand. "You went toe to toe with

Flex, and now I'm hearing that it wasn't even the first time." He almost jumped up and down. "You're a fucking rockstar."

I laughed some. "Most people say idiot, but rockstar has a better ring to it. Either way, I'm likely getting the boot because of it." Kevin shook his head. "Dunno man. The other members are pissed, but they also know Flex kind of provoked you. So, don't sweat it."

I shrugged as Kevin held his fist up and they began to glow with pink energy. "When the heat dies down, I want to see if I can hang with the mighty Hunter Monroe." He dipped and moved like he was a boxer. "We'll have to train together. You know, make it legit and not some brawl like you're used to," he said as he laughed loudly.

I shook my head and agreed. "Get some rest man, I'll catch up with you later." "Assuming I'm still here," I added. He laughed and then darted back up the hall. I opened my door, and slouched into my room. With my stomach being full now, all I needed was to rest, and that was what I had intentions of doing. I took a quick, hot shower, changed into some sweats and a shirt, and then fell onto my bed and found myself looking inside of my own eyelids.

My peaceful sleep was interrupted by a text coming through. Before I even opened the message, I saw the time. Only a little after nine, which was good because I had much more sleep that I needed. I glanced at my message and saw it was from Danielle, again. At first, I thought she was still trying to win my forgiveness. I was wrong. She wanted to tell me she wasn't going to be able to make it to the Young Pyro show tonight. She felt it would be more complicated if we went together, or saw each other, so she just wasn't going.

I refused to be a jerk, so I did at least text her back, and told her Flex and I got into it again, but that I would give her details on what went down later. Then she said she couldn't wait to hear about it, and that she missed me. I thought for a moment, and sent back that I missed her too, but it didn't change how I felt about us. Then I told her goodnight, and put my phone to my side.

I couldn't believe that I forgot about the concert tonight. With the speed at which I got dressed again you would think I had a fifth power. Super speed like my dad, or Impervious.

Once I was dressed, I looked at the door, as if I was afraid to touch it. Should I really be sneaking out for a concert after what just happened? I rubbed my chin and paced a little. It wasn't really sneaking out, though was it? I had never been told I couldn't leave after a certain time, and unlike at home, I didn't have a curfew here as far as I knew.

My decision was made, as if there was ever any doubt. I was going to the concert. After the night I had, I needed some relaxation anyway, and the bass and lyrics of one of the biggest rappers in the world was a good way to start.

I pulled my phone out and sent Jen a text. She said she was down to go. No surprise there. Then she sent a follow up text saying she would need a few minutes to get ready. We had an hour before it started, and I could fly us there in no time so that worked.

Even though I didn't have a curfew, I still felt like I was breaking out of a high security prison. I stepped onto the hallway and look around before actually coming out and closing my door. It was empty. I made it past a game room, but was caught off guard as I saw Flex, walking into the library. As if he could read, that jerk.

After a few minutes and he was well and deep inside, I quickly ran by the door. All this sneaking around was causing me to sweat. I had a red shirt on, that visibly showed off the moisture of my armpits now.

There were two problems though. One, was I didn't exactly know where Jen's room was. I didn't see where Prism took them to. I sent her a message and asked what her room was near. I knew it was on the same floor as mine, but that was it.

The next text from Jen came through and she said her room was near a gym. This made sense. I remembered hearing Flex tell Zeva her room was near a gym, too.

Eventually, after a few wrong turns, and narrowly dodging being seen, I found the gym. I would have likely missed it, had

I not heard the loud grunts coming from inside of it. I slowly walked around the corner and looked inside at the source of the noise.

The room was smaller than a normal college level, or franchise gym. Stretching about the size of a two- bedroom apartment, it was still pretty large. One section had some weights, and cardio equipment, while the other side had a literal ring with several dummies and punching bags that extended from the roof.

The overpowering chill in the room was a strong indicator of who I would find there. Sure enough, with her headphones in her ears, Zeva was going full blown amazon warrior on the punching bags. Despite the chill she was giving off in the room, she was still sweating. She had on a loose fitting white Imperial Lords tee shirt, and some mesh workout shorts that showed off her toned legs.

Seeing her here, sweating, and working out made me feel like I was being a creep of some sort. I never really saw Zeva train before. Heck, I barely saw her use her powers. I knew of her optic powers, but how often did a person really need enhanced or x-ray vision? Her Ice powers however, were on full display now, and was as beautiful as she was.

She was so fast as she delivered several attacks to the bags around her. Attacks that seemed to be almost fluid in motion. She would land several punches, and then switch to her ice powers, one bag had large shards of ice impaling it, which caused sand to fall to the floor into a puddle that was forming from the melting shards. The next bag she attacked, ended up completely frozen and encased in ice. Then once she was done, she sprinted, to the last dummy in the ring, this one was made out of wood. It was one of those dummies you see a lot in the kung fu movies.

As she ran, her fist and arms became encased in ice. It almost looked like a form of armour, and she sent blow after blow at the wooden dummy, causing it to splinter and crack. Then she suddenly stopped, and the ice on her melted, leaving a large puddle near her feet.

Breathing hard, she walked over to a large pink gym bag, and grabbed her towel. Noticing the temperature change in the room, I clapped my hands loudly and caused her to jump as she looked in my direction. She glared at me.

"You're pretty good," I said as I slowly walked towards the ring. "You want to fight me next too?" she snapped. "Two Greene's in one day?" I shook my head. "It's not like that. I would apologize, but your brother is an ass." She was still breathing heavily, and I tried to not look at her chest moving up and down, she slowly shook her head. "Maybe, but he is still my brother."

I shrugged. "We, you and I, I mean, are still partners now so, let's just leave that behind us." She twisted her mouth some as she thought. "Sorry for what he said. About your parents and all." I put my hands in my pockets and shrugged again. "Like I said, he's an ass."

She dried herself off under her shirt, with her towel, I felt like I enjoyed this way more than I should have. Then she reached inside her pink bag and pulled out a large sweatshirt. She put that on and then removed some sweat pants from her bag, and put those on as well. "Where are you going?" she asked as she looked at me.

"Looking for Jen's room. We're going to the Young Pyro concert." Her eyes got wide. "Is that tonight?" I shook my head with a smile. "You like Young Pyro?" I asked her. She didn't say anything. Instead she put her earbuds to my ear and allowed me to hear the music. As I suspected from the gesture, the music playing was Young Pyro.

"Okay, I'm impressed with your taste in music." I said. "She pointed to a door literally across from the gym. "That's my door, and Jen is the next door down." I nodded and began to backup and turn around to head to Jen's door.

"Can I come?" I heard her ask as I was almost out of the gym. I formed a smile and then released it before I turned around. "To the concert?" I asked. "Zeva, are you asking me out on a date?" "Don't be a creeper," she said. She may have said that, but I did see a hint of a smile.

"It's not a date. It's three groupmates going to a concert." I checked my phone. We don't have much time for you to get ready." Zeva stretched out her arms, and shrugged. "I'll wear this. It's not like I'm going to impress people anyway."   I grimaced. "You, don't want to shower or anything?"

She sniffed under her arm, and then shook her head as she shrugged. I thought it over. I could still fly three people there, but not as fast, so we would be on a time crunch.

"Sure, I don't mind if you come, and you and Jen seem to be getting along better, so she will be cool with it I'm sure." Zeva smiled, and ran ahead of me, opened her door, slung her pink bag inside, and then shut the door again. "All set." she said.

I knocked on Jen's door, and instantly it opened up and she placed a finger to her lips. "How in Atlas are we gonna sneak out with you knocking on doors like the damn police?" Jen said as she came out.

She had on some blue jeans and a black Young Pyro shirt. Her hair was down, and of course, she had on a ball cap that matched her shirt. Both her pants and shirt were a little too tight for my liking. I didn't say anything, but made a mental note to keep an eye on her, and the guys, or girls, she spoke to at the concert.

Jen gently closed the door behind her. "We aren't sneaking out." Zeva said. Jen looked at Zeva, and then back to me." She wanted to come." I replied. "I figured you would be okay with it.' "I am," Jen said. "But can you get us all there?"

Before I could even answer, I heard another voice behind us. "What's going on?" I turned and saw Picasso standing there in front of us. He had on the same clothes from earlier when I meet him in the hall and, as before, he had his sketch pad in his hand.

Jen sighed. "Is this the busiest hall in the base or something?" We all looked at each other, then back to Picasso. He looked at us all with his brow raised. I could have told him a lie, but something inside me decided to be honest with him.

"We're going to a concert." Then something else inside me continued to push me to say something I didn't really agree with, but it felt like it was only right. "You, should come with us." I didn't even have to look at them. I could feel Jen and Zeva shooting glares at me so strong that for a second I thought they both had an Impact Blast aimed at me.

His hand tightened around his sketch pad. "Um. Okay." We all looked at him in surprise. "Really?" I questioned. "You want to go?" He shrugged. "Not really. But I have been thinking about our conversation earlier. Maybe I do need to get out some. Lose that serial killer vibe you said I have." He avoided our eyes as he said the last part.

"You told him he had a what?" Zeva asked. "Ignore that part," I answered quickly. "Plus," Picasso said. "Jen is my partner now. If she is going then, I'm going too." I looked at Jen and then back to Picasso. This was an odd plot twist if ever there was one. For some reason, if we did get in trouble, maybe having the son of Mr. Impervious in our company, would reduce the damage. That's finding the gray zone at its finest.

"Okay, only problem now, I can't fly us all there. We would be hovering at best." I said out loud. "I can drive." Picasso slowly said. "You have a car?" Zeva asked. He shook his head but avoided her eyes too, and stepped back from her as she asked the question. "Several. I just never use them. I never leave. I collect them more as a hobby."

His finger began to glow, and we all stepped back. Once again, he drew a large rectangle in the middle of the hall. Suddenly, before us, was a single door in the hallway. "Damn," Jen said as Zeva and I looked around the door.

"It's like magic, right?" I said out loud. Picasso opened the door, and even though it should have been just the hall behind it, what we saw was clearly a garage. "Wow," Zeva said as she stepped through. We all followed her, and Picasso shut the door behind us, and it faded away.

Now we were standing in a large, and I mean large, garage. It was easily holding over two dozen cars of all shapes, sizes, colors, and models. Picasso walked slowly to a black Audi sedan, and opened the door to the driver seat, while pressing a square remote on some keys.

As we all piled in, a garage door opened up. Jen tried to sit in the back with Zeva, but I stopped her. She rolled her eyes and shook her head at me, as she walked around the car to the front seat. "It's downtown," I said to Picasso as I shut the door to the back seat and buckled up. "Okay," he replied as he put both hands on the wheel.

"Wait," Jen said as we slowly pulled out. "If you never leave, how do you know how to drive?" There was silence in the car. "Picasso," I said. "I really don't know how to drive exactly." Zeva and I exchanged glances at each other. Jen sighed and took off her seatbelt, and got out the car.

"I'll drive," she said as she walked around the car. Picasso looked at her, and then got out and let her behind the wheel. She slid her seat up some, and once Picasso was in, she slowly drove out the garage.

At that very moment, fireworks began to dance in the sky. Even from here, on the edge of town, we could hear the bangs as the many colors caused the skyline to glow. "That's the warm up for the crowd. Show should start in fifteen minutes or so." I said.

Jen must have heard this and assumed I meant, *get us there as fast as you can*, because at that moment she slammed her foot to the ground causing the tires to screech as she pushed the Audi to its limits and zoomed in the direction of the fireworks, and Young Pyro himself.

CHAPTER 16

OLD FRIENDS...KIND OF

I opened the back door of Picasso's Audi and never was I so happy to be alive. I had never driven with Jen before. Never really had to, because I could fly. It never dawned on me to wonder how she got around when I wasn't there to be her personal flying escort. Apparently, she had learned to drive like she was evading the police.

Picasso, and Zeva piled out of the car too. Picasso was breathing hard from fear, and Zeva was actually leaning on the car with her eyes still wide. "Where in Atlas's name did you learn to drive, Jen?" I asked her.

"I took a class in the academy." she replied casually as she shut the driver side door, and adjusted her clothes. "A class?

As in one?" I asked. "And they taught you to drive like that?" Zeva added. "I thought I was going to hurl between all the dodging and sudden stops, followed by the sudden acceleration."

Jen shook her head and laughed. "Nah. Accelerated and Angry taught me that." I held my hand up. "Wait. Accelerated and Angry? You mean the movie series about street racers turned bank robbers?" Jen gave me a wink and made a pointed gun with her hand. "You know it. Now come on let's go. Plus, it's not like we didn't make it safely."

Picasso and Zeva looked at each other with brows raised. Jen had a point, albeit a small one. She did get us here in record time. Less than ten minutes in fact. We had to park in a parking garage downtown, then walk to the amphitheatre where the concert was going on.

There were legions of people around us. I took a few deep breaths and prepared myself to walk through the tight crowd. My claustrophobia, was bad in crowds, but not to the same degree as when I was inside my force field and it was too small. The people around were at least constantly moving, so that helped. If things got really bad, I also had the strength to push them aside, or the ability to just fly up and get some breathing room.

Every person I could see was sporting Young Pyro clothing in some form or fashion. Even if you didn't have his clothing you could purchase it at several of the booths leading up to the venue.

As we made our way from the parking garage and up the street, Picasso gripped one hand around his sketch book, and the next hand disappeared in his pocket. He removed a pencil and twirled it in his fingers, and seemed to observe everything around him. His gaze would stop on certain people longer than others, but he never tripped or stumbled as we walked.

We lost Jen for a moment as she stopped at a concession stand to grab a pretzel, but she returned just as fast as she was gone. "These damn pretzels are orgasmic," Jen said as she took another bite. "Noted," I replied as I decide to make sure I grabbed one before we left the concert. "I do enjoy a good orgasm," I said. I unintentionally looked at Zeva when I said this, and quickly jerked my head away. "Such a damn perv," Jen added as she took another bite of her pretzel, and rolled her eyes and smiled.

Zeva was now walking in front of me, and she began to move a little to the loud bass that suddenly began to fill the air. My eyes followed her hips back and forth as she danced and walked at the same time. I could feel myself smile as I inadvertently licked my lips. Maybe she enjoyed the orgasm joke more than I thought.

I felt a strong nudge in my side. "What?" I said as I looked at Jen who was putting a large chunk of pretzel in her mouth.

She grinned and raised her brows repeatable. "You like her," she said. I was a statement, not a question. Thankfully, because of the loud music around us, Zeva couldn't hear her. I made a gesture with my thumb and index finger to show that I agreed with Jen only a little. She laughed, then caught up with Zeva.

More fireworks went off, and we could finally see the amphitheatre ahead in our view.

"This is it," I said loudly as we got closer. People around us were camped out on street corners in lawn chairs. They didn't care to see Young Pyro, they just wanted music, food, and beer, but not me. Not us. I wasn't a groupie by any means, but it was Young Pyro. I had to see him. A thought ran through my head, and I realized that is exactly what a groupie sounds like.

"I think we are on the wrong side." Picasso said as we stopped and looked at the stage. For a guy who didn't leave the base, he was handling everything very well, despite it being new to him. From where we stood, we were on the side of the amphitheatre. We could totally see the concert, and could hear it well, we just wouldn't be able to see Young Pyro himself.

"Screw this, we have to get in front. I can't see him from here," Zeva said. I was thankful that she voiced what I was thinking. This way, it didn't look like I just had to see Young Pyro. "I agree," I replied. "We came here, and survived Jen's driving, may as well be able to see the performance."

I lead the way around the side of the amphitheatre as we broke through the crowd. It would have been easier to make a large force field around the four of us, and then just push people out of the way as we moved. Instead, we formed a line and continued on. Me in the front, Jen and Zeva in the middle, and Picasso bringing up the rear.

The base continued but the fireworks were slowing down. Just as I could see a portion of the front I heard a booming voice roar over the crowd. "Make room, make room." We all turned around and saw several men the size of trees walking towards us in a small circle. The lead man who was talking, was the largest of the group. Standing at just under seven feet tall, with a beard that stretched down to his chest, and muscle that even Flex would envy. His skin was pale and his head was bald. Just like the other half a dozen men with him, he had on black slacks with a tight black shirt that had the word *security* printed on it in white.

One random person from the crowd ran up to the security guard screaming. A skinny guy with curly red hair. "Young Pyro. Young Pyro." He had his phone out and was trying to snap a picture between the massive security detail. He failed.

Before he could even take a picture, his phone was snatched by one guard and thrown on the ground. The next guard, the one who was talking with the massive beard, used both hands and grabbed the young man. As he lifted him in the air, his large arms seemed to want to explode from his security shirt. The fan was tossed back into the crowd with ease, and I couldn't help but laugh as we watched.

"Damnit, I said move. Back up." The bearded man screamed again. We all did so and the security team moved in front of us. I squinted and was surprised to see that it was in fact Young Pyro in the middle of these man mountains.

It was hard to see him but it looked like he was eating a pretzel too. He came all the way through this crowd for a pretzel? Must have been a damned good pretzel like Jen said. Still why risk the harm from a stampede of fans? Then again, he was an extremely powerful Icon himself, that as a bonus, had his own security detail. He could handle himself.

Downside was, he couldn't just go around using his powers on fans that got out of line. Doing that would result in legal issue, and make him damn near a villain. So, despite being a powerhouse, he had to have the security detail.

As they moved by, Zeva and Jen began screaming his name, too. They were in full fan mode now. Picasso, however, said nothing. He just looked. Then, it happened. I almost screamed in excitement, and was ashamed of myself instantly. Young Pyro looked our way. He looked at me. Young Pyro himself, looked at me. Chunk of pretzel in hand, he looked directly at me, and then he said something. My heart felt like it was going to explode from my chest.

His moving guard escort stopped and created a hole in their circle. There he was. A slender black kid with thick hair and a five o'clock shadow on his face. He had on a large striped shirt, blue jeans, and wheat colored boots.

He was older than me by a few years, but I looked like his elder. Why had he stopped? Was it Jen? Or Zeva? Maybe he was into guys, and it was me. Guys weren't my thing, but still how cool would it be if Young Pyro was feeling me. It sounds bad I know, but it's Young Pyro.

He shoved the rest of his pretzel in his mouth and chewed quickly. As he did so, he laughed and clapped his hands together. The crowd went nuts as they saw him move.

His security was earning their pay now, as they kept people away. He stepped closer and leaned in as he squinted. "Picasso? Shit, that is you." We all turned to look at Picasso. "Hey Jason." Picasso said casually. As if he wasn't talking to one of the biggest music stars in the world.

"I can't believe you left the base," Young Pyro said as he moved towards Picasso with his hands stretched out. Picasso stepped back some. "Forgot," Young Pyro said as he retracted his hand. "No hand contact."

"Sir, we have to get moving." The large guard said as he bent down to speak. Several other large men in his employ had surrounded behind us as well to keep the crowd in check. Young Pyro shook his head, then snapped his fingers, and another guard gave him several lanyards with laminated badges on them.

He gave Picasso a badge. It had *VIP Backstage Access* written on it. My eyes followed that badge leaving Young Pyro's hand, and I fought the urge to snatch it from Picasso. "How many are here with you?" Picasso looked to the rest of us, and we all looked at Young Pyro, trying to contain our excitement for what was coming. He handed us all badges. Backstage access, VIP, I'm better than you badges!

I held the plastic badge in my hand and looked down at it. For a moment, everything faded away. The sound, the crowd, everything. I took in a deep breath, swallowed hard, and looked back to Young Pyro. I wanted to says something but excitement and shock had rendered me speechless. I was a groupie. No doubt about it now. But, I was also a groupie with backstage access. It was worth it.

"Jim," Young Pyro said, "make sure they make it to the stage so they can see the show close up." Jim, another larger than life guard, escorted us behind Young Pyro and we all made it to the stage. Jen and Zeva were as excited as I was. We all kept looking at the badges and held them tightly as if they were made from some valuable metal, instead of paper and plastic.

Young Pyro walked up the stage steps, and so did we. I didn't even know if we were supposed to, but nobody stopped us. "Hang here and we'll catch up after the show. You can tell me how everything has been," Young Pyro said to Picasso as he removed an afro pick from his pocket and stuck it in his hair.

A blond lady appeared and handed him a microphone. "Enjoy the show guys," Young Pyro said to the rest of us. A grand finale of fireworks exploded in rapid succession, and Young Pyro looked up at the sky, moved his hands, and the fireworks all began to take shape and spelled out his name on the nights sky.

The crowd exploded and screamed as he ran on stage and his music started. Instantly we all turned to Picasso. "How do you know, Young Pyro," Zeva asked. He shrugged. "He was a member of the Imperial Lords for a short time."

"Short time?" I repeated. "I read it was for less than a week. Then he quit to pursue music." Picasso shook his head as he began to draw on his sketch pad. It looked like he was drawing the scene around us. "Before that." Picasso suddenly pause as he drew an outline of the crowd on his sketch pad.

"Focus, focus," Jen said as she snapped her fingers. "Before that he was an intern just like you three. I met him then. He always was nice and spoke of his music. He never teased me about my sketching, or awkwardness, as some do."

This made me feel hollow inside. Picasso was weird, but he was a nice guy. I personally felt like he was underutilized in the

Imperial Lords. All that power and he just, hangs around doing nothing. Either way, I hope he knew I wasn't trying to tease him. If it wasn't for my suggestions, he wouldn't have even been here right now, meeting old friends. Well, sort of old friends.

"I'm just glad you came," Zeva said as she and Jen started dancing and saying the words to the current song Young Pyro was doing. I looked at my badge again, and felt myself start to move to the music. "I'm glad you came too," I said loudly over the song. Picasso simply nodded and continued to draw the crowd on his pad.

Three more songs were performed and then, everything stopped in the middle of the fourth song.

Literally, everything stopped. The hyped crowd suddenly stopped moving. They appeared frozen. So did the people backstage with us. "What's going on?" Jen asked. I looked around. All the security, stagehands, and anybody else excluding us four were frozen as if somebody had paused them.

Young Pyro turned and looked at us from his center spot on stage. So, five of us were able to move it seemed. Zeva and Jen ran to him. I walked closer to a guard and realized that his eyes were moving, and he was still breathing. "Blink' if you can hear me." I said to him, and he in return blinked rapidly.

"Blink once for yes or twice for no." I said to him quickly. "Can you move?" two blinks. I placed my hand on his arm. "Can you feel that?" Two blinks again. His eyes became glazed, and tears rolled down his cheeks.

I grimaced. "Are you in pain?" One blink. I took a deep breath. Total, painful paralysis that seemed to only effect Voids. Why did that sound so familiar to me? I walked on stage and told the others what I had found out. Then I looked at the crowd, and even the people in the vendors section.

All statues. All apparently in pain as they were unable to move. The five of us. Icons, were able to move. "We need to get help." Jen said as she pulled out her phone. "I'm calling dad." Then she screamed as a single bolt of electricity struck her phone, causing it to fall to the ground.

Another bolt of electricity hit the stage and a man appeared from it. He was tall and broad shouldered. Dressed in all black, with a matching black trench coat, his face couldn't be made out because he had a white mask on that covered it. I looked at him. Where had I seen him before?

"Ah, Young Pyro." he said. His voice had a rattle to it, and he tilted his head. "Look at how you glow. How you all glow. All of you, but two are different. No bother, can't say I'm not surprised." His head turned as his white masked face stopped on me.

"You again." Then it hit me. He was the same guy I saw getting out of the elevator at Danielle's apartment. Why was he here? I glanced around again. Was he the reason everything was paused in place?

"Who the hell are you?" Young Pyro asked. "Your end," was all that the masked man said. Then he rose in the air, and lifted his hands. As he did so, two things happened. First, anything around him that wasn't secure, and wasn't a person, began to float in the air. Second, his raised hands began to glow red and pulsed with energy.

Young Pyro, didn't seem to miss a beat, and instantly transformed himself into a living blue flame. The heat he generated was intense. Even after his years of being in music, he still looked formidable, and almost demonic. Following his lead, Zeva encased her body in her ice armour, while Jen turned invisible, and I heard her move away from us.

I looked for Picasso, but he had retreated off stage. He hid behind a vendor cart, and was visibly shaking. Fear had him now. He would be no use in a fight. He likely had no experience with confrontation. I flicked my hand to form a force field around him. He sat under the force field, still shaking.

I then called a force field forward and surrounded myself. Leaving enough room so that I wouldn't be too enclosed inside. I glanced back to check on Picasso. I expected to see him shaking, instead I saw him draw a door and vanish. "Coward," I said through gritted teeth.

I didn't have time to worry about that though. Something worse was happening. The others may not have noticed it but I did. Pausing people, electric manipulation, flight, telekinesis, and what seemed to be some energy- based power. Five powers. Five of them. That was impossible. Wasn't it? Before I was born, nobody even had four powers, and here this guy was flexing five of them.

Surprise and awe, washed over me, as he floated above us. I wish I could say I wasn't impressed with his power, but my gaping mouth said otherwise. My surroundings turned blue, as I felt energy course through me, and then the unexpected happened. The impossible happened.

He used a sixth power.

CHAPTER 17

ASHES

As the man dressed in black hovered in the air, he turned his head to his left, and let out a sonic scream. Funny. For it to be a scream it didn't hurt my ears. It didn't even sound that loud. It was apparently strong, though.

The scream caused his mask to shatter at the bottom, showing only his white chin. The scream was so powerful, that you could even see the waves of sound as it traveled, and collided with something unseen and caused it to crash to the ground. It was Jen.

It knocked her out of her invisible state, as she was thrown back several feet. She was holding a long pipe in her hand that I could only assume she intended to use as a weapon on our attacker.

Now, she found herself unconscious on the ground. I didn't understand how though. How could he have seen her. She was clearly trying to sneak up on him, but still she never got the chance.

Jen was almost cat- like, no ninja- like, when she was invisible. She made virtually no sound, and was utterly impossible to see. Yet he knew. He knew she was there. That usually only happens with people who have enhanced senses, or powers that allowed you to see thermally. Either way this was not a good sign. I could feel my heart skip as realization came to me.

Did this guy have more than six powers? How could that be? Was he created in a lab or something, because this was becoming unreal.

"Jen," I screamed her name as I flew to her. She was sideways on the ground, with her arms tangled under her. I was leaning over her now. Mouth dry with shock. She was surprisingly not bruised or bloody. Her hat seemed to be the only thing that would never be the same. I checked for a pulse, and felt her breathing. "Good," I said to myself as I formed a force field around her. "This will keep you safe."

Before I could turn around I felt a cascade of heat roaring behind me, mixed with an intense chill, then the stage was the home of several random lightning bolts falling from above.

Our attacker was moving from location to location. This lighting power made him some sort of short- ranger teleporter that was hard to lock down. When he finally did stop moving, his hands were pulsing with energy again. I didn't know what this power could do, because if he used it before, I was too caught up in Jen being down to see.

Before he could use this power, several shards of ice were sent his way. Hell, they just barely missed me as they searched for their target. I had to dip my head some to stay out of their way. Zeva didn't seem to care. She had a frightening smile on her face as she continued to use her powers.

At the same time, Young Pyro, had flown in the air, and created several beachball sized, balls of fire, and hurled them at our attacker. He followed this attack with a constant, flamethrower style, stream of fire that came from his mouth.

The masked man twitched his head, and with the wave of a hand, a wall of red energy was blasted in the air, destroying the balls of fire. This same wall, after consuming the fiery attack, kept moving, overpowering the second flame attack, and still moved towards Young Pyro, who had to fly out of the way for his own safety. As he moved, a trail of blue fire followed in his wake, and painted the night sky.

The same shards of ice thrown by Zeva, were floating helplessly in the air, trapped in our attacker's telekinetic power. If our attacker was anything, he was fast, and he was powerful.

To stop one attack with your mind, while physically fending off another was no small feat.

The shards were then sent flying back to Zeva, but she created her own extra layer of ice around her current ice armour to protect her. The shards shattered on contact and fell to the ground.

"Pathetic," the man said as he disappeared in a flash of lighting again, and reappeared beside Zeva. He raised a red hand of energy to attack her, but I was in the fight now. I formed a force field around Zeva, and used my control over it to pull her towards me. It wasn't telekinesis, but it got the job done.

While pulling her, I let my Impact Blast fly. A solid beam of blue energy rushed towards our attacker. He, in return sent a beam of red energy towards my blast, and they both exploded on contact with each other, causing the stage to shake, and some of the paused, helpless people, to fall over.

"Hunter, let me out," Zeva screamed. I did so instantly. Not for her own well- being, but because we were out gunned with this guy, and needed the help. As I released the force field around her, I flew towards the attacker. With all the strength I could gather, I swung at him, but just before my attack landed, he phased.

The bastard phased. Another power. What was that? Eight? I was starting to lose count and with each new power displayed I grew more concerned, and even a little jealous.

His phase was short lived, maybe for a second or two, and while I couldn't see his entire face, I could see his lower jaw and mouth, and he was breathing hard. Phasing must really take it out of a person.

Young Pyro landed in front of the heavy breathing man, in all of his firey glory. He stretched out both hands and literally engulfed the man in a sphere of fire. He should have been burned alive, but instead, a powerful scream came out again, punched through the wall of fire, and hit Young Pyro square in the face.

The reaction was instant as Young Pyro fell to the ground and reverted back to his normal self. His fire form was no more. "Pyro," the man said as he looked down on him with a disapproving, and mocking tone. "This. Was. Fun." Then he sighed, and without even looking, the man stretched out his hand, and I heard Zeva scream as she was lifted off the ground.

She continued to scream as quickly her ice armour became cracked. Tiny chunks of it began to fall, as she was slammed to the ground several times. Each time shattering a larger portion of her armour until she passed out. Once she was out, her armour melted away. He held her limp body in the air like a child holding a doll.

Then he coughed and tossed her to the side as she landed close to Jen. I was stunned. Standing there like an idiot. Caught between fearing for my life, and the life of my friends, while still being in awe with what this guy could do.

I called my force field once again, making it large enough for two people as not to feel trapped, and looked at my attacker. He placed a foot on Young Pyro's chest, and looked at me with a smirk formed on his lower, exposed, mouth.

"Just stop," he said casually. I ignored him, and flew directly towards him. As I moved, he screamed again, but this time it was different. It wasn't high impact, and it couldn't be seen. It wasn't even aimed at me like his previous attacks.

It was different. It couldn't hit me physically. What it could do was hurt my ears so bad that I grabbed them with both hands, as I literally came crashing down and my force field faded away.

My force field could stand up to extreme physical attacks. Made me almost invulnerable actually, but sound could still get through, and this sound was like some sort of death cry. As I pulled myself to my knees, I could see what he was doing to Young Pyro. He lifted him off the ground with one hand.

This guy wasn't overly large, so the act alone suggested some sort of enhanced strength. Yet another power. As he lifted him up, he looked Young Pyro in the face. They looked like they were going to kiss for a second.

I tried to use my Impact Blast, but the area around us merely flickered blue. "Your glow is now mine, Pyro. Worry not. They all will join you soon" the man said. Then he took in a deep breath and something came from Pyro's mouth.

He began to literally glow, a pale white glow, for a second and then it faded as it left his body, and seemed to flow from his mouth into our attackers. Pyro began to come to as his head moved and eyes blinked a few times.

"No need for that," the man said and then he casually snapped Young Pyro's neck. The sound of the crack was followed by the sound his body made as it fell to the floor and rolled. Our attacker brushed his hands together as if he was removing the last remnants of Young Pyro's dirt from them.

He looked around, then saw me as I slowly moved. I had been trying to get to him, trying to attack for the last few minutes, but couldn't get it together. That death cry was overwhelming. My head was still spinning and as I touched my ear, I felt something warm and sticky. As I had assumed, I found blood when I looked at my fingertips. "Don't fear me boy. I don't kill my own kind. Not often anyway."

I could feel my face grimace. "I didn't expect to find a Spellborn here. Seeing two of you here was even more surprising." he said as he looked around. He spoke slowly as if he was talking to a child.

"A spell what?" I muttered. He ignored me. "Hm, I could have sworn there were two of you but the other one seems to have gone." the man shrugged his shoulders, and then walked towards me. "I only came for the boy and his fire, but you and your friends proved to be an annoyance."

He looked around at all of the people, still seemingly paused in place around us. I had been so wrapped up in the fight that somehow, I had forgotten all about them and their condition. "Collateral damage," he said as he glowed red. Much like the energy from his hands earlier, this red energy pulsed, too.

I didn't have time to think. With the little energy I had I stumbled over to Zeva and Jen's bodies, but I fell before I could get to them completely. I was still close enough. It took all I had, but I called a force field in time to surround us all. As the force field went up, my attacker exploded as the energy pulsing from him dispersed in a single effort.

As the energy expanded from him, every person that it touched vaporized, but not completely. While their bodies turned to ash and were blown away, their bones remained. I watched in horror as by the dozens small piles of bone scattered. The entire crowd or fans, the people behind stage, and even the vendors, were all gone. Dead. I had seen fake skeletons before in school, but never had I realized just how many bones were in a person's body until I saw this.

"Yes, that's better," he said as he lifted a skull from the ground and tossed it up in the air a few times as if it were a ball. Ashes from the vaporized bodies floated in the air around us like snow now.

He actually, held out his free hand and allowed a few chunks of ash to fall on them. He smirked some. Then in a flash of lightning, he was gone. Leaving only Jen, Zeva, and I on the stage, and the skull spinning from where he just stood.

CHAPTER 18

OFFICER JACKSON

As my force field faded away, I rolled over and looked up at the night sky. My head still felt like mush from whatever that death cry did. Jen began to stir and slowly, so did Zeva. "My head. My everything," Zeva said as she sat up. Her eyes darted from side to side slowly as she looked around. It was as if she had forgotten where she was before she blacked out.

"Where is he?" she said. "Gone," I replied as I pulled my phone out. I hit three numbers and was instantly connected to a person on the other end. A woman with a tired voice answered. "I'd like to report several dozen murders at the Young Pyro concert in downtown Atlas City. Send everybody."

On her end she likely wondered why I sounded as I did. It wasn't that I was calm, I was just drained, overwhelmed, and still afraid to look around me. As I hung up the phone I just dropped it to the ground beside me.

There was silence for a few moments, then it was replaced by people screaming and running. The people who were paused by our attacker, yet were out of reach of the blast had been freed now.

Jen was the first to find her way to her feet and was standing now as she stretched her hand out to me to help me up. It was visibly shaking. For the second time in a short period, I was seeing Jen without her hat. I know it's an odd thing to notice, but it was so rare, and now to have it happen twice so close to each other stood out to me. Maybe noticing this was a way my mind tried to deal with the chaos of my surroundings.

She may have helped me up, but Jen was clearly rattled. The shaky hands, and her heavy breathing despite standing still, were clear giveaways.

I grabbed her hand as she slowly pulled me up. Now that I was close to her, I could see that her face was pale, and her eyes were red. Zeva was standing over Young Pyro's lifeless body. He hadn't been dead long but his skin was oddly waxy and stretched. Not only that but his neck was twisted in a way that just didn't seem natural.

What was even more confusing, was that he hadn't been vaporized. Best I could figure, the power only effected living people that were voids. Jen moved to look at Young Pyro, and then suddenly bent over as bile came from her mouth.

"Sorry," she said as she stood up and used the bottom of her shirt to clean up. "It's just," Jen said as she searched for the words. She was standing on the edge of the stage where only minutes ago she was enjoying a performance from one of the music world's biggest stars. Now, as I stood beside her, I could see the piles of bones scattered in front of us. It looked like a graveyard had been done in reverse, leaving the remains of the dead on the surface.

The view was worse than I could imagine. Surely being a villain didn't mean you had to kill so many. My father was infamous, yet his body count was incredibly low. While Jen and I were taken aback at the scene around us, Zeva was handling it well. She was almost passive to the human remains around us. She must have had nerves of steel or something.

I jerked my head to the distance. We all heard it at the same time. Police sirens were headed our way. Zeva looked in the direction of the sirens and for a second, her irises flashed to a bright pink color. Her enhanced vision. "They're a few miles out. You'd think with what happened they would have sent more," Zeva said as her eyes returned to normal.

"Should I call dad?" Jen asked. I shook my head slowly. "Atlas no! Cops get first dibs." I wasn't a model student at school, but that lesson I did take seriously.

We had both shared a class where the teacher loved to tell us all that while we had power, we were never to think we were above the law. Only villains think like that. That same teacher later was fired for sleeping with a student in the academy. Clearly villainy comes in all forms and not just the superpowered kind.

Several black and white, sleek cop cars finally came into view. Red and blue siren lights flashed and touched almost every corner around us. As if the lights from the concert weren't blinding enough, now we had siren lights to add to the mix.

The officers opened their doors quickly and drew their weapons. Jen and Zeva instantly put their hands up. "I called you guys here. No need for the guns." I said as I gestured for them to come on over. None of them moved, and none of them lowered their weapons. I could feel my eyes roll, and yet again, despite being low on energy, I called upon my force field again to surround the three of us. I didn't survive a fight with a murdering, powerful, Icon to just be shot by a trigger- happy rookie.

As my force field expanded, several of the officers looked in awe as they lowered their guns.. A few officers from other cars, slowly approached us, eyeing the piles of bones scattered around as they passed. "It's a damn freak show," one officer said. He was young with brown skin and a thick black mustache. He looked so young he could have been in high school, not a police officer.

After a few minutes of looking around, one officer looked at me directly. He was visibly older than some of the other men. His skin was more wrinkled, his mustache was gray, and his eyes were sunken in. In honesty, he seemed a little too old to be a normal beat cop.

He holstered his weapon and then rubbed his chin as he glanced around at the bone graveyard. Then, he screamed to his men around him. "Put your guns down." Nothing really happened. "Did I fucking stutter? Put the damn guns down." he screamed once more as spit flew from his mouth.

He looked around at all of his men, and then back to me. The three of us still stood on top of the stage while the officers were where the fans once stood, several feet below us. "Now, son," the screaming cop said as he slowly raised his hands. The universal gesture of not meaning harm. "Are all three of you, Icons? Or just you?"

Had she not just had a brush with death, I was sure Jen would have flexed her invisibility, but instead she just stood there. Zeva barely reacted also. "My name is Hunter, not son."

The officer shook his head. "Fair enough. Hunter." "Yeah. We're Icons, but we didn't do this."

The officer shook his head and then turned to a fellow officer and said something. I was too far away to hear what though. The officer he was speaking to nodded as he listened. Then finally, turned and ran away. "Hey, we didn't!" Zeva said. The older officer began speaking to another one of his men. They kept talking as if they couldn't hear us. "I'm calling dad," Jen said as she pulled her phone out. I didn't stop her this time.

The screaming officer spoke into the walkie on his shoulder as he moved closer to the stage. "Dispatch, we are going to need Jackson over here. It's going to be a long night," The officer then snapped his fingers and the rest of his men began to get to work. Some pulled out phones, while others went and got crime scene tape.

"You just wait here. Jackson is on his way." Before I could even ask who or what Jackson was, the officer turned away and began yelling at another member of his team. "Dad's on the way, but he said they will take a minute."

"Is Flex coming too?" Zeva asked. Jen shrugged. "Can you let us out of here?" Zeva said to me. It was worded like a question, but the tone of her voice made it seem like a command. I canceled my force field as she sat down on the edge of the stage. "They don't train you for something like this in Purgatory," she said as she looked at the cops at work. "No shit," Jen said as she sat beside her. The two of them slowly, began talking as I tuned them out.

I didn't know what it was but something wasn't sitting well with me. Whoever this guy was, he had said some off the wall stuff. Called some of us Icons, and others Icon like. Then he referred to me as a, what was it, Spellborn? What in Atlas was a Spellborn?

Suddenly, and I mean so sudden that some of the policemen drew their weapons again, a man standing on a large slab of rock descended from the sky. "Sup' guys!" he said as he got lower to the ground. He was an average height black man. He wasn't slim, but wasn't overly large either. He was a solid build, and had a smile that was stretching from ear to ear.

The fact that he was descending from the heavens on a rock lead us to believe he was an Icon, yet he had on a police officer's uniform. As the officers saw him, they once again went back to work. Only then, the screaming man moved towards him. "Jackson," he said as the man stepped off the rock.

"These three are Icons. Figured they would be more comfortable talking to one of their own." Jackson nodded, and bounced on the balls of his feet slightly as the man spoke to him. Jen, Zeva, and I all exchanged glances. This Jackson guy seemed too relaxed and too upbeat to be an officer. Let alone, an officer surrounded by several dozen dead people's remains.

"Just get as much as you can and see how we can get to the bottom of this." he said to Jackson. "You got it! That's what I do. Now go ahead, beat it," Jackson said as he smiled. "I got this, man!" The other officer just looked at him, shook his head, and then walked away.

Jackson watched him then turned to look at us. "That guy gives me the creeps. Screaming all the time and stuff. Like damn, chill man." We didn't say anything. "So, what's with all the bones?" Jackson asked us, then shook his head. "Wait don't answer that yet. Don't think I want to know just yet."

He raised his hand, and several portions of the large rock he was floating on separated into five smaller sections. All floating in the air. He stepped on each rock and made his way to the stage. "Mind if I join you?" he asked as he sat down beside Jen.

Once he was down, he closed his hand into a fist, and the rock chunks formed one large piece again. "So, who is first?" he asked as he looked around. "Tell me how all this came to be." He said as he shook his head and looked at the scene around us. "Tragic." There was a moment of silence and then we all began speaking at one time.

"Whoa, whoa, whoa." Jackson said loudly. "You three trying to make my brain explode. Take some breaths, relax, one at a time." We all stopped talking. "Sorry," Zeva said. Jackson nodded. Then he looked at me. "Hunter I'll start with you. Then Zeva, and then Jen." We all looked at him.

I was worried for a moment, and was curious what would happen if I attacked an officer of the law. "How do you know our names?" I asked him. "Oh sorry. I know that comes off as a little creepy. I read your files at the start of the school year. I like to keep up with the new Icons going on internships. They usually get into some sort of trouble. Not on this scale, but still."

"You read just our files by chance?" Jen asked him. Jackson shook his head as he pulled some candy from his pocket and tossed it in his mouth. "Yes. Well, no. I read all of the files, of all the students for the year." He said this as he pointed to us.

"Jennifer Reid, invisibility and phasing of items. Daughter of Life-Line." Then he pointed to Zeva. "Zeva Greene, ice powers, and ocular abilities, but no fun ocular abilities. Well known family of purestock, but just a F.Y.I., I hate the term purestock. Also has a brother in Imperial Lords who is making a name for himself." Zeva's head jerked.

Then he finally pointed to me. "Last but not least, the most popular young Icon around it seems. Hunter Monroe. Son of a villain and heroic Icon. Strength, force fields, flight, and ocular abilities of the fun kind. Also, sadly, known as a troublemaker, abomination, half breed," I raised my hands to stop him from talking. "We get it, we get it. Enough with the names."

Jackson nodded his head. "My bad."

Over the next ten to fifteen minutes, we told Officer Jackson what had happened. How we came to the concert, how the people were suddenly paused, and how the person attacking us had more powers than any other reported Icon. What was strange is that he didn't take notes like a normal officer would. He just nodded and ate his candy, making faces and gestures here and there

"So, wait a dang-on minute," Jackson said as he looked at us all. "Your friend just left you guys? Picasso, I mean." "I don't think friend is the word I would use," I said. "Either way, that's some messed up shit to do. You've given me a lot of information." He stood up from sitting down beside us.

"Some I will have to share with Icon supergroups, while other portions I will have to share with the police. Being both Icon and officer allows me entrance to both worlds of the crime fighter. Cool ain't it?" Jackson said with a smile.

"Later, Kids," he raised his hand and the rock slab on the ground floated to life. "Wait." I asked him. Zeva and Jen looked at me. They likely thought it was about what had just happened, but it wasn't. Officer Jackson was much like Young Pyro to me. He had decided to do what he wanted to do, and not just become a hero or villain simply because that was what was expected of him.

"What's up?" Jackson asked. I glanced at the girls and then back to Jackson. "Can I talk to you for a second?" I asked as I jumped up and walked over to him. Zeva turned back around and slowly, so did Jen. "Sure, what's up? Wait. This isn't some question about sex or something is it? That's not in my job description man." "No," I replied quickly.

Jackson nodded his head, and exhaled as he put his hand on his chest. "Good. Okay then, ask away." I cleared my throat some. "Why a cop?" He looked at me. "Why a cop what?" I paused for a second as I searched for what I was trying to say.

"I know it's not the best time, but what made you want to be a cop? Like most of us either go hero or villain. You went on to be a cop. Which is a hero, but not to the degree of an Icon." He likely thought this was a random question. Which, in honesty it was. I didn't get this chance often, and the only person I ever was able to ask before was Mrs. Reid.

"I get it. You don't know which side to take. Hero or villain. I suppose you have a little bit of both in you. Well for me, I wanted to do what my abilities helped more in. I was born with geo-kinesis, or the ability to manipulate earth, and with a memory on the supreme level." He laughed a little. "Like I can even remember what my mom ate when she was pregnant with me."

My eyes bulged. "I know, trippy right?" Jackson said. "With my earth powers alone, I could have been an Icon who went the traditional way, but I never wanted to, yet I knew I wanted to be a hero of some sort." He took a deep breath and for the first time, his smile faded some.

"I had a younger brother whom I lost to a car accident when I was younger, and it opened up some points of view for me. There are tragedies happening every day that go under the radar of Icons because they are so common. Car accident, neighborhood violence, and so on. All important, but not on the level of a plane falling from the sky, or stuff like the Battle of Ages. So, I put on the cop uniform and found my purpose. I feel more powerful than ever when I have this bad boy on," he said as he stood comically proud in his uniform.

Surprisingly, I laughed some. "In a nutshell, I followed my heart. I know your file, and I can admit your path is more public than others, but still it's your path. Do what you feel is right." "What if I don't know what I feel is right." I asked him, and for a second I felt like a kid.

He reached in his pocket and pulled out a card. I thought he was looking for more candy at first. "You will when the time is right. If you need any advice or a person to talk to, or even help getting out of a speeding ticket, you give me a call, okay?"

I took the card from him and nodded. Officer Jackson smiled at me, and then jumped off the stage, and landed on the large floating rock nearby. I watched him float away and then heard Jen call for me.

I turned around and saw her and Zeva looking at a door on the stage. It wasn't there before, and it lead to nowhere at all. I took a deep breath and immediately became upset. This was one of Picasso's constructs. I had seen this door before.

I walked up to it and opened it slowly. On the other side of the door, at a large white table in a gray room sat Detach, Picasso, and Mr. Impervious himself. Detach looked very passive. It was hard to tell if she was angry or not. I also was curious if this was a clone or if it was the original, I mean Prime, Detach.

Picasso didn't even look up at us. He looked like a helpless dog or something. A helpless dog that knew he was in trouble and avoided our eyes at all cost. "Come in and sit down." Detach said. We all glanced at each other, but none of us moved. Then Mr. Impervious finally spoke. "The shit is about to hit the fan for everybody. You have no idea what you have stumbled across."

CHAPTER 19

INFINITY

As we sat with Detach there was silence for a few moments as she looked at some papers in front of her. I glanced at Mr. Impervious, who looked blankly at us all. The only sound in the room was that of Detach moving her papers back and forth. This sound, this casual action was driving me crazy inside. You can't allow Impervious to lead off with a statement like *the shit is about to hit the fan* and then keep us in suspense like this.

I casually cleared my throat, and in the silence, it sounded like a bomb going off. "Are you rushing me, Mr. Monroe?" Detach said without even looking up at me. I shook my head, but didn't answer. "Good," she said once more, even though she still never looked my way. I guess she knew the answer to that already.

I turned to Jen and Zeva who were both looking as nervous as I felt. Jen had even taken her hat off and had it resting on her lap. I had seen her do this several times before at our home when Mr. Reid was on the warpath.

Zeva, unable to stay still and visibly uncomfortable, was glaring at Picasso, as she cradled a dagger made out of ice in her hand. I was upset with him too, but I honestly think she wanted to stab him. He had retreated and, for all he knew, was leaving us to die, so maybe he deserved a little pain.

Detach put all her papers in order and dropped them on the table a few times to get them straight.

She placed them in front of her and leaned over and clasped her fingers together. "To say you fucked up, is an understatement. You four stumbled into an ongoing investigation of the Imperial Lords, for several months now." She took a deep breath and exhaled as she licked her lips and adjusted herself in her chair. Then Impervious took over and began to speak.

"No doubt you have seen the report of Icons being found dead around Atlas City recently. Well the truth is that we have been containing the media to prevent panic. While it may seem like only a few Icons have been found dead, the number is really in the double digits."

I felt myself frown as I clenched my hands into fist and then relaxed them under the table. I was also a little upset that

Mr. Reid kept this from Jen and I. A damn Icon serial killer is running loose and he lets us causally go back and forth to school. Sure, he tells me to keep my eyes open, but at what cost?

"Your families were told to keep this detail confidential in order to prevent word from getting out. Our best empath has been working around the clock to erase memories and create new ones for witnesses." Impervious said as he glanced at Detach, who cracked a smile. Wait, was he implying that Detach was an empath with mental abilities? If he was, why was it kept a secret? The general public surely didn't know.

"But," I went to speak, but something slapped me in the back of the head. "What the hell?" I said as I turned around. Another Detach was standing behind me. I didn't even know she had created a clone. I rubbed the back of my head, and turned around in my seat to face the Detach in front of me.

"Don't interrupt Prime," the clone said to me. "Thanks," Detach said as she smiled and winked at her clone. "I can't go into too many details, but the Icon you encountered goes by the name Infinity. He has so far, had around twenty- five documented powers, and could have more for all we know." Detach said.

I could feel my mouth drop open, as my brow frowned. Jen let out a slow whistle. Twenty- five powers? Twenty- five? How is that even possible. Detach seemed to be in my head as she responded to my thought. "We don't even know how that's possible. The body shouldn't be able to contain that type of power, yet he has found a way. The only saving grace of your encounter is what you saw of how he reacted with Young Pyro. Tomorrow, myself or Impervious will do a thorough memory recall and interview with each of you to go over what was said or done so we can get to the bottom of this." Impervious nodded his head as she finished speaking.

"Memory recall?" I snapped as I formed a force field around me in my chair so not to be slapped by the clone again. "Screw a memory recall. We have to get out there and stop his guy. Do you realize how many people he killed? He barely broke a sweat and left nothing but the bones behind. We can't just sit in here and talk. We have to stop him!" I was almost yelling now.

How could these two be so relaxed about this. Jen and Zeva seemed to be stunned to what was going on and Picasso, well he was Picasso. Detach cleared her throat. "No matter what?" she asked casually. "As in kill him?" I nodded and bulged my eyes. "Damn right if we need too. Some psycho Icon shows up, talking about how we glow, then wipes the floor with us, and kills dozens of people? Yes, we put him down."

Impervious' head jerked up at my words. As if he was listening for the first time. He had a grimace on his face as he glared at me. Detach, on the other hand, nodded. "That's a mighty villainous thing to say." "No, it's a realistic thing to say. You want to act like this is fine and have reviews, but the fact of the matter is that this guy is still walking free regardless of where he is, and that's not right."

"I appreciate your candor, Hunter. I really do," Detach said. "But my decision is made and is final."

Then she snapped her fingers and her clone walked over from behind us, and stood behind her. As the prime Detach stood up, her clone pushed her chair in under the table. The clone then smiled at Detach and in return Detach kissed her. Full on, on the lips, with tongue kissed her. A part of me found it gross, but another part of me found it hard to turn away. Once the kiss was over, Detach turned and looked at us all.

The only two who didn't seem shocked were Impervious and Picasso. "That's disturbing," Zeva said as she grimaced at Detach and removed her pill bottle from her pocket. Zeva shook it a few times, and nothing came out. Her pills or vitamins must have needed a refill.

The clone smiled and Detach herself laughed. "Nonsense. I like to think of it as, enhanced masturbation. The common person often finds pleasure in touching themselves, I just take it a step beyond because of my abilities."

Even though I was still angry, I unintentionally nodded my head. She made a good point there. "Zeva," Detach said, "You may return to your room. Your brother is waiting for you there to discuss your actions tonight. He will also review footage of your skills displayed as an Icon with you."

"What footage?" Zeva asked as she stood up. "We have footage of the fight with Infinity tonight. You show promise. Flex will go over it with you, but not in detail. Then get some rest, you and Hunter will have your first mission as interns, tomorrow morning." Detach looked at her watch. "About nine hours from now actually. Now run along." Zeva glanced at the rest of us sitting down, and then walked out of the room.

"I should have told her to shower first." Detach said. Jen and Picasso, you are dismissed too. My clone will take you to your rooms. There is no footage to really go over for you two. Picasso," Detached hesitated some as she searched for the correct words. "Well Picasso retreated back to base, and Jen you were knocked out too fast."

Her words came out harsh and disproving. I instantly felt bad for Jen. Picasso, that coward, deserved to feel bad. "This is why you both have been assigned recon duties for the Imperial Lords. You will learn to play to your strengths. Life-Line, can't out damage Flex in a battle, but his role to the team is essential nonetheless. In time you will find your common ground, but you have to make better decisions in the future. Dismissed."

The Detach clone opened the door of the room and casually said "This way," and Jen stood up, while extending her fist to me. "Later, bro. Give em hell in the morning." I bumped her fist back. "Always," I said. She left the room and Picasso walked by me. He stopped for a second and then, under his breath said two words. "Thank you."

I looked at him from the corner of my eye, but I didn't reply. "For shielding me with your force field." I looked up at him and then turned around in my chair. "Sure thing," I said without looking at him. He exhaled some and then left the room as the clone followed and shut the door behind them.

"You may want to go easy on him," Detach said. "For running and leaving us there to get our asses handed to us?" I said as my voice rose again. "Well, look at it from his point of view. Picasso has left the base, maybe three or four times in his life, and he was young then so he likely doesn't remember. Then you show up, and somehow convince him to leave and he crosses paths with perhaps the strongest Icon in existence. It was natural to be scared. Fight or flight kicked in, and he doesn't know how to fight."

I glanced at Impervious who still had an off look on his face. You'd think he would have something to say about his son being put into danger, but he didn't. I knew what Detach was saying, and some of it made sense, but the fire in me wasn't having it. Not now. She had already shut me up about stopping Infinity, she wasn't about to make me feel pity for Picasso.

"That's the supergroups fault. How can he have powers like he does and not know how to use them? Detach eyed Impervious.

"I have always wanted to keep Picasso close. Out of danger and never wanted him to even use his powers, let alone use them to fight." Impervious finally said. "Hunter, are you sure Infinity said you were glowing. That you all were glowing?" Impervious asked. I nodded. "Yeah. said he had two Icons and Icon- likes, then he called me something. A Spellborn or something."

At these words Impervious took a deep breath, and Detach swallowed loudly. In an instant Impervious stood up. "I'm going to investigate the scene," he said to Detach. "I don't want to be wrong, but I have to know for sure." Detach said nothing, but nodded as she stepped closer to the wall. Mr. Impervious looked at me, and then in a blur he was gone.

I said nothing for a minute, and then looked Detach in the face. "What was that about?" She remained quiet. "So, am I dismissed to my room too?" Detach shook her head. "Not yet. I want you to think about something before you go. Before the fight broke out, according to Picasso, you assessed the situation and talked to one of the paused victims." I narrowed my eyes at her.

Even this made me upset. While I was fighting for my life and watching people turn to piles of bone, Picasso was here giving her details. She continued to talk. "Then, you used your force field to cover Picasso." "So." I said as I tried to follow where she was headed with this. "In short you acted like a hero would have acted. In this instance, at least."

I felt my head jerk. I hadn't expected this, especially after she told me how villainous it was to want to kill Infinity, but she was right. Maybe I was meant to be a hero after all. "But then," Detach continued. "You formed a force field around yourself. Keeping your phobia of tight spaces in mind, you formed one large enough to keep yourself at ease. You didn't form it around all of the others. You only worried about yourself."

I knew where this was going now. "In short, you did what a villain would have done." She shook her head. "You continue to show aptitude for both heroic and villainous profiles." She walked to the door and opened it for me. Oddly enough, Prism was flickering into existence on the other side.

"Hello again, young Lord," he said as he bowed. "There will come a day when lives depend on you deciding which side you give your allegiance too. I've never in my days seen somewhat walk the line between the worlds of good and bad like you Hunter." She paused for a moment. "Well, maybe one other person. Now, you are dismissed, and good luck tomorrow."

She walked out leaving only Prism and myself standing there. "Seems you have had quite the night," Prism said. I looked at the hologram. "How do you know?" I asked him. "I'm connected to everything in the base. Effectively I see everything. I am happy you all made it back safely."

His words shook something up in me. "Prism," "Yes?" he responded. "You were able to see our fight as it happened?" He stood there for a moment, flickering slightly in and out. He finally came back to full view.

"Yes." he answered. "So, if you could see it, anybody connected in the base could have seen it as well?" "That is correct, young Lord." I thought for a moment. I knew Detach said Flex would go over the video with Zeva, but I had assumed they acquired the video. "So, either all of the base or somebody in the base, watched our fight with this Infinity asshole. They knew how powerful he was, yet they didn't step in to save the new interns. To save the young Icons that clearly stood no chance."

Why? What did they gain from watching? Not only that, why were we spared? Something didn't feel right. Sadly, I was beginning to think the Imperial Lords saw us as expendable. "We really should get going, young Lord," Prism said.

I didn't respond. I was still trapped in my head, but I followed the flickering hologram anyway.

255

CHAPTER 20

MISSION ONE

True to her word, Detach had an assignment for Zeva and me rather early. The entire setup for detecting crime for the Imperial Lords to deal with was impressive. All of the entire base, worked as one large computer with a host of servers, networks, and data centers. Various emergencies filtered through the computer system and were eventually given to a member to handle. Think of a police scanner but on a much larger scale.

Many occurrences around Atlas City were below what an Icon group like the Imperial Lords would handle. Things like robberies, police chases, cats in trees, and so on, were more for low level Icons or the normal police department. The Imperial Lords worried about larger scale stuff.

Nuclear reactor about to explode? Imperial Lords. Volcano about to cover a small village in lava? Imperial Lords. Icon running around with more powers that several supergroups combined? Imperial Lords. Events that could send a ripple effect around the world, was where the Lords stepped in.

This only changed if you were an Imperial Lord intern like Zeva and I. While we both seemed to show promise after our encounter with Infinity, that could have been a fluke fueled by circumstance. Our evading of death could have been dumb luck or simply, as I believed, Infinity didn't really want us dead. He was only there for Young Pyro. Either way, we were on our way right now to one of those various small incidents that the Lords usually didn't even get out of bed for.

The door to the carrier opened slowly. Once again, Zeva and I were inside of the R.M.F.C headed into the heart of the Diamond District. We were both dressed alike. Black combat boots, that matched our tactical cargo pants and black mesh compression shirts. Even our ear pieces to talk to each other were black. I wasn't a stick figure by any means, but Zeva looked considerably more in shape in her compression shirt than I did. While I was still sleep this morning, Zeva had worked out for two hours. With dedication like that, it's no wonder I could see her abs through the shirt.

"Good luck, young Lords," a voice came from inside the carrier. I looked around and then locked eyes with Zeva. "Prism?" she said out loud? "The one and only," responded the voice. "How?" I asked. I realized I was talking to the wall of the carrier as if Prism was hiding inside it.

"All of the carriers are on the same network as the base, so I can reach you here as well." I nodded. "Any idea where we are headed?" I asked. Before he could answer, Zeva pointed out in the distance over the city. "There, I'm guessing."

I followed her out- stretched hand as she held onto a portion of the carrier to keep her balance. From where we were, I could see dark smoke clouds billowing into the sky. A small apartment building, maybe four or five stories high, was engulfed in flames.

In typical Diamond District fashion, it was sleek and modern looking. Surrounded by lush grass, trees, and even a fountain in the front. The Fire department was on the scene but didn't seem to be having any luck with the fire. Barricades had been set up to keep people back, and from where we now hovered in the R.M.F.C I could see those same trees, and lush grass lean back from the fire, as to not get burned.

I was surprised the trees hadn't run away yet. They certainly had the power to do so if they wanted to.

"A burning building?" I said out loud. "Seems a little cliché, doesn't it?" Zeva grimaced at me. " Cliché or not, heat messes with my powers if they have to cross paths. The dry air makes it hard for me to form my ice."

I exhaled. "Okay," I said as I looked out below us. People on the streets had started to look up and point at our hovering craft. Some were even jumping up and down, while others clapped. I rolled my eyes. They assume we were experienced heroes here to save the day.

Wrong. Two teens trying to figure out what the hell to do is more like it. "Okay," I said to Zeva, "Are there any people in the building?" From where I stood in the carrier, I could only see the building, but with Zeva's powers she could enhance and x-ray.

Her eyes glowed pink for a moment and flickered back and forth in her head as she scanned. "Several dead animals on the upper floors, a fireman carrying out an elderly man on the first floor, but they almost are out." Her eyes blinked as she continued to look at the building. She gasped as her glowing eyes faded away.

"There's a child on the third floor, far right side. I don't know how they missed him but they did." I felt my throat get dry and it had nothing to do with the heat from the building. I had honestly hoped the building was empty. Then even if we failed to stop the fire, we could have avoided people dying.

"He, must be saved." Prism's voice came through the carrier. "I got it," I grabbed Zeva's hand and leaped from the carrier. She screamed as I called my force field to surround us and she began to fly alongside me.

"Shit!" she said as she slapped me with her free hand. "Give me a warning next time." I ignored her rant. We didn't have time. As I flew down, the onlookers screamed louder. The only people not worrying about us were fire fighters. They were still trying to control the blaze and were having no luck.

I landed on a building across the street from the apartment that was more flames than building now. "I need you to guide me to the kid." She nodded at me as she turned to the building. I could see her neck move as she swallowed and leaned towards the blaze.

Then her eyes glowed again as she positioned her gaze on the burning buildings perimeter. "And form the largest ice construct that you can. Right here and right now." Her mouth opened as she held her hands up and they turned frosty.

I ran and jumped off the building before she could speak. Regaining control as I hovered in the air above the people below. Glancing over my shoulder, I saw that in a short time, Zeva had already formed a large chunk of ice about the same size as an office desk.

With her hands still stretched in the air, slithers of ice, and frost manifested in the air around her. Swirling almost like smoke and then adding to the mass of the ice in front of her.

I turned and faced the building again. "Third floor, right side," I heard Zeva's voice come in my head through the earpiece. I counted from the bottom and found the third floor, and looked at the center of the building. Flying in the air, I formed a large force field around myself and watched as the building turned blue.

I had to control my Impact Blast as much as possible to not cause the building to collapse due to the fire and the weak frame. I released a small beam of energy from my eyes that punched a four- foot hole in the side of the building. The fire men below scattered as debris fell. "Sorry," I screamed out as I floated inside the building.

Fire surrounded me on all sides and smoke filled the air so much that most of the inside was either flames, or a dark cloud. Even though I couldn't feel the heat inside my force field, it was still hard to see. Still hovering in the air, I stretched out, and lowered myself to the ground. With my oversized force field around me, I looked almost like a submarine moving through an ocean of smoke.

"I can't see shit," I said as I quickly moved out of the way as some of the ceiling fell down. "He or she is directly in front of you. You lucked up and blew a hole in the wall of the same unit. The kid should be two rooms over." Zeva said. I could hear it in her voice. She was straining. I just hoped she could hold out a little longer, and that my plan worked. "Hurry up, Hunter." She came back again.

"It's harder to form as it gets larger." I thought to myself *what sense does that make*, but I kept my mouth shut. Like a rocket, I increased my flight speed and hovered through the first door. It was an office of some sort. A couch, desk, and bookshelves all burned around me as a stream of water came through a window. The firemen were still trying, but had no luck. I stretched my force field some to push the burning desk out of the way as I kept moving.

"Next room you should see the kid." Zeva said slowly. She was breathing heavily in my ear now. She sounded like she had been running or something. I moved quickly into the next room, and there, on the ground stretched out was a little girl. She couldn't have been more than five years old, and her blond hair was in pigtails and ash colored. I hovered over her body and created a hole inside my force field as I descended on her.

As I reached for her, more of the room began to crash down. Chunks of the floor around us fell apart, beams from the roof above us fell down, and despite their efforts outside, the fire raged on. I closed my force field some, and instantly felt myself shiver as the space got smaller. Smoke quickly began to filter inside the force field as I opened a hole to pull her inside with me. My arms wrapped around her body, and I couldn't tell if she was alive or not.

As I held her close, I closed the force field again. Instantly the heat faded. "The building is empty? You're sure?" I asked. "Yes," Zeva's faint voice came back. Wasting no time, I exploded from the right side of the building like a pale blue bullet. Holding the child in my arms as I lowered us to the ground.

The crowd around us erupted in cheers. Cheering yet they didn't even see the child I was holding yet. Honestly, they didn't even know why I was in the building, but people love to be around when an Icon is doing something good or bad. A larger fireman ran to me quickly, as two more firemen appeared. The first man had olive colored skin, that was covered in sweat and ash.

I handed the child to him and he quickly placed her on the ground and began CPR. Not too far away, I could hear a woman scream. I was willing to bet that she was the mother to the child I had just handed off, and even among the cheering crowd, her sobs were easily heard. I wanted to see if she was okay, but I wasn't done yet.

I flew into the sky again, quickly leaving the crowd of people below. When I made it to Zeva on the neighboring building she was kneeling on one knee but still forming the chunk of ice.

My eyes widen as before me, in the air was a damn iceberg. Zeva had created a chunk of ice almost as large as a public bus.

I flew under it and placed my hands firm. Last thing I needed was for her to lose control and this plummet down to the crowd below. "I got it," I screamed as she dropped her hands and fell on her back. She oddly closed her eyes, and started laughing. Like a creepy laugh, and I wasn't sure why.

I was no Flex, but I could hold this up a little bit with my enhanced strength. To give me a little more of an edge, I created a massive force field to surround myself and the chunk of ice. With my gravity control inside my force field, the iceberg was easier to move.

Back into the building I flew but this time on the top floor. "Zeva." Nothing came back from her in response. "Zeva, get up." I heard her grumble through our ear piece. "You got your breath, now focus on this ice and hold it here. Just like you did a few seconds ago."

"Okay," she said. This time she sounded a little better. "Ready?" I asked. "Ready," she responded. I removed my force field and instantly felt the weight of the ice in my hands. The gravity boost was missed already.

I held my breath, and flew from under the floating ice, and as I did so, I could see my plan coming to life. I flew back out through a hole in the wall of the apartment building, and could see the ice had already melted down to half its size from the intense heat.

Not only that, but the water from it had created damn near an indoor waterfall that flowed through every hole, crack, and floor of the blazing building. Still hovering in the air, I summoned a force field large enough to encase the entire building.

I couldn't recall ever making a force field this big, and it was no easy feat that required maximum effort. I couldn't let the building come crashing down on the people below. As the massive amount of water served its purpose, the building became more and more unstable, and in minutes it was nothing more than a mountain of ash, brick, and metal.

I removed the force field slowly, allowing for the water to exit in more of a focused stream to avoid the people standing nearby watching.

"I think we are all good," I said as I landed beside Zeva and coughed a little. "Thank Atlas," she said as she slumped over. She looked at the spot of the former building and smiled as she wiped sweat from her brow. I stretched my hand to her, and she grabbed it quickly.

With my force field, I took her in my power, and we stepped of the building to the ground below. As we fell, I could see cars had halted in the streets. More fire trucks had come and even police were on the scene now.

Then I saw what I had been looking for. The girl from the building, sitting in her mother's arms. Wrapped so tightly that she could barely move, but she was alive. "That's her," I said to Zeva as I pointed slightly. She looked at me, and then, she hugged me. A hug that I didn't expect, but didn't shy from either. I breathed in deeply, and smelled her sweetness again, then instantly felt like a creep for doing so.

"We did it!" she said. "Maybe I'm not such a bad influence." I said with a grin. "Perhaps the mighty Flex was wrong about you after all," she replied. At that time, several news vans arrived on the scene. This I hadn't expected, but wasn't surprised by either. "Well, time to shine," I said as I prepared to tell Atlas City viewers of our victory and bravery.

"I'm pretty sure that *we* can't talk to the press." Zeva said as she looked at the woman dressed in red approaching us as she pulled out a microphone. "Why not? We're Imperial Lord members." I said as I nudged her with my elbow. "Now, act casual and smile."

"Don't you say a damn word to that reporter." I heard a voice go off in my ear. A voice that didn't belong to Zeva. "Mr. Reid?" I asked with a twisted look on my face. "Who else would it be?" he replied. "You didn't think Prism was the only one who was in on the feed did you? I'm watching over your first mission. I can see and hear everything. Now, smile, wave, and get out of there."

"But," Mr. Reid cut me off. "But nothing. You haven't been trained on how to handle public relation stuff like speaking to the press." Zeva, hearing everything Mr. Reid said, grabbed my hand. She seemed as ready to fly out of here and back to our carrier as Mr. Reid was.

I looked at her, as she raised her brow to give me the signal to leave. The woman was about five feet from us, now and a red- haired cameraman was only seconds behind her. I decided to do the right thing. I called my force field to life again, and was greeted with hollers and clapping from the crowd.

I was about three feet off the ground when she screamed at me. "You're Hunter Monroe, aren't you?" the news lady said. "I'm Misty Gettings, channel five news. You and your friend really saved the day."

Her microphone was pointed at me as if she was a witch and the device was her wand. "Back to the base. Now!" I heard Mr. Reid go off in my ear. "I take it you've heard of me." I said as I slowly dropped back to the ground and canceled my force field, while looking at Misty.

Zeva groaned. "No. Just your story. Everybody knows about the half- villain, half- hero Icon. The world is going to be on the edge of its seat to see the legacy you create. Care to give a statement about today's rescue.? You saved that little girl's life."

Misty licked her lips and then turned to the crowd. "Following in mom's footsteps I see." As she said the words, the group around her began to clap again. I knew she just wanted a story but it was a good feeling to be in the spotlight for a good reason, instead of just because of my parents, for once.

"I. I," the rest of the words wouldn't come out. I wanted to speak but didn't know what to say. "No comment," Zeva said as she leaned over and grabbed the microphone from Misty and turned it into ice.

She then dropped the microphone on the ground, causing it to shatter. "Oops." she said in a tone that was a clear indicator that it was done on purpose. "We really must get going," Zeva said loudly as she looked at me. I nodded, and then with my force field back, flew up into the carrier.

As soon as we landed inside the carrier began to move again. "Thank you, Zeva," Mr. Reid said through our ear pieces. "Had you not been there he surely would still be on the ground, ignoring rules and talking to the media." Zeva glared at me and then found a seat.

I opened my mouth to defend myself, but before I could Mr. Reid spoke again. "As for you, Hunter, see Impervious when you return. He wants a word."

CHAPTER 21

THE FAMILY TREE

Our flight back to base was much more different that when we went to the mission. Between our success, saving a life, and our albeit brief encounter with the local news, we were feeling like full-fledged Imperial Lords. "Imagine feeling like this all the time," Zeva said. "It's a little bit of a rush. Like a high or something."

I nodded. I couldn't recall seeing Zeva this happy before. While I was fond of her normally, I could see how seeing her smile, and being this happy on a regular basis would make me crazy about her. Then, I blurted out words that I didn't even truly mean to say. "I bet it's even more intense for villains." The words had left my mouth before I realized what was being said. The mood in the carrier shifted instantly as Zeva blankly looked at me. Her eyes narrowed. "What do you mean?" she asked.

I shook my head. "Nothing. It's just. Villains must get this feeling too. The rush from a completed job. The high from the infamy. Not to mention the paydays from their line of work." If what my father left me was any indicator of potential income for some upper level villains, then good paydays were plentiful. I glanced at her and swallowed some. Perhaps I should have toned down the appeal to the villainous side.

She looked at me for a long time, and then she eagerly nodded her head and smiled from ear to ear. "I suppose you could be right. I never thought about it that way." I could feel my head jerk and face turn as I looked at her. I wasn't expecting this reaction. When I expressed my feelings of how the bad side is appealing, people usually turn away from me. Zeva, however, seemed to see the point. Not only did she see the point, she embraced it. I could see her thinking as she bit her lip and continued to smile to herself. I didn't expect the thought of being a villain would have excited her so. Or her agreeing with me to make me feel so good inside. She was perfect.

She glanced at me, and casually sat down a little closer to me in the carrier than she did on the way there. For the first time in ages, I was in a small space, and didn't feel uncomfortable about it at all.

As the carrier reached the base my phone went off with a text alert. I opened it to see that Danielle had sent me a message asking if I was still going to the end of year dance at Purgatory. Originally, I had invited her, just to make people feel awkward, plus at the time she was my girlfriend.

She also added in that she felt like we should talk face to face to clear the air, and that she promises everything wasn't as it seemed. Finally, she sent a third text saying that E-Rase was just being a dick, and that she hadn't talked to him since, after he told the lie about him and her. She event sent me his phone number to call or text him, so I could hear it from his mouth.

I thought about replying to her. She really did seem to be trying, and I did miss her. Terribly so. I missed our talks, our times at her home late at night, even the casual dates of just looking at something on tv as we had pizza. I missed it all. My anger had faded some, and I didn't know how to handle my feelings now. On top of it all, I couldn't help how I felt around Zeva either.

Against my better judgement, I sent her a text back, saying that we can talk later, but I had a lot of Imperial Lord stuff going on. She replied back quickly. Her reply made me laugh. She said she wasn't sure I would even text back, seeing as how I was saving kids from burning buildings and stuff now.

Our heroics of the day must have made it to the news fast. "Hunter," I heard my name called out as Zeva snapped her fingers. I looked up out of my daze She was standing outside of the carrier on the ground already. "You getting out?" she asked as she held her hands up.

"Oh. yeah. Just thinking about something," I replied back as I made my way out of the carrier. "Scared?" she asked. "Of what?" "Your meeting with Impervious." I snorted. "Hell no.' I replied as I dropped to one knee to tighten my boot. "Flex had his talk with you about what happen to Young Pyro. Jen had her talk with Life-Line," I said as I made air quotes when I said Mr. Reid's true name. "And now our fearless leader wants to have the same talk with me. No big deal."

"If you say so," Zeva added as she pulled out her pills and looked at them. At some point she must had gotten a refill. She looked at the bottle and then, to my surprise, she put the pills up. She didn't take any. Instead she just continued talking.

"Flex made our talk seem like it was a big deal. He went on and on, about how we represent the rest of the family, as much as the Imperial Lords, and yada- yada- yada." I was two seconds from saying *that's because Flex is a dick*. Instead I just shook my head and said, "well you know how Flex can be."

With my boots secure, I began to hover in the air. "what are you doing?" Zeva asked. "I'm flying to Impervious' floor." You sure you don't want to, like go the traditional way? Knock on the door and stuff."

I shook my head. "I'm ready to get this over with. I'll catch up with you later." Then I looked up and shot into the air.

While everybody else in the Imperial Lords had a room, or suite to themselves, Impervious, as the leader, had an entire damn floor dedicated to him. Inside this floor he had everything he could need. Bedrooms, yeah- more than one. A private kitchen, several bathrooms, a library on Icon history that would make several schools jealous, and even a tailor for his suits. Now, this was all guess work on my part. I knew where his floor was, everybody did, but only certain members were allowed inside, or so I had heard.

Everything I just listed was a combination of rumors, and hearsay. None of it had actually been proven. As far as I knew, none of the current Imperial Lords even went inside of his room. That's why randomly showing up on his luxury patio appealed to me so much. I wanted him to know that I wasn't impressed by any of it. Not to mention all the secrets about his floor were uncalled for and creepy.

In seconds I was several stories up in the air. This floor was one of the highest of the facility. I landed on the patio and was greeted by a massive grill, several comfy looking chairs and a wall tv. It was nice, and this was only the patio portion. The wall separating the patio from the rest of the floor was solid glass inside of a cherry wood frame.

Just standing from here, I could see inside pretty well, and was surprised to see that the living area was mostly hues of whites, grays, and olive green. Everything from the furniture, to light fixtures, were ultra- modern and sleek. To be honest, it looked like it belonged on a magazine cover. Seems some of the funding provided to the Lords was spent to good decor.

As I walked to the door to knock, I was surprised to find Detach. So apparently at least one other person was allowed on his floor. She was wearing a casual dress now instead of her usual pantsuit. She was talking to Impervious, who was yet again in a navy suit, and they both looked stressed. Detach was moving her hands around wildly, and Impervious was shaking his head but letting her talk. I couldn't hear what all the fuss was about but I was curious.

Lover's quarrel was the first thing to come to mind. Did I know if they were seeing each other? Not at all, but I could see them being an item. They were so close, and spent a lot of time together anyway.

I knocked on the door several times loudly. Detach jumped, but Impervious reacted. In a blur, he was standing in front of me with his hands around my throat, and had me lifted off the ground. When he realized it was me, his eyes grew wide and he placed me back on the ground.

"What the hell?" I said as I coughed. "Sorry." Impervious said as he looked at me. "I don't usually get random people arriving here on the patio without warning." Judging from his tone he was telling me, *so don't do it again.*

"I'll leave you to it then," Detach said. She said in a hiss, and somewhat glared at Impervious before she turned and left. "She okay?" I asked. "As much as Detach could be," Impervious said. "She's my closest friend. We both grew up here. Myself as a Lord, but a young one, and her as the daughter of a member. Being the same age helped as we didn't have much in the way of friends."

His gaze lingered on the door she just left out. "As a result, she calls me on my bullshit more than anybody else. Even when I don't ask her to. She knows my darkest secrets, and fondest memories." Using his super speed, he darted through the home and the returned with two glasses.

One was holding a brown liquid, and the other was a clear liquid with bubbles in it. He handed me the clear liquid- filled glass. I sipped it and found soda. My favorite soda actually. What were the odds that he knew my soda of choice? "Come on, follow me," he said as he turned and lead me through the house. Seconds later I found myself in the kitchen.

Several cooks all dressed in white were at work in the massive kitchen. I didn't know what they were cooking but it smelled good. Despite the several cooks in the kitchen, there was a large pizza box on the counter. "Ignore my workers, they are cooking meals for the people of Ebony District that can't afford to eat. I drop them off myself to several shelters. It's not much but it all helps.

He lifted up the pizza box and spun it around, revealing circular, oven baked goodness. "Double pepperoni, extra cheese, mushrooms, and thin crust." Impervious said. I looked at the pizza and then back to him. That was my favorite food. Nothing odd there, plenty of people loved pizza, but this was my favorite pizza, from my favorite pizza place.

Now I was worried. Impervious removed his blazer and rolled up his white sleeves. Then he grabbed a slice and devoured it in seconds. "Come on, I know you're hungry after that burning building." he said. Right on cue, my growling stomach roared in betrayal. Minutes later I had down three slices, and another cup of soda before I asked the question on my mind.

"What's going on here?" I said. "My favorite soda. Favorite pizza." He avoided my gaze for a second. Then he exhaled. "Follow me," he said as he wiped his mouth with a napkin and left the kitchen. I grabbed one more slice to eat along the way and then followed him.

The entire floor of his home seemed to have a sweet smell, and just as with the living room, everything seemed to be professionally designed. The furniture was sleek, the paintings on the wall were vivid splashes of colors, and from what I could see no surface had dust on it.

We passed through a library, living room, and even walked by a room that seemed to house nothing but shoes from floor to ceiling. "Wait a minute," I said as I saw a statue down an adjoining hall.

"Hm?" Impervious said as he looked at me. "What's this doing here?" I asked him as I walked to the statue. It looked like the statues, heroes received for their deeds, but it was of a young boy. Not an adult. The statue was only a little under five feet tall, and the youths face was smiling at me. "This is my son," Impervious said as he exhaled. "Was my son," he followed up slowly.

"Why do you have a statue of Picasso?" I asked him as I looked at him. To my surprise, his eyes were red. I touched the statue and looked at my finger. A thick layer of dust was there. Clearly this statue didn't get as much attention as the rest of the house.

"No," Impervious said as he blinked slowly. "This is Will. My first born. My son." "I didn't know you had another son." I replied. "Not many do. I lost him in the Battle of Ages. I made the ultimate sacrifice. After all this time, I still miss him every day." He said as he touched the statue slowly. "I try to avoid the statue to spare myself the pain, but now and again, I find myself looking at it from afar, or even talking to it."

I shook my head. "How have I not heard this before? About Will." "Empath" Impervious replied. "I had his memory erased from the world. The only people who remember him now are Detach and I. It's easier that way." He cleared his throat, and continued up the hall.

The entire world forgot his son even existed. I found that a tad disrespectful to the memory of his son. Judging from the redness in his eyes, and the catch in his voice, I was seeing something for the first time that our fearless leader wasn't Impervious to. The pain from the loss of a child.

I stood alone there looking at the statue for a few more minutes, before I left and found my way to his office. Unlike the rest of the house, his office wasn't modern at all. It was the opposite. There was an older looking sofa against the wall. The large wooden desk looked several years old, and the book shelves had more toys on them than books. Even the walls were unexpected. Several movie posters were framed and covered most of the area.

"Whoa." I said as I looked around. "Didn't expect this." Impervious laughed a little as he walked behind his desk and sat down. He stretched his hand out for me to sit across him. "So, now you tell me about how I did in regards to the Infinity fight, huh? Our little one on one? I still think we should be out there looking for him."

Impervious shook his head as he shuffled through his desk drawer. "Oh, we are. We have several Imperial Lords, and some independent Icons searching every inch of Atlas for him.

Even Detach's clones are on the hunt." "But why aren't we?" I asked him sternly. "We have some things to discuss first," he said as he pulled out what looked like a photo album. He flipped the book open and pulled out a single picture and spun it around to me.

"Dad?" I said in surprise. I quickly grabbed the picture and looked at it. It *was* my dad, but, it wasn't. Yes, it was Donald Monroe, I knew the face and the grin I had seen several times on articles I read over the years about Blue Rush. What was confusing was that the picture wasn't of dad in his Blue Rush outfit. He was wearing some blue jeans and a plaid shirt. He was also, easily, in his late teens or early twenties.

"Why?" I stumbled over my words as I looked up to Impervious. "Why do you have this?" He didn't answer my question. Instead he pulled another photo out. Yet again, it was my dad, and this time he was standing beside another man. His arm was around the man's neck and they both had beers in their hands. They were smiling. They were happy. I looked at the picture, and then back to Impervious, and then to the picture again. The other man in the photo was him. His hair wasn't peppered with gray and his face was smooth but it was no doubt, a younger him. He too was in his early twenties. "That picture was taken three years before I joined the Imperial Lords." He said casually as he adjusted in his chair. "When times were good."

He sipped his glass of brown liquid. "When *he* was good. There was no Mr. Impervious or Blue Rush. Just Davis and Donald Monroe." His words hit me like a punch from Flex himself. I looked at him, and all he could do was shake his head as he avoided my gaze. Impervious, and my dad?

I dropped the photo to the on the desk as I frowned at him. "You two were?" "Brothers," he said as he placed his glass on the desk. He paused as he looked for what to say next. His fingers tapped the desk and then just clasped around each other. "I didn't know how to," I stood up quickly from the desk. So fast that I actually nudged it some.

"No." I said as I shook my head. "Mr. Reid would have told me. Hell, anybody would have told me. The world wouldn't just ignore that one it's most famous heroes had a brother that was a villain." I found myself breathing hard.

"I understand the surprise, but it's not so black and white." I found his words ironic, seeing as how I prided myself on living in the gray area as much as I could. "Nobody has told you, because nobody remembers." He said to me. I could feel my brow raise. "What?"

He let out a long sigh. "Detach. She is the *empath* that you may have heard mentioned here tand there, and the one I told you that made the world forget my son. Mind reading, and memory alterations are her prime abilities. She is, to this day, the strongest empath I've ever known. The entire clone thing is simply a secondary power. It's also why we are so close. I'm the only person immune to her gifts."

Impervious leaned on his desk and rubbed his forehead. He was Impervious to mental Icons as well. Damn could nothing hurt this man? I still didn't follow, though. In fact, none of this was making sense to me. So, Detach had a power she had been hiding all this time? What kind of sense did that make? "Who would do that?"

I had said my thought out loud without meaning to. "Do what?" Impervious asked. I shook my head in return. "Just, start from the beginning. So, my dad and you are brothers. You're my uncle and Picasso's my cousin." He paused for a moment, as if he had to think, then he nodded. "In a way, yes." In a way? What the hell did that mean? It's a simple yes or no answer.

"So why doesn't anybody know?" I asked. "Detach erased the memory of every person in Atlas City and the surrounding area when I asked her to. After the original Imperial Lords never returned from that mission, I didn't want anybody to know. Seemed easier seeing as how I was suddenly propelled into leadership."

I remembered something Detach had said when I first arrived here with Zeva and Jen. We were in the Hall of Heroes or Hero Hall, I can't remember what it's called, but she said Impervious joined because his brother was a well- known Icon.

In reality, it was because his brother, my dad, was a villain. The villain!

No wonder she looked at me funny when she told us the story. She knew. She knew the entire time. What a bitch. A secretive bitch. A secrecy bitch that could wipe minds apparently. "So why tell me now?" I asked. My surprise was fading and was being replaced by rage.

"After all these years. Why now?" I repeated. He pursed his lips. "It. Felt like the right time. Your age now is when the decision is made. Hero or villain, and I want to see you do good. I want to make sure you do good."

I shook my head. "But why now? Why after all these years?" I said as I slammed my fist on the table, causing cracks to come alive in the wood. "I really don't have an answer for you. Not a good one anyway, and not one that will make any of this less painful." I slumped back into my chair, and took a deep breath.

My uncle was Impervious. Davis Scott was my uncle. "Wait. Why is your last name Scott then?" I asked him. My last name, just like dad's, was Monroe. He shrugged. "Wanted to distance myself from your dad as much as possible. People didn't know we were brothers, but I still knew. Near the end, those final years he went down some dangerous roads. As the eldest brother he made some decisions that I didn't agree with, nor could I stop."

He looked away from me. "You have to understand that; your father was faster than anything or anyone. His speed made mine look slow. For Atlas' sake, he could cross the globe in less time that I could cross the damned road."

"Decisions?" I asked. Impervious nodded.

"What decisions? You mean to be a villain?" "No." Impervious replied back. "Some of the worst things he did, the world never even knew of. Blue Rush could move so fast that at times he seemed invisible, and many of his deeds weren't even attributed to him. Then," Impervious paused. "He fell for your mother. He loved her, and she loved him. Even though he was bad for her. Following his lead, I found love too." He closed his eyes for a moment and then opened them. "Love was our downfall, and set things in motion that would change the world forever. Love, wasn't why we were sent here."

I could feel my eyes squint. "Sent here?" I repeated. Impervious stood and walked around the desk and found a seat on the couch. "Contrary to what people say, think, or call you, you don't have four powers because you're a half breed. It's because of your heritage."

Sent here. My heritage. What in Atlas's name was he talking about? "Hunter, your dad and I, weren't born on this planet, or even in this dimension. We, like you, belong to an elite class of a race called Spellborn. While you were born on Earth, your father and I were born on the world of Mo'eizus.

CHAPTER 22

SPELLBORN

"'This is why Infinity puzzles me so. He not only seems to know you are a Spellborn, but it is very likely that he is one himself." I thought it over for a moment. It was a lot to take in. "So, I'm an alien is what you're saying?" Impervious shook his head and laughed. "No, that would be a little cliché don't you think?

Well, on the plus side, at least I wouldn't be adding alien to the list of names people like to call me. "So, what in the world is a Spellborn?" I asked him. He looked at me and seemed to be trying to figure out his next words. "Maybe we should pause right here," he said? My mouth gapped open. Pause? As in stop? He must had been crazy if he thought I was going to let this go. "Maybe we can pick this up later. It's time we focus on Infinity. But later, I'll tell you more, and you can tell me how things are working out with you and Zeva?"

He said this last part with a smirk. "Me and Zeva?" I repeated. Impervious shrugged. "It's clear you like her." I shook my head. Then thought about it. "Well, maybe a little." Impervious burst out laughing. "Flex is going to have a field day. His nemesis dating his baby sister."

"Nobody is dating anybody," I said. "Plus, I kind of still have a girlfriend. I think. I mean it's hard to say at this moment." "Oh, you mean the villain?" My eyes bulged. Where did he get all this information?

I could tell he was grasping to talk about anything except what I wanted, but I wasn't going to let him. He had kept a secret from me, and the world for over a decade. Now, to feel better or to connect with the only ties to his brother he could find, he wanted to tell me the truth. Well, all in. I wanted to know everything, and I wanted to know it now. I had nothing but time, and for the first time I felt the hunt for Infinity could wait.

"What is a Spellborn? I asked once more. Impervious sighed, leaned back on his couch and crossed his legs, as he clasped his finger. "Well the better question is who. As I mentioned, since you refuse to learn about your heritage in baby steps, Spellborn are a race of beings from another dimension. A race you partially belong to, and inside that race our family is considered to be elite." "Elite?" I repeated as I tried to understand.

"Yes, elite. It's just a word. Here we prefer to use terms like royal, or noble. Well on our home world, we use the term Elite. Elite families do tend to be more powerful that other Spellborn, though. In many ways we are very much like humans and Icons. It's even long believed by some that we even share a common ancestor."

Just at that moment, Prism flickered into existence. "Sir, Flex would like a word. He needs help with his speech for his statue ceremony." Impervious nodded, and Prism flickered away. "Well, duty calls. Looks like we will have to pick this up later after all. His ceremony is later today and he needs to be ready. He always gets nervous at these things."

Impervious stood up and began to fix his clothes. He tucked in his shirt tight, and rolled his sleeves down. "So, you're going to go help him? What about Infinity?" I said. Impervious shook his head. "Oh, no. I'm not helping him at all. He's got to do these things for himself. He'll either do great, or crash and burn. Either will be good for him as he progresses. Plus, as you mentioned, Infinity is priority. There are some questions I want to ask him before he meets justice."

Meets justice? Surely, they didn't intend on trying to capture Infinity alive? Where would they put him.? Even the jails made for the worst villains likely couldn't hold him. "Well, nephew, you are welcome to look around some if you want. You can even go and find your cousin to connect. He is aware of his heritage, but not of you. So, go easy."

Using his super speed, he was gone in an instant. Then in another burst of speed he was back. "Think about this until our next talk. It will give you and Picasso something to talk about." He smirked at me, and muttered three words. "Magic is real." I could feel my face frown. "Not only is it real but it is the source of a Spellborn's power." He smiled at me once more, and then was gone again.

Magic is real? Surely, he wasn't suggesting that what he could do was magic- based. IF he was, then that meant that this magic, or at least some of it, was passed down by my father. I decided to make a mental list of questions to ask, but didn't know if I could wait that long. What I needed was a person who would know some answers. A person who would have been able to avoid or dodge the mind- altering abilities that Detach apparently possessed.

Then the answer came to me so fast that I was actually surprised. The Honor Hand. If anybody knew, their leader would. I returned back to my room, grabbed a shower because I could still smell smoke on me from my mission earlier, and then got dressed.

I hadn't been to see the Honor Hand in about a year, but last time I was there, I was told I was always welcomed.

Grabbing my phone, I opened my door and almost jumped from shock. "Hey," Zeva said as she stood in my doorway.

"Hey?" I repeated. "Why are you lurking around my door?" Even now I could smell her sweetness. She had changed clothes, too. She now had on some shorts and a button up shirt that had a few buttons opened on the top.

"I'm not lurking. I actually came by to talk. I wanted to ask you something." My heart skipped. Was she about to ask me out? Or if I liked her? In theory it sounded good, but what would I do, if she did ask me?

"Right now? I have some place I need to be." She bit her lip some, and then nodded her head. Her eyes looked away as her shoulders dropped . *Idiot* I thought to myself. "What was it?" I asked her. "Never mind. I just need to clear my head I guess. Too much on my mind. Can I come with you? Partners stick together you know." she said with a grin.

"Sure." Zeva followed me out of the base and in no time, we were in the air in my force field above Diamond District. Holding her hand, we zoomed around buildings, punched through clouds, and even flew outside of the domes that encased both districts.

As we hovered in the air, above the domes, I told her everything Impervious had told me. At first, she was quiet. Then she was a little surprised that Impervious had done so much to keep a secret. "Makes you wonder what else the heroes will hide." She said. Then she admitted that it was kind of cool. In her eyes I belonged to some super race of alien- like beings, and that even weird Picasso, was a little cooler now.

Then there was silence again. She glanced at me and bit her lip a little. I didn't want to read too much into the situation, but I think she wanted me to kiss her. Here I was floating in the sky with a beauty like her, and I didn't know if I wanted to make a move or not. No that wasn't it. I wanted to, but Danielle's face kept coming to mind.

"What did Jen say when you told her?," she finally asked. Just like that, my moment was gone as fast as it came. I cursed to myself severally as I answered her question. "I haven't told her yet, actually." Her brow raised. She was surprised I hadn't told Jen yet. In reality I tried to before I grabbed my shower, but wherever she was on her mission with Picasso made her unavailable. Her phone kept ringing and ringing, but she didn't pick up.

"I may be a little late to ask now, but where are we going?" Zeva asked as I descended to the ground below us. We landed in the area where the dome of the Diamond District and Ebony District touched. This area was commonly known as The Abyss. It was never day, and yet never night. What it was, was always gray and misty. Some reason, when the domes touched it created a dense haze of gray and silence.

This area as one could imagine was very vacant. Nobody wanted to live in the Abyss. For one, it was creepy. Two, it was just depressing. There was only one building in the Abyss that actually saw people. Everything else was abandoned from failed attempts of capitalizing on cheap real estate. The building in question, was a large church that had been renovated to serve the purpose of the Honor Hand and their leader.

Several stories high and made of red brick, the building looked like a place you would see in a horror movie. The same place you would yell at the main character in a movie not to go into because the monster was in there.

"You have gotta be shitting me. You came to see the Honor Hand?" Zeva said as she stepped back. "It's okay. I know their leader." I replied as I walked towards the church. I stopped and turned to see that Zeva hadn't moved an inch. "It's okay," I said as I motioned for her to come on.

Slowly, she followed me as she looked around like something was going to leap out of the gray mist and attack us. I doubt that would happen, but anything was possible in the Abyss, I supposed.

"I heard this guy was insane." Zeva whispered. I laughed. "Let me guess. Flex told you that?" I asked as I glanced at her. Her silence, mixed with a shoulder shrug, was all the confirmation I needed. Per usual, Flex was being a judgmental bastard.

The Honor Hand was led by a man called Cornelius Love. An Icon with precognitive powers on a supreme scale. Using his abilities, he was able to see the future anywhere from four hours up to forty- eight hours. On top of that he was also able to sense people's inner urges.

Some people compared it to mind reading but it wasn't as finely- tuned. Mind reading almost made a person's mind and thoughts an open book. One where an Icon could casually sift through your thoughts until they found something they deemed important. What Cornelius could do was feel your desires and emotions. If you were overly happy about something, he could tell but he couldn't tell you what it was for. On the flip side, if you were overly happy, he could glance into your future and see if anything would be contributing to your happiness.

Cornelius also knew my father from back in the day, when Blue Rush was a name to be feared. Out of respect for dear old dad, Cornelius offered me a free pass in the Abyss where his men wouldn't harm me. I didn't see him often, and because like Zeva said, he had a reputation for not being wrapped too tight.

Constantly seeing the future and being able to sense a person's true nature would do that to anybody I'd assume.

Zeva stayed behind as I walked up the steps to the large front door. Despite the renovation, the original church doors remained.

I balled my fist up to knock but before I could touch the door, it opened. Two men, dressed in long robes answered the door. The robe was split into three colors. One side was black, the other white, and in the middle a strip of gray. Naturally these colors represented the two districts and the Abyss.

Both men were bald and had smooth faces. They also had swords on their backs. Large swords that, according to rumor, could chop a man in half if they needed to. Both, the swords and bald heads were required of their order. The Honor Hand also didn't believe in using guns. Swords apparently were more personal.

"Cornelius is expecting you." one of the guards said in a slow dull voice. He looked at Zeva. "You as well." I could hear Zeva swallow loudly. This place really was messing with her.

"Well. Hard to surprise a man who can see the future, huh?" I said jokingly, as I hoped to ease the mood for Zeva, and to show the guard that he didn't have to be so serious with us. The guard in return acted as if I wasn't even there, and said nothing. Instead he turned around followed by his companion, and walked inside the church.

I looked at Zeva whose eyes were wide as she shook her head. She didn't speak, but in my head, I felt like she was saying. *Get out! Get out!*

The outside appeared to be a church. That is where the similarities stopped. Inside was more of an upper- class style training facility almost on par with Purgatory Academy. For one thing, there were no walls of any kind. How this was structurally sound, I have no idea. Instead each room just flowed into the next.

From where we entered we saw a good two- dozen Honor Hand members going through sword drills. Each man was bald and clean shaven on their face, and they all had a real sword for practice too. Last time I was here I asked about getting a sword, but Cornelius looked into my future and said Mr. Reid would take it from me so why bother.

Beside the sword drill was a section with several dozen chairs and tables. All positioned in the center of various book shelves that formed a circle. Each table had members reading a book or in some cases several books at once. Besides that, was an eating area. The most disturbing part of the entire place, was the lack of sound.

Even the members practicing drills were oddly quiet, except for the sounds of their slashing swords. The rest of their movements, and footsteps were silent. Not only were they quiet, but they were Voids. Every single one of them. Cornelius preferred that, apparently. I never knew why. "Hunter Monroe! You little shit." A man said several feet away. Our guard escorts stepped aside and allowed the man to approach us.

This dark- skinned man was the polar opposite of his members. While his men were bald, he was sporting a head full of curly dark hair. While his men were smooth- faced, he had a beard several inches long and thick. Lastly, his men carried long swords, while Cornelius had two medium- length swords by his side.

"Hey CL" I said as I opened my arms to embrace him. "Good to see you, man." Instead of responding he withdrew from our hug and looked at Zeva. His eyes grew wide some and she stepped back instantly as if to avoid his gaze. "Zeva Greene."

He said slowly. Zeva raised her brows. "Yes?" She asked slowly as she took another step back. "Think about your brother. How he would feel. How it would alter his life. Before you make any decisions, also think about your family. I can feel your inner battle. I feel your pain, and from your future I see why." Cornelius said to her.

He closed his eyes and tilted his head slowly. Frowning as he did so, as if he was looking for something in his head. He shook his head, and opened his eyes. "I'm sorry," he said as he looked at Zeva. "Uh, okay?" Zeva said as she glanced at me.

Then, just like that, it was as if he said nothing. He wrapped his arm around me and showed me to a place to sit in the eating area.

As we walked off, I looked at Zeva over my shoulder. She shrugged at me and then slowly followed. He pulled a seat out for both Zeva and I, and allowed us to sit first. He however, just leaned on the table. Being over six feet tall and lanky, it was likely more comfortable for him to stand instead of squeezing into a little chair.

"Are you two hungry?" He asked and then his head jerked to the side and his mouth hung open. "Course they're not," he responded. "You knew the answer. Why ask?" Zeva looked at me with her face turned. Maybe I should have told her about the talking to himself thing. I figured that would freak her out too much, but seeing her here now, it couldn't be worse.

"Ask him," Cornelius said to himself. "So, Mr. Impervious, in all his glory finally came clean huh." Cornelius said. I shook my head. "CL," I began. "What I don't understand is how were you able to avoid your mind being altered by Detach."

He pulled out a comb and pulled it through his beard several times. Then he looked at his watch on his wrist. "Hunter, I really am sorry for the decisions you will have to make." "What?" I asked him. He shook his head.

"Sorry, too early." he replied. Then he said nothing. He just looked at us, and ignored my question. When he finally spoke, it was so random that it made us jump a little. "Detach, that over loyal bitch, did and does, everything Impervious ever asked. When I saw that she was going to alter the minds of people in the city, I had a little over twenty hours to prepare, and so I did. Hired a technopath to make me a helmet to guard my thoughts."

He pointed a finger to his head. "I have so many things going on up in here. Between vision flashes, and seeing people's true nature, it's crowded as it is. Last Thing I need is some empath up in here screwing shit up. Cost me half a mil but the helmet worked. I didn't take the easy way out either."

"What do you mean easy way out?" Zeva asked. Cornelius looked at his watch again. "Still have a few minutes." he said to himself under his breath. Then as if he didn't just speak to himself again, he answered the question.

"Well, Impervious and Blue Rush were brothers, and for a while people knew. Even as Blue started down the wrong path people knew. It wasn't until the original Imperial Lords went missing that Impervious wanted memories wiped clean. That was the first time. The second time was the Battle of Ages. Impervious did something, hell, all of the Imperial Lords did. Agreed to it anyway. They wanted to have their memories erased to ease their guilt, but not Impervious. You see, they took the easy way out."

I thought a moment. So, there was a secret. A secret that the Imperial Lords knew about, but wanted to forget. What did they know? Plus, how bad could it be that one of the most popular groups in the world wanted it covered up. It dawned on me that Mr. Reid was involved, too. He was like a father to me, and I didn't want to distrust him, but I could feel that lack of trust growing inside of me like a weed already.

"So," I asked as Cornelius checked his watch. "Why didn't Impervious want his mind altered?" Cornelius laughed. "Oh, he did. The pain he felt on the Battle of Ages was the first time he had ever truly been hurt." I knew where CL was going but I let him explain, so Zeva wouldn't be left out.

"You see *Impervious* isn't just a name for him. It's what he is. What he truly is. Normal Icons can be invincible or invulnerable. Take Flex for instance, or Dynamic. Both are hard to harm, but if you try you can do it. Impervious is literally Impervious to everything. Something about him being an elite Spellborn amplifies his invincibility and makes nothing harm him physically or mentally. So, Detach couldn't alter his mind if she wanted to because he would be immune to it."

"Impervious," Zeva said under her breath. Like me, I think she was beginning to see the full scope of Mr. Impervious' powers. How did CL know about Impervious being an elite

Spellborn, though? Before I could ask the question, he cut me off.

"Time is running out." Cornelius said. He clapped his hands twice and every member of the Honor Hand stopped what they were doing, and began to form lines and exited the area through various side doors. Now it was just us three in the main part of the building.

Zeva and I looked around. "What's going on?" she asked slowly. I could feel a chill in the area now. "You want to know how I know what a Spellborn is," Cornelius said looking at me. "I know almost everything. Downside to my abilities. I know your phone is going to ring in exactly one hundred seconds and you will answer it. That single action will change everything for you, Hunter. I'm sorry."

I looked at my phone. "You see," he said. "Despite knowing the future, it is ever changing. It has a way of making us feel like we are in control. Right now, you're prepared to answer the phone because I told you. Yet had I not told you, you would still answer the phone. Regardless if you knew or not, you would still answer. No matter how we see the future, it will always have the same outcome."

He stepped away from the table and did a fancy bow. "Keep your friends close, Hunter." He glanced at Zeva. "Dark times are ahead. Be well. You are always welcome here." Then he turned and walked away, talking to himself as he did so.

I had several questions but as I stood up to call out to him, my phone rang. I looked down at it and saw Jen was finally returning my call. I grimaced. Why would Jen calling me change everything for me?

"Answer it," Zeva said. I tapped my phone and put it to my ear. "Jen," I said. Then I heard a voice on the other end that wasn't Jen's at all. A voice I had heard before that sent a chill over my body that had nothing to do with Zeva or her powers.

"Hello," Infinity said from the other end of the phone.

CHAPTER 23

PHONE CALL

I could feel my eyes pop open, and judging from how Zeva was looking at me like I had horns on my head, my concern was evident. I moved the phone from my ear for a second and mouthed *"it's Infinity"* to her.

"Shit," Zeva said as she rubbed her hands over her face while exhaling. "Where is Jen?" I asked back into the phone. I wanted to scream, but I had to keep my emotions in check. It's funny, I always assumed I learned very little while at Purgatory Academy, but more and more, the little life lessons drilled into my head there, were coming to the surface when I needed them.

Mainly, to always keep focus, keep calm, and keep control in a tense situation. Common sense practice, but often overlooked in times of crisis. If this didn't qualify as a crisis I didn't know what did.

A slight laugh came through the phone. "Jen is fine. I have no intentions of hurting her. I already have powers similar to hers so it would be no point in taking them, thus it would be no point in harming her."

That confirms it. From the mouth of the man himself. He was in fact stealing the abilities of the people he killed. How in the name of Atlas was he able to do that? Was it some sort of leach like Icon ability? For all I knew, it was a Spellborn thing, if he in fact was a Spellborn.

"While she isn't going to be harmed, I can't, in good faith say the same thing about this one you all call Picasso." I gritted my teeth. "You see he is a Spellborn, and one that plays a role in my plans. I had to be sure. It could have easily been you."

What was he talking about? "Look, don't hurt them." "Don't hurt him," he replied. "I already told you, this girl you call your sister is fine." I could hear a lot of noise in the background where ever he was. Noise that sounded like wind blowing, and children being ordered to find their seats by a woman.

He sighed on the phone. "Once the cards are on the table, and you know the truth, I want you to join me. You will never be as powerful as I am, but still you are powerful in your own right. We are alike you and I, we can accomplish much together."

I could feel anger flow through me. "I'm nothing like you. I'm not a murderer. You killed for your powers, I was born with mine. See the difference?"

His response was a slight hiss. "When you find out how the Battle of Ages came about and how it was halted, you'll feel differently," Infinity said. I was confused. How did the Battle of Ages have anything at all to do with this?.

"Looks like people are starting to arrive," Infinity added after a few seconds. "I believe the one you call Flex just landed on the stage. My, my, my, isn't he an unusually good- looking fellow. His outfit is horrendous, but he himself looks almost plastic like."

I could feel my eyes dart back and forth. Flex landed on a stage? I thought to myself. Then it came to me. Impervious said Flex was getting a statue today. "Damnit," I said out loud. Zeva raised her brows at me. She didn't react well to being left out the loop. I removed the phone and put Infinity on speaker.

"You should have figured out where we are by now," he casually said to me. "I gave you credit for being that smart. We have a lot to talk about you and I. Spellborn to Spellborn, I mean." I looked at Zeva. She didn't understand the magnitude of what Infinity just said. He confirmed what Impervious had suspected. Just like me. Just like my dad, and Impervious. His roots also, come from another dimension, and were wrapped in magic it seems. This didn't make sense at all. Why tell me that? Why give such a thing away?

"The Imperial Lords aren't the saviors the world thinks they are." I could feel my face twist. "They never claimed to be saviors. They do what any heroic Icon does. They save lives. They help people." Zeva said.

"Lies." Infinity shouted. It was so loud that Zeva and I jumped and I almost dropped the phone. "Think about this," Infinity said calmly again. "I murdered, what was it, several dozen people only last night. Yet here I sit, only several blocks away and people are gathering for a statue event as if nothing happened. More so, have you even heard it mentioned on the news?"

Zeva and I looked at each other. We both knew that he was right. Had I not seen it for myself, I wouldn't have realized some many people were dead. I hadn't even heard about Young Pyro's death yet and he was a superstar.

"I take your silence as an agreement." Infinity said. "The Imperial Lords, and their empath work very hard to keep up their godlike images, and their funding. That changes today. More and more people are arriving. There are going to be more here that at the concert I'd imagine. Pity."

He was going to kill them. He was going to kill them all. Zeva shook her head. "Flex won't let you hurt them." she said to the phone. Infinity responded by laughing loudly and hard. Then the phone went dead. We looked at each other. "Where is Flex getting his statue?" I asked Zeva as I shoved my phone in my pocket and then looked for my earpiece.

"At the Atlas City aquarium." She responded. "A pillar cracked a few weeks ago and Flex held the entire center tank up, as it got repaired. Saved an entire sixth grade class, and teachers in the process. So, they are giving him a statue in the viewing garden beside the building."

I shook my head, inserted the bud in my ear, and scooped Zeva off the ground in my arms. She squealed a little, and then looked at me. She felt so light in my arms as I began to rise in the air. The room turned blue, as I used my eyes and blasted the entry door off The Honor Hand entrance.

CL would be pissed, but I had the money to cover the damages, and knowing him with his precog powers, he has already ordered the new door to be replaced. I continued to hold Zeva in my power, while calling out through the earpiece. "Prism. Prism." I said.

There was silence for a second, before his voice came into my ear. "Yes?" "Thank Atlas you were listening." I replied. "I wasn't *listening*. As I have told you, I am the system. I see and hear everything."

"Sure, fine whatever. I need you to tell the Imperial Lords that Infinity has Picasso and Jen, and he is at Flex's statue ceremony. Zeva and I are already flying there now, but we need everybody we can there."

"Transmitting message now," Prism said, and then his voice went away. In return I could hear a faint click several times. I looked down at Zeva who was holding her arms around my neck, I expected to see her eyes red or glossed over, but they weren't. She was calm and passive. Talk about nerves of steel in a crisis. "It's going to be okay." I said to myself.

She shook her head. "I don't think it is." she replied. "You've seen him. He can't be stopped. The Lords won't stand a chance. He has too much power. Too much freedom."

"We have Impervious," I responded to her. "Not only that," I hated to even admit it but I did. "We have Flex. He may not be as hard to harm as Impervious, but he's likely the strongest Icon alive, so that does help."

She didn't respond. She just looked at the city below us as the ocean surrounding the edge of The Diamond district came into view.

"They're on their way," Prism said as he returned. "Thanks, Prism." I said. "If you don't return, Young Lord, know it has been a pleasure." "I didn't know you cared Prism." "I don't," the program replied. "I am programmed to say such things to all members of the Imperial Lords, and their Interns if they are tasked against odds with little chance for success."

I exhaled. "Thanks for the honesty, I guess." I used my finger and tapped the ear bud off. In seconds a large dome-shaped building came into view. The open ocean sat behind it, and on both sides, were massive gardens of flowers of all colors.

Each garden had a center area for events. Usually the events only were weddings, or some sort of outdoor play, but today it was home to the statue ceremony for Flex. In front of the actual building itself was something standing over six feet tall with a drape covering it up. It was safe to say that under said drape was the life- like replica statue of Flex, along with a plaque detailing his heroics that earned him the statue.

On the stage was a podium, a few chairs, and Flex standing reading some cards to himself. His outfit was different today. I had never seen the color scheme before, and to be honest it was rather ugly. A splash of lime green over black. As I began to land on the stage, I looked at the chairs in the audience. There were almost a hundred seats in the area.

In the back were several news station vans, two school busses, and one police car. Infinity was right. With such a massacre last night, you'd expect more security at this event. Even if Icons were going to be there. Many of the chairs were empty except for a small section that contained the children and their teachers. "Flex," Zeva said as I placed my feet on the ground.

She leapt out of my arms and ran to him. Flex stepped back some and looked at his sister. "Z, you look, odd. Pale." His eyes narrowed, and I could see his hands grip her arms a little tighter. "Are you taking your pills?" "Yes," she quickly replied. It was odd for her to lie to Flex, because I knew for a fact she wasn't taking them anymore.

I didn't have time to think about this, or to address Flex, nor did I want to. Zeva had that part covered. Instead, I scanned the area around us, looking for Jen and Picasso. Nothing. Even Infinity was nowhere to be seen. All I could see besides the school children, were three older people sitting in the front row. Two of them, a man and a woman, were still as they looked up at us. The man between them however, had his legs crossed and a smile on his face as he watched us.

"Infinity is here. Now." Zeva said to Flex. His jaw clenched as he sprung into hero mode, and hovered about six feet in the air, letting his index cards and his notes drop to the ground. A chill rushed around us, as Zeva formed a layer of ice armor around herself, and a large ice mace was crafted in her hand.

Even under the armour of frosty ice, I could see her eyes glowing as she looked around. Her eyes returned to normal as she shouted, "I got nothing." Apparently, her vision powers couldn't find them either.

"He has Jen and Picasso," I shouted up to Flex. His chest rose and nostrils flared, as he nodded to me. I had to give it to him. He wasn't afraid. Even with knowing how powerful Infinity was, he was ready to take him on. Not to leave myself at a disadvantage, I called forth a force field around myself and floated a few inches off the ground. I didn't know about all Icons, but I reacted easier in the air, as oppose to on the ground.

Just then, a glow erupted on the stage as yellow light pulsed around us for a second. The children stood up and looked at us pointing and screaming. From within the yellow glow stepped a singular red boot.

I squinted my eyes and looked. He was standing tall as a red cap billowed around him. His entire outfit was silver, and on his forearms, were golden bracers. Every muscle seemed to pop from under his outfit, and a scowl was on his face as he looked around. I felt relief pass over me as Impervious stood on the stage.

The light faded away completely now, as Life-Line, Detach, Power Prince, and Solar Goddess, all stood beside Impervious. Flex landed on the ground beside them. Seeing them all together, ready to take on whatever came their way was impressive.

The all looked so regal. Hell, we all did, to be honest. We really did look like Lords. Mr. Reid, I mean Life-Line, had waves of green energy pulsing from both of his hands. If anybody was harmed now, they would instantly be healed by his power.

Detach called her clones to her aid and stood ready with her troops. Secretly, I'm sure she was mentally ready to assault Infinity too, if he showed. The golden aura and energy of Solar Goddess burned brightly beside Detach. So bright that I could barely make out her face. Power Prince was at the ready as well. Sparks of pink energy dancing and glowing around his fist, so intense and rapid, that they each looked like plasma balls. I had never truly seen Kevin in battle mode. The laughing and jokester face I had grown to know, was gone. Instead he stood determined, in an outfit of black and orange as he scanned around him.

Lastly, Impervious and Flex, the powerhouses of the team stood side by side. The news crews had finally seen us all on stage and began moving closer to start filming. Even if the ceremony wasn't set to start yet, it seems they couldn't resist. "Stay back," Flex shouted to them. I was surprised. I had never really seen this side of him. Serious and stern. Not being a dick at all. Maybe he did have what it took to lead the Lords.

"We got your message, Hunter," Life-Line said as he looked around wildly. "Where is Jen? Where is she?" Before I could respond, one of the older people in the front row, stood up and clapped. "Well done." the man said. As he moved closer to us, his body rippled and shifted into a man I had seen before.

Where the older man once stood, was now a tall man dressed in black with a white mask on. Infinity could shape shift too, apparently. He snapped his fingers and the other people in the front row with him instantly changed. The older woman was now Jen and the other gentleman was Picasso. Both had red bands of energy around their ankles and wrists.

"Let her go you son of a bitch," Mr. Reid said. "Or what?" Infinity said in a mocking tone. "You'll heal me to death?" he laughed. "Don't embarrass yourself, Marcus."

How did he know Mr. Reid's first name? Did anybody else find this as confusing as I did? Infinity stretched out both hands and, similarly to my own ability, he formed a massive green force field that encased the entire stage and half of the chairs in the audience. Inside the force field, I could still see outside, but everything seemed to be moving in slow motion.

As the other children outside the force field ran, and officers ran to the dome, they were moving as if time had come to a halt for them and only fractions of seconds were passing. "Well, nothing like some privacy." Infinity said.

The room in front of me turned blue as I stood with the other Imperial Lords. My eyes hurt a little as I flooded them with energy. In return Infinity balled a fist, and almost twenty of the students screamed as they were lifted in the air.

Flex went to move, but Impervious held his arm out and stopped him. "Flex I'm sure you recognize these kids as the ones you saved only weeks ago. They wanted to see you get your statue. Now look at them." Infinity said as he shrugged.

"Put them down." Mr. Impervious said. As soon as he spoke, the entire posture of Infinity changed. His relaxed movements became rigid. He was breathing heavier now and he cracked his neck as he turned to Impervious.

"What did you say?" Infinity asked. "Let them, Jennifer, and my son, go." He bellowed. "Son!" Infinity screamed as he removed his white mask, showing his full true face. His face looked oddly familiar. Like I had seen it before, but I didn't remember where.

The other Imperial Lord members remained as they were, ready to move if need be but otherwise they didn't react. Impervious and Detach however, both gasped. Detach allowed her clones to fade into her as she stepped away from Infinity.

"Will?" Impervious said out loud. "It can't be." I looked at Impervious as my vision turned back to normal. Will? I searched my brain to figure out what was going on. Then it came to me. "Your son that died in the Battle of Ages," I said slowly. Then I looked at Infinity. He was an older version of the statue I saw in Impervious' living quarters earlier.

"Died?" Infinity said. "Tell him the truth." Impervious seemed to be unable to talk. Flex looked at Impervious out of the side of his eye while at the same time stepping to the side to put most of his body in front of Zeva.

"Davis, what's going on here?" Life-Line asked. "Don't play innocent," Infinity said. "You knew. You let it happen and did nothing. None of you did."

A bolt of lightning came crashing down and Infinity vanished in it, reappearing behind Life-Line, he placed a hand on his head and instantly, Mr. Reid fell to the ground and began to scream.

Jen shouted, as I watched the body on the ground. Then Solar Goddess pounced and came crashing down on Infinity landing a blow to his face and sent him down to the ground. She didn't let up, as she formed a knife out of golden energy and stabbed the spot where he was.

He phased quickly, allowing the knife to pass through him. Detach called her clones to life and they ran for Infinity. Before they could reach him, he was back and solid once more.

Lighting rained down from the sky, through the force field he created and struck each clone. They fell to the ground and faded away. Solar Goddess summoned several floating orbs of energy. "Stop." Mr. Impervious screamed. Solar Goddess looked at him. Her golden face twisted in anger.

She stopped, Infinity didn't. Instead his eyes became living flames.

He moved his hands and from his flaming eyes came a large cone of heat that consumed the glowing woman. Solar Goddess screamed as a ball of fire overpowered her. In moments her lifeless body was on the ground as her remains crackled. Without Mr. Reid to heal her she stood no chance.

Infinity clapped his hands as if to remove some dirt from them. I pulled out my phone and sent a text message and hoped the person on the other end received it, and took it seriously. It may be the only way out for any of us.

"One of your precious Lords is dead," Infinity said. "I don't want to kill any of you just yet, but she attacked first. I needed answers first. I just want to know why." Infinity said as he paced back and forth. His words came out calm, but his posture was tense, and his eyes were alive with passion. He didn't seem as calm as his words were.

"Why what?" Power Prince asked. "Ask them." Infinity responded. "Ask them how they ended the Battle of Ages at the cost of my life." "What is he talking about?" I asked Impervious. He avoided my gaze. "Davis," Flex said as his brow raised. "What did you all do?"

There was silence for a second. Outside of the still squirming Jen, nobody said anything. Infinity snapped his fingers and one of the children yelled. "Okay. Okay." Impervious said. Instantly the force field faded away. Allowing the other students, as well as the two officers and the news vans to move freely.

True to their nature, the reporters didn't miss a beat and began filming. Every second from here on out, the entire area of Atlas City would see. The officers drew their weapons, but instead were lifted in the air and held as helpless as the first part of the class was.

"You know what, I'll tell the world how you saved them. How the mighty Mr. Impervious so easily halted the enemy at the Battle of Ages, and then how you and your Lords covered up what you did."

Every camera shifted to Mr. Impervious as Mr. Reid slowly stood back to his feet. Had more people been here, I'm sure everyone would have had their phones in the air recording.

Mr. Impervious took a deep breath and exhaled. "Restore Life-Line's memory," Impervious said to Detach. She wiped sweat from her brow and looked at Mr. Impervious, who in turn just nodded. A faint purple pulse came from her body and then Mr. Reid's eyes rolled back in his head for a moment and when they returned to normal he looked at Infinity. "Will!" He said as he looked at the man in front of him. His eyes bulged and the he looked back to Impervious. "You removed the mind block?" he said to Detach.

At that moment, Infinity's hands glowed red, and the bands of energy restraining Jen vanished. She jumped up and ran to Mr. Reid and hugged him. He returned her hug for a moment, and then stood in front of her.

Infinity looked at Picasso who was still bound by energy. "A father and his child. Loving isn't it." Infinity said. Impervious walked closer to him. "Will, we can talk, it doesn't have to be this way. We can make it right."

"That time has passed, father." Infinity vanished in a bolt of lightning and reappeared near the floating children and police officers. A faint purple pulse, similar to the one that came from Detach, exploded from Infinity, and every floating victim he had in the air instantly froze. They just hovered lifeless in the air.

"Their minds are in my power now. Think of it like a light switch," Infinity said. "If I decide to turn the light switch off," One of the cops twitched in the air as blood came from his nose. "They will die." He walked towards one of the camera men. "Just to make sure none of you try anything while I explain how we all ended up here."

"No." Mr. Impervious said as he stepped forward. "It was my decision, my actions, and it should be my words." Infinity glared at him as my phone went off in my pocket. I checked it quickly and then placed it back.

"Very well. Tell them how you intended to conquer this world, and then backed out at the expense of my life."

CHAPTER 24

SINS OF THE FATHER

"Is that what you think?" Mr. Impervious asked. "That I just gave you to them without worry or remorse? It was the only way to save this world." I could feel my eyes narrow. "You gave him away?" I asked. Impervious snapped his head in my direction, as if seeing me there for the first time.

"It's not that cut and dry," he hissed at me. "Yes, it is." Infinity said as he spun and looked at the camera. As he turned, the same red energy surrounded him, causing portions of the stage to warp and distort.

"The Battle of Ages only ended because your glorious Mr. Impervious struck a deal of peace with the Spellborn people, because he knew their magic could destroy this world if they saw fit."

Spellborn people. I could feel my eyes dart inside of my head. He couldn't mean what I thought he meant. "The invaders, were Spellborn?" I asked. I didn't direct my question to anybody. I didn't care who answered, I just wanted answers. "What in Atlas is a Spellborn?" Flex said. "Good question," came Jen's voice. I couldn't see her though so I had no idea where she was in her invisible state.

"We are Spellborn," Infinity said. "My bastard father. Picasso. Hunter. And even myself. All Spellborn or half Spellborn. Wielders of passed down magic and might." Flex made a mocking face. "Magic?" "Be quiet, Flex." Mr. Impervious said.

"The Spellborn were intent on taking this world. That's what we did back then." Impervious said as his head slumped some. "We conquered worlds. Used them until we didn't need them anymore. When the royals arrived here, we fell in love instead. In love with the people, the culture, the world itself. So, we stayed."

He exhaled as her massaged his eyes with his fingers. "My brother enjoyed the freedom this world offered." Impervious continued as he shook his head. "He found love in only two things. A woman and his freedom to use his powers how he wanted, and the villain Blue Rush was born."

Impervious looked at me. His eyes were red. "Blue Rush, was your brother?" a reporter asked from behind her cameraman. Impervious ignored her as he sobbed. "I soon found myself a father for the first time. Years went by and the Spellborn returned. Their power, our power, was unmatched. Some of them were able to see the aura of a person. Their *glow* as we called it. This allowed them to channel the power of their victims for short periods."

In the back of my mind, I couldn't help but notice that Infinity seemed to channel his victims power indefinitely. "They found me and my brother, but even then, we refused to leave. Instead we fought. Fought our fellow Spellborn. Fought for our freedom, for our loved ones here in Atlas City. These were the early days of the Battle of Ages."

I looked at him, and slowly, began to turn on him. Everything that I thought was good about this man was beginning to unravel. Where a hero once stood, now seemed like a selfish child who only cared for what he wanted. "How many people died because you two refused to leave.? Because you two wanted Freedom?" I asked slowly.

"Hundreds did." Flex said as he looked on at Impervious. "He didn't have a choice." Detach said as she stepped up." "Yes, he did." Mr. Reid said. "We all did." Impervious held up a hand to silence them both.

"Their new leader was from another Royal family. He offered me a way out. To halt the war. He offered a trade of peace. His son for mine." Instantly I looked at Picasso who seemed as surprised by this as anybody else did. His brow was raised and his head was turned slightly.

"You gave your son away?" I asked him. "You could have just gone back home to your world, but you decided to stay, fight, and what, make-" "The world forget I ever existed." Infinity added.

Nothing seemed right now. My father could have been alive if they just left. Sure, we would be on a different world, but we would have been together. Then he went and got killed before the war was even halted. "How?" I began to speak then paused. "What gives you the right?" I asked Impervious. "Then you," I said as I looked at Detach. I know you knew each other when he was younger, but to blindly follow his madness. To play with minds of the people in the entire city."

I had never felt such disgust for people that I respected. "And you agreed to this. To him giving his son away." I finally asked Mr. Reid. A man who raised me in the absence of my father. A man I loved. How could he have felt like it was okay?

"When he came to us and told us what was going on," the war had already started and we were not winning. We did what we had to do, in order to save lives. To save Atlas City. The world."

At some point, Flex, Zeva, and I had distanced ourselves from the three The Imperial Lords that were responsible for what happened. Power Prince soon followed. It seemed that none of us wanted to be close to them anymore. "Now you have to decide, cousin." I heard Infinity say to me. "You all do. You can stand with these, so- called Lords and accept what they did, or you can join me." He looked at us all. Flex was the first to speak.

"I'm a hero. My purestock goes back generations. It's in my blood. I can't say I agree with their methods, but for now, I'm an Imperial Lord, and I'll stop you, even if it kills me." Just like that, he stepped beside Mr. Impervious.

Flex had chosen his side. Zeva didn't even speak, but stood still for a moment. She had been oddly quiet this entire time now that I thought about it. Then, she simply moved between her brother and Detach, and looked at me. Infinity simply smiled. He had enough powers that he really didn't need us on his side at all. "Hunter." he said to me.

I swallowed as everybody looked at me. Hero or villain. It was always the question looking down on me. Now I had to decide. Lives, including mine depended on it. I moved away from the Imperial Lords.

"Hunter. Son." Mr. Reid said as he stretched a hand out. Beside him, Jen became visible. I stopped moving, and looked at Infinity. My cousin. A half Spellborn just like myself. "I'm not with them, but I'm not with you either."

Infinity shook his head and clasped his hands behind his back. I felt the energy ripple from him as he performed this simple gesture. "I spent the better part of the last year collecting the abilities needed to bring you and this city you hold so dear to its knees." He said as he looked at us. Then he narrowed his gaze to his father. "You picked this world over me, and now I'll take it from you. You can't be hurt, but you can be broken."

He exhaled and shook his head. Infinity quickly opened his hand and created a miniature ball of red energy. The ball formed into a sharp spear and hovered in the air. "Well, let's begin shall we.?"

It happened so fast. He thrusted his hand towards the still-restrained Picasso. As he did so, the spear of red energy pierced his chest. Everybody gasped as blood flowed down Picasso's chest and he slumped over.

The red spear pulsed and his body slowly began to turn to ash, leaving nothing but bone visible. He looked up from his wound to us, as tears rolled down his face. "No!" Impervious screamed as he shifted into super speed. I thought he was going for Infinity. For his son, and in a way, he did. When his speed faded away he was holding the limp body of Picasso in his hands as what was left of him turn to ash, and slipped through Impervious' hands.

"You see, dear old dad can't be hurt. He is *truly* Impervious. But his heart is weak. As people die around him, he will break."

Infinity looked at Impervious as he held what was left of Picasso's skeleton.

"He loved the wrong son." Infinity said. Then slowly, each and every child he held with his power began to twitch and fall to the ground lifeless as their eyes turned black.

CHAPTER 25

LORDS NO MORE

Life-Line was the first to react. His glowing green hands came together as he covered the fallen children. He stood in the middle of them, and allowed his green energy to flow over their bodies. He would heal then and, in theory, they should be okay.

Flex lifted in the air, balled his fist and went for Infinity. As he moved, Infinity sent both a cone of fire, and red energy his way. Flex flew right through the attack unharmed. His fist was several inches away from the stomach of Infinity, and then it stopped midair . Infinity was using his telekinesis again as he smiled at the trembling Flex.

The smile faded away as Flex slowly began to move again. "How,?" Infinity asked as his eyes grew wide and he looked at the moving fist. He may have spent years gathering powers, but still one thing that he couldn't match was the uncapped power that was Flex's strength. His face contorted as he continued to move closer to Infinity.

I looked for Impervious, but he was still holding Picasso's remains, rocking back and forth crying. I had never seen him so vulnerable. Nothing else seemed to matter to him as he held his son's remains.

"A little help here." Flex shouted as he was hit by a wave of sound from Infinity. In that moment several Detach clones appeared. Materializing out of thin air and were on Infinity in mere seconds.

The clones had no additional power, they were nothing more than shields. As one fell, the real Detach would form another. I summoned force fields around them all to give them extra support, and I moved to help Flex fight Infinity. "It's not working," I heard Mr. Reid scream.

I glanced over to him and saw him leaning over the children and police officers. "They're mentally being harmed, not physically." I glanced at my watch. My ace in the hole should be here any moment now. Just had to hold Infinity off.

"Let me try," the prime Detach said as she went to assist Life-Line. For the first time I was thankful for her mental abilities. Then something unexpected happened. Her clones began to scream as they all fell and faded away. Flex didn't have room to breathe as it was, and now his support was gone.

Why had the clones screamed? I looked for the original Detach and then I saw what was going on. She was slumped over, covered in her own blood as an ice shard several feet long was sticking out of her chest. My eyes grew wide as I watch Zeva pull the ice from Detach's body.

"Zeva," I screamed to her, "What are you doing?" She looked down at Detach and grinned a little. "Picking a side." she said calmly as she slashed her ice blade in the air to remove blood from it. "This is why I wanted to talk to you in your room earlier. I've noticed for a while now that the Lords weren't the heroes we thought they were. Their events at the Battle of Ages and the cover up confirmed it."

I shook my head. All I could think was how could she have killed Detach. I was the one who didn't know which road to take. She was the favorite born of purestock. "They were no better than the villains they were supposed to stop." She said once more as she raised her hands and several important-looking ice structures came into existence. All standing around four feet tall and transparent. The imps held their hands up, and they formed into sharp edges.

How in the world, had she thought that was true? I didn't' agree with the Imperial Lords actions but that didn't make them villains. She had gone to a place there was no coming back from. "Z," Flex said from a distance. I glanced at him to see that Kevin, Power Prince, was in the mix now. Slinging glowing hands of pure energy.

Flex had seen what was happening and paused mid- fight. It was all Infinity needed, and he wasted no time. He screamed and sent Power Prince flying, and then he ran towards Flex. He then turned into a bolt of electricity, and struck Flex right in the chest. Flex screamed out as Infinity reformed and leaned over him, and looked him in the face,

I knew what was happening. He wanted Flex's power. I wasn't sure why because he was holding his own against him, but it was a process Flex wouldn't survive. He would end up like Young Pyro. Quickly, I stretched my hand and a force field slowly formed over Flex. As soon as it was complete I used my manipulation over the force field and yanked it closer to myself, pulling Flex out of Infinity's path. Then one of the ice imps hit me square in the back.

I fell face first and I could feel my force field go away. I rolled over quickly, flooding my eyes with energy and released it on every imp Zeva had summoned. I didn't stop there. I liked Zeva, but as far as I was concerned, she was no longer on my side.

I sent another burst of my Impact Blast to her, but she created a solid wall of ice to hide behind in seconds. She stepped from behind the ice wall smirking. Then, unexpectedly she turned in a cloud of crystallized mist, and floated in the air for a moment and then flew away.

I realized two things then and there. One was that Zeva had been misrepresenting the true strength of her powers all along. Her purestock heritage, in my mind, put her on par with what the Spellborn considered elites. Two, I couldn't let her get away. As I watched the mist float away, Flex ran to my side.

"Catch her, but don't hurt her, Hunter." Flex said as he looked at me with pleading in his eyes. "She's still my sister. She's just confused." I was confused, too. If Flex was here, then who. Then I saw him. Impervious was dashing around with his superspeed, landing several blows to Infinity. Power Prince was back on his feet, too. For every ten punches Impervious landed, Power Prince would land one. Punches so fueled with energy that they sounded like amplified static burst going off.

"Go," Flex shouted. "I'll stay here and help them." Flex wasted no time, as he flew back into action. When he landed, Infinity laughed, and then several other versions of himself stepped from his body. He seemed to have acquired the ability to multiply, likely to balance the scales when Detach became a problem. One copy, turned invisible. Another copy created weapons of fire, two other Infinity copies floated in the air, and one copy literally grew to about eight feet tall, and had muscles larger than anything I had ever seen.

Still, more and more copies came to life as Impervious, Power Prince, and Flex, were outnumbered. Unlike Detach, it appeared that Infinity's clones came with powers of their own.

"Hunter, go." I heard Jen's voice come in my ear. I could only assume she was hiding invisible somewhere. Waiting for my plan to work. She only had to hide until, the help I summoned got there. Then she would help them.

I rocketed myself in the air and followed Zeva. It wasn't hard. She had a head start, but her misty form was slower than my ability to fly and it left a fog like streak behind it. I tracked her to the top of the sports club near the aquarium. From there, she landed in the middle of the field, and caused a baseball game to halt.

I crashed on the ground more than I landed. As I collided with the earth chunks of dirt flew, causing the baseball players to scatter. "Go go." I shouted as I waved hands to get them off the field. Zeva was breathing hard now. Her gaseous form seemed to take a lot out of her, as most abilities did when they turned you into a phased state.

"Just let me go, Hunter," she said calmly. As she spoke I could see her breath, as if she was standing in a freezer. "You'll slip up and then it will be over. I don't want to hurt you. I want you to join me." she said.

"I don't want to hurt you. If I do, I'm sure I'll have to deal with Flex and I don't want to go a third round with him." She turned into her misty form and flew directly into my chest. The pain was instant as the cold consumed my body, causing me to fall to one knee. The mist entered through my nose and mouth, causing what felt like every inch of my being to be in pain.

She reappeared standing before me, and hurled several ice shards my way. I summoned a force field just fast enough to block most of them, but one made it through and pierced my arm. As I screamed I heard Jen's voice in my ear.

"Dude, everything is going to shit. Power Prince's hands seem broken. Flex is down, my dad is down, and Impervious is slowing down. He's taking everything Infinity sends his way, but can't contain him. It's like he is toying with them before he kills them. Your guy better hurry."

I shook my head as Jen's word gave me an idea. *Contain.* I created a force field around myself and Zeva. It was tight. So tight that I felt like the walls were closing in on me and it was becoming harder to breath. Like I was going to be stuck inside of my own power. I gritted my teeth and held out.

She punched an ice- covered fist into the force field and her ice shattered. "Just you and me now," I said as I allowed the force field to lift us in the air. She tried her mist form, and simply bounced back around the inside. When she returned to normal she was wearing her ice armour and looked at me.

I ignored her pretty face, and the nausea in my stomach, as I released an Impact Blast on her. I was tired already and that burst of energy had done it for me. As the energy from my eyes punched through her armour my force field involuntarily faded away.

She fell through the sky, unconscious from my blast. I stretched my hand out to form a force field around her, but it was no luck. She continued to fall. I flew towards her but I wasn't moving fast enough. She was going to crash into the ground. She was going to die because of me.

I stopped flying, and then I began to fall, but because I had stopped flying, now I had enough energy to save her. She was feet from the ground now, as a pale blue force field came around her, only seconds before she hit the surface.

"He's here," Jen screamed in my ear. It was so loud that I almost removed the ear piece. "Good." I replied. He knows what to do, and he'll hold up his end if he wants his one hundred grand I promised him. Just turn him invisible." I'm on the way.

I wanted to check and see if Zeva was okay. I couldn't waste time though. I had to hurry. If Jen messed up, Infinity would kill her for sure, regardless if he had her powers already or not. I left Zeva in the force field. Her own pale blue prison.

As I ran I slowly began to get some of my energy back, so my running became a hover, and my hover became flying. As I came back into view of the garden where everybody was I saw several cop cars in the distance parked, but none were advancing the scene. This fight was being broadcasted live, and if The Lords were having a time, then the police knew they would fail. So, why even try?

I did find it odd, that no other supergroup had come to help. Had their actions made the rest of the Icons turn their backs on them?

When I landed on the ground, I could see Flex. He was bruised, bloody, and his eyes were closed. Mr. Reid was in some sort of trance and looked almost like a zombie. Kevin was unconscious, and bleeding badly from his hands. Not only that, but Impervious was now actually down.

I didn't know how, but he, the Icon who could withstand anything was down on the ground and Infinity was on top of him. Leaning over. "You're precious Lords will be no more when you wake up, father." Infinity said. He said the word father like it was a curse, or that it caused him disgust to say. "You will be alone, just as I was when I arrived on that new world that turned me into who I am today."

"You don't want to do that," I said as I walked towards him with my eyes glowing blue. "You're still here, cousin?" Infinity said as he stood tall and looked at me. "I thought you had run after that ice girl. I really must thank her for killing one of the Lords. Even I didn't see that coming."

He looked around at the destruction around him. The children that were lifeless on the ground suddenly came to, and ran in all directions. "I told you, it was only ever about the Imperial Lords." Infinity said.

"I will kill them all. Sadly, that includes your adopted father." I shook my head. "I can't allow that. "Allow?" he said and laughed. "How do you intend to stop me, cousin? What you should be doing is joining me. I could teach you about that power inside you. That power you don't even realize you have. We could go back home. To the world of Spellborn. To Mo'eizus, or we could rule this world. My offer still stands, cousin. You played no role in what they did to me, but stand in my way now, and you will fall just as they did."

"Almost in position," Jen said in my ear. "Just keep him talking." I swallowed. "You know where you messed up, cuz," I said in a mocking tone. "You focused so much on power, that you stole from people with powers that other Icons would envy. You ignored the little people and that is how I'm going to stop you."

I released a burst of my Impact Blast, and Infinity opened a small orange swirling portal in front of himself. My blast flew into that portal and then the portal closed. "I got that power from a girl two cities over about three months ago." he said as he laughed. "I have no need for pointless powers. I couldn't stand up to Flex and Impervious with pointless powers."

"Do you even have powers of your own?" I asked him. "I do. Father hated them though. This ability to leach others powers, was my power. I didn't learn of the true potential until he traded me off like I was nothing. The Spellborn showed me how powerful I really could be. Just as I have offered to show you."

"Ready, on your word." Jen said in my ear. "Now," I screamed. Infinity squinted at me. My random scream confusing him. As I screamed, I also ran away. He watched me, and then he turned around and saw Jen standing in front of him, with an old enemy. She had concealed none other than Eric Rasenburg, aka E-Rase.

Danielle had given me his number to validate her claims that nothing was going on between them. I was glad I saved it. He was the only way I could think of to halt a person like Infinity. He, for a small one hundred grand fee, had agreed to help us out. Then he was going to take his money and leave town.

As he walked towards him Infinity, looked at him and them back at me. He laughed and then snapped his fingers. Nothing happened. Infinity snapped his fingers again and again, but nothing happened. He flinched and looked to the sky, but no lighting came down. He was powerless.

Before I could move, Flex stood up behind Infinity, placed both hands around his head, and snapped his neck with such force that the pop made almost an echo. He fell to the ground, eyes still open, but unmoving just the same.

He was dead. Infinity. Will Scott. The most powerful being in this world, taken down by a low life thug because his powers were considered small while compared to others. E-Rase looked at me and then pulled out his phone.

I did the same and transferred the money to his account. "Awesome," he said as he looked down at his phone. Jen went to help her dad, as E-Rase walked towards me with his hand out.

"Hey man, sorry about the other day. I wasn't going to really shoot you or anything. And, it wasn't what it looked like. We never slept together. To be honest, I haven't seen her since Lobo showed up. Now, thanks to you, I'm headed to Emerald Canyon for a fresh start."

I shook his hand. "Thanks for the help." I said. He nodded, and then screamed, "I'm rich," as he ran off. I laughed. I was guessing that in three months he would be back to doing petty acts of crime to get by.

"Where is Z?" Flex asked me. He was removing some of the blood from his face. "In the baseball field near here. She's trapped in my force field. She tried to kill me, too." Flex sighed as he shook his head from left to right.

"We thought, we thought she was better." he said. "What do you mean?" I asked him. "Z showed signs early on of being a villain. She found pleasure in other people's pain, and even went through a killing animals phase. Well, in her case, freezing them. She had several doctors, a pile of pills, and special classes she had to take, but we thought she had worked it out of her system. She would have urges, but as long as she took her pills, she would had been okay. I guess we were wrong."

"She needs help Flex. That and a cell. Her powers are," "More than she let people believe." Flex finished my own sentence for me. "Yeah. Her pills keep her powered down. I don't know why she stopped taking them suddenly after all these years." His eye became glazed over. For the first time ever, I looked at Flex and didn't see a showboating jerk. Instead, he was a big brother, who felt like he failed his sister. I wondered if my casual attitude towards what was right, and what was wrong had an influence on her.

"I'll take care of it." he said as he flew off into the air.

I looked around. Cops had finally come close to the scene and were talking to Jen and Life-Line near the children. Mr. Reid looked at me and nodded. I quickly turned away. I still wasn't ready to address his part in what happen when Infinity was given away.

Mr. Impervious was standing over the body of his son. His real son. "He was like this because of me." he said in a broken voice. "He made his own decisions," I said with a grimace. "Then again, so did you. You covered up deaths, lied, chose your happiness over what was right, and on top of it you gave your child away in some back- alley bargain."

It was odd, but right now I hated my uncle more than I did Infinity. All of this could have been prevented had he, and my father, just gone back home.

"You're right." he said as he removed a small silver device from his suit, and clicked a button. As he did so, a green, swirling portal opened. I gasped, because I hadn't seen one of these since the invaders came. I mean Spellborn. The same portals were used during the Battle of Ages.

"I'm taking them home. To our world. They both deserve a proper burial, no matter what, they were still my children. One by blood, and one by love." I wanted to say something but I couldn't find the words.

He shifted into super speed and in a blink of an eye, the remains of Picasso were gone. Then Impervious was back, bending over and picking up the body of Infinity. "Seems the Imperial Lords are done for now. Tell Life-Line and Flex to handle everything and to keep a low profile until I return."

I fought the urge to tell him that he doesn't get to leave us in this cluster fuck while he goes to another world, but all I did was nod as he stepped into the green portal that closed behind him.

I looked around and realized there was nothing left for me to do. Flex was handling Zeva, and what was left of the Lords were either speaking to police, or getting healed by Life- Line. I had brushed Mr. Reid off when he tried to heal my arm. I just didn't want to be around him, not yet. Now, he was with Jen and they were talking to the police. It was best if I just headed back to the base, took a shower, downed some food and went to sleep.

I rose several feet in the air and then was suddenly stopped by several screaming voices. I turned and looked down on them. Reporters.

"Can you tell us what happened here?" A blond woman said as she held a tape recorder in my face. "Where did Mr. Impervious go? Was that a portal from The Battle of Ages?" A large white man with red hair asked.

Then between them all, a short black woman forced her way to the front of the crowd. "Forget all of that, just tell us your name!" she said. I landed back on the ground and walked towards them.

I didn't have a true name. I never really thought about getting one because I didn't know if I was going to be a hero or a villain but now I knew. I knew I was a hero. I wanted to save lives and not end them. I wanted to protect with my power, not enslave. Then, from who knows where a name came to me.

I smiled and looked at every reporter, and cameraman in the face. "Call me, Paragon."

EPILOGUE

"**P**aragon?" Danielle said as she let her head fall back in laughter. "That was the first thing that came to you? You just help defeat a crazy ice bitch and a super powerful Icon and that was the first thing that came to mind?" I shrugged and continued to rub her feet.

We were sitting in my room. Not my real room at the Reid's house, but my room at the base that once belonged to the Imperial Lords. "It's been about a month now you know? You'd think the name would have grown on you." I replied as I put some more lotion in my hand. "Nope, not even a little, but the media seems to love it."

She was right. Since the fight with Infinity and Zeva, I had become somewhat of a celebrity for a variety of reasons. While many still knew me because of my villain dad, and hero mom, now they knew me for what I really was. Hell, they knew my family for what we really were.

Impervious confessing to everything like he did on live television shed some light on some very old questions. Questions like why the invaders came to our world in the first place, and why they left so fast. Knowing all of this and being the only Spellborn left on our world made me a celebrity of some renown for most people. I had also been warned by several government officials to not try and start any trouble.

The Imperial Lords were officially disbanded, and the name was even retired. Yet, a majority of the base was still left open. Mostly the lower levels. The shops and stuff up top were closed to the public and would eventually be demolished.

Speaking of demolished, my relationship with Mr. Reid wasn't what it used to be. With the Imperial Lords gone, he decided to retire from hero work and opened a small healing clinic for the sick at a price and was doing rather well. Over twenty grand a month in profits was the expectancy for the first year of business.

Finding out that he agreed with the events of trading Will Scott off as a bargaining chip didn't sit well with me. I found it even harder to look at him, or Mrs. Reid in the face. Turns out she knew and agreed to it too. Apparently, she was a member back then that worked alongside The Mechanic. Another surprise to me. We all still talked here and there but not like we used to.

I decided to move out of the house permanently, and not just for my internship, to live in the base. Jen spent most nights here, unless she was out doing recon for other supergroups like she was now. She was dating a girl from Up, Up, and Away and was on mission for the next month with her. Even with her schedule, she still went home more than I did. We were both handling things well, seeing as how we technically were still on our internships. We were just given a lot of slack since we had helped with Infinity

Danielle had become my roommate, and girlfriend again. After E-Rase came clean, and came through for us, I gave in and gave her another chance.

I had missed her more than I let on and she knew it. For the last month we were almost joined at the hip. I saw her face at the start of every day, and the end of every night, and I wouldn't have changed it for the world. "You know," I said looking down at her, "I guess we could be considered vigilantes, now couldn't we?"

She looked at me with a grimace. "Well think about it. We aren't really affiliated with a hero group, yet we aren't villains." She cleared her throat. I raised my brow. "We aren't villains, right?"

She sighed. "Yeah, we're not villains," she added again with a grumble. "Whatever you say Paragon," she said. Before I could respond a knock came to the door. "Come on in," I shouted. The door opened slowly, and Flex stuck his head inside.

"Hey. Got a minute?" he asked. I moved Danielle's feet from my lap and slid off the bed. "Hey Flex," Danielle said as she began playing with her phone. "Hello," he replied casually. Since Zeva went off the deep end, Flex had become more relaxed and less of a dick. I liked him better this way and we actually got along pretty well now. I hated that his sister had to become a murderer to bring out his better side, but life happens I suppose.

With Impervious still gone to his home dimension, Flex was also the unofficial leader of whatever we were, and Power Prince was his second in command. Me, Danielle, Power Prince, and Flex often trained together, ate together, swapped stories, and even occasionally went on random patrols together.

Flex had the most experience, so it made sense to follow his lead. He was unbearable to deal with the first week after the fight, though. Zeva had been placed in Vincula, a maximum-security prison for the worst Icons around, and since then, Flex and his family pretty much disowned her.

If I didn't know Flex, I would have never known he had a sister. It was sad because they were always so close. I always assumed they loved each other. In reality, Flex was making sure her darker side never manifested. Keeping tabs on her under the ruse of brotherly love.

We all left my room and walked down the hall a few feet before we stopped in a lounge area. The area was small and only had two tables, some chairs, and a tiny kitchen area. "Where is Double P," Danielle asked. That was her nickname for Power Prince. "He's still helping with that power outage in Emerald Canyon," Flex replied. "Two thirds of the city's power is coming from him, until they get everything up and running."

I sat down in a chair and leaned on the table. "What's up?" I asked him. His eyes darted around. "Nothing. What's up with you?"

I twisted my face. "Really? You lured me here to ask how my day was? What, did your trip to see Zeva go bad?" Flex shook his head. "No, she is still as violent as before. Refusing to take her meds, you know the usual."

I raised my hands a little with my palms out. "So, what's wrong because I don't know if you noticed, but I was in the middle of rubbing lotion on my hot girlfriend." Danielle cleared her throat again, as I laughed. He shook his head.

"Prism," he called out. In a second the holographic butler appeared beside us. "You called, young Lord?" "Stop calling us that," I said quickly. He was having a harder time adjusting than we were, and with The Mechanic working out of The

Ebony District now, he hadn't had the time to update his system yet.

"Play the audio we received earlier today." Flex said. Various speakers in the lounge made a loud clicking sounds as they fired to life. A high pitched male voice began to speak from the speakers. *"Why do only Icons get to be heroes?. I'm a normal guy, with a drive to save the world. I'm going to do it or die trying. My name is Brandon Strome, but the world will know me as Mighty Defender! My legend begins now."*

The audio suddenly stopped. "I looked at Flex and then smirked. "Okay? Am I missing something?" "This was sent to us, by an Icon friend of mine. Apparently, this idiot is her boyfriend. He tried to stop a mugging, and nearly got killed. She wanted to know if we could go by and talk to him."

I shrugged. "What's this have to do with me?" "He saw Paragon on the news." Flex replied. "Paragon," Danielle said as she laughed. I glared at her, but she continued to laugh. "Apparently he is a fan. Look just talk to him. He's at Atlas City General." I protested for a few minutes, but ultimately, I gave in and figured I would talk to the guy. I had nothing else to do after I spent some time with Danielle, and he was a fan after all.

"Sure. Anything else?" I asked as I slowly backed up to head to my room. "Next time don't be so secretive." Then as

I turned around a swirling green portal sprung to life right there in the base.

"Impervious is back, it seems. Good, now he can figure out what he wants to do with this place." Flex said as he sat down. A body fell out of the portal and came crashing into several chairs and Flex.

It wasn't Mr. Impervious. Instead it was an olive skin girl with spiky blond hair, and vibrant green eyes. She had on some large blue goggles around her neck, a black shirt with a brown vest, and some black boots.

"Who the hell are you?" Flex said as he stood up and grabbed the girl. She looked around quickly. "Is this the Imperial Lords' base?" She asked. "It used to be, up until about a month ago," I replied to her.

Tendrils of dark energy sparkled around Danielle's hands that slowly moved and twisted up her arms.

"My name is Perkins," she said as she found a chair to sit on. "Impervious tells me that you may be looking for some new talent to join the crew." I looked at Flex who shook his head, and then to Danielle who shrugged her shoulders. "You want to be an Imperial Lord?," I asked her.

"That's right," she said as she clapped her hands together and grinned. "So where do I sign up?" Flex stepped closer to her. "The Imperial Lords aren't a thing anymore. The group has been terminated." The smile on her face slowly faded.

Just at that moment, Prism flickered into existence once more. "Sorry, young Lords," we all glared at him. "Sorry all," he continued. "There is a," the hologram paused, and vanished. It reappeared again beside where Perkins stood. She jumped as she saw the hologram beside her. "Who is this?" Prism asked. Flex snapped his fingers. "Prism, there is a what? What's going on?"

"Sorry. There seems to be a massive power struggle going on in Emerald Canyon. The power outage wasn't an accident, and Power Prince has requested backup." We all looked at each other and then Flex glanced at Perkins. "Looks like your trial period starts now." and he turned and dashed down the hall. "Welcome to the team," Danielle said as she slapped Perkins on the shoulder and walked down the hall.

"Get a move on Paragon," she shouted over her shoulder in a mock tone. I took a deep breath and held back a laugh, as I glanced at Perkins who to my surprise was standing inside her own, pale green force field. I nodded at her, and called my own force field to life, and flew down the hall to catch up with Danielle and Flex, with Perkins behind me.